Sirens and Sea Monsters

Blue Moon Australia - Book 2

S.C. Stokes, Steve Higgs

Contents

The Scales of Luck are Turning. Sunday, April 23rd 2030hrs

KYLE'S LIFE HAD CHANGED the day he'd won that Olympic Gold Medal. Well behind the other racers when he hit the pool, he brought home the gold in the men's relay. Overnight, he went from unknown nobody to town hero.

News outlets pursued him. He sold his story for a small fortune and landed a number of lucrative keynote speeches. The day he'd opened his swim school, he struck pay dirt and, for the last two decades, he'd been teaching young Australian athletes to swim. Parents paid whatever he wanted to charge in the hopes their children would grow to be the country's next Olympians.

It was good to be a winner.

Today it was especially sweet. So much so that even Kyle struggled to believe his good fortune.

He set his beer down on the bar and enjoyed the ambiance of his favorite hangout, The Watering Hole.

The bar was located at the Spit, the Gold Coast's northernmost beach. It was a peninsula of land that together with South Stradbroke Island, sheltered the Broadwater from the Pacific Ocean. The Spit protected the Gold Coast's harbours and expensive waterfront living from the harsher elements of coastal life.

The unique geography of the Spit also meant that there was saltwater on both sides of the narrow stretch of land, and the ability to see the water from the bar was one of Kyle's favorite things about The Watering Hole. That, and it was almost exclusively frequented by beach bums and young backpackers.

Kyle started drinking there years ago, buying rounds and endearing himself to the barkeeper, Phillip, and a whole lot of the locals. Didn't hurt to have a few wingmen around who could tell stories of Kyle's glory days.

As he looked about, Kyle caught the eye of a young woman at the end of the counter. She smiled at him, her blue eyes twinkling with mischief. She couldn't be more than twenty-five. He had a good decade, almost two, on her but that didn't seem to be putting her off.

Kyle dyed the grays. He didn't want his clients to think he was getting old. However, try as he might to stay in shape, he was losing ground. Perhaps it was the drinking. He worked hard and felt he deserved to let loose when the mood took him, though it had got him into trouble more than once. Most recently with that troublesome brat, Kaley Winters.

Kyle pushed the thought from his mind. That mess was over now.

The ancient jukebox clacked as it changed tracks, and the Beach Boys flooded the bar. Good music and the smell of the salt air relaxed him.

He glanced back at his young admirer. Her attention wasn't particularly unusual, and she was far from the first Olympic groupie he'd run into. His medal had ensured he was seldom without companionship. Sure, he was carrying a few extra kilos but he still spent hours a day in the water coaching others, and doing plenty of laps for cardio.

Celebrity might allow you to get away with a great deal, but a fat and flabby instructor didn't fetch a premium price. Women weren't keen on it either and Kyle Cruz loved his women. He'd seduced his share, and largely avoided reprisal at the hands of their angry husbands.

Yes, he was winning at life and things were going his way. Even the courts had sided with him. And with their judgement, his contract to coach the nation's swim squad was safe once more. Preparing for the Commonwealth Games had him in the spotlight again.

There were certainly worse jobs in the world than coaching a squad of gorgeous twenty-year-olds in peak physical form. Coaching had been going splendidly until that wicked little viper Kaley Winters had gone after his paycheck and livelihood.

She'd cited sexual harassment and crusaded to get him sacked. The scandal right on the back of the me-too movement had looked like it would destroy his career, but the courts had seen the light and tossed it out on its merits.

Kaley Winters had been cut from the squad for her lackluster work ethic, not for rebuffing his advances as she'd asserted in court. Fortunately, the jury had seen right through that.

Kyle Cruz was an Olympian, a national treasure, and with no evidence of foul play, they had summarily dismissed the whole matter.

He sipped his beer. He hadn't laid a hand on her. Sure, he might have thought about it once or twice, but a man couldn't be jailed for what was in his mind. If he could, the prisons wouldn't be able to keep up.

Kyle drained his cup and waved Phillip over. The barkeeper had a shaved head but sported a well-kept brown beard that hung from a firm jawline. His shoulders were broad and well defined, lending the impression that his neck was almost non-existent. He had a barman's rag over one shoulder and moved with purpose as he approached.

"Another for me, and a drink for the young lass over there. Give her another one of whatever she's having."

"Righty-o, Kyle." Phillip grinned as he fetched another beer.

The Watering Hole was the scene for much of his misspent twenties, and it was a stone's throw from the sand and surf. It was his love of the water that had paved the way for his Olympic performance.

Phillip set down a beer and a martini. "Good luck, Kyle."

He bustled off down the bar.

Picking up the drinks, Kyle made his way down the bar and paused at the empty stool beside her. "Mind if I sit here? I come bearing gifts."

The pretty brunette toyed with her long curls as she smiled back. "Not at all."

Kyle handed the woman the martini, and she took a long sip.

That's it, lass. Drink up. Only good decisions follow a few martinis.

"Somebody knows how to have a good time." Kyle chuckled as he planted himself on the stool beside her. It wasn't his smoothest line, but she smiled, nonetheless.

"Oh, you have no idea." She broke eye contact as the colour rose a little in her cheeks.

Tonight was looking more and more promising by the moment.

"I'm Kyle. Kyle Cruz."

It never hurt to use his full name. Worst case scenario, they had never heard of him. On more than one occasion, his name had worked in his favor.

She sipped at her drink as she processed the name. He'd seen that look before. A look that said she recognised the name and was trying to work out where she had heard it before. He watched the thoughts play across her face like it was a screen.

She held up a finger. "You're that swimmer, right? You won gold at the Olympics."

Ding, ding, ding. We have a winner.

"Back in the day, sure. Now I mainly teach. Fancy a lesson?"

She laughed. "I really am a terrible swimmer, but I can appreciate talent when I see it."

Kyle tried not to choke on his drink. The girl would have had to have been ten or twelve when he'd been at the Olympics. Still, she was laughing and giggling along, and it seemed the fates were smiling on him, so Kyle pressed on. Who knew? Maybe a midnight skinny dip was on the cards.

"Never too late to learn," he replied, "but perhaps another time. I've already had a few."

"I'm Dayna." She held out her hand. "It's nice to meet you, Kyle. Would you like me to get the next round?"

"Oh, it's on me." He reached for his wallet and signaled Phillip.

Kyle drained a beer for every martini Dayna sipped and as the night went on, he grew more and more impressed she was still upright. She could certainly hold her liquor, and she was all smiles and giggles.

She rested a hand on Kyle's knee. "You still haven't told me what you are celebrating."

"Just a great week," Kyle answered, noting her hand. *Getting your sexual harassment case thrown out of court* wasn't the sort of line that got women hot and bothered for you.

"I just found a new job, so I thought I'd take this chance to cut loose while I still can."

"Oh yeah?" Kyle's eyes lingered on hers. "What are you doing?"

"I just landed a job at Gold Coast Hospital. I'm a nurse."

"Wow, way to go," he replied. "Best have some fun before you start then."

"That's the plan." She raised her drink before downing it. With a giggle, she said, "I've probably had quite enough."

She certainly seemed to be throwing herself at him and Kyle wasn't the sort to say no to a good thing.

"Why don't we get out of here?" Dayna placed her hand on his arm. "Would you mind walking me home? I don't live far."

It was about the most forward any woman had ever been with him. Well, apart from one of the eager mothers last year. She had known what she wanted and went for it. It was a quality Kyle admired. He'd never been one for beating around the bush.

He slid off the stool and held out his arm.

"I wouldn't mind in the least." He flashed a big smile.

"Such a gentleman," Dayna cooed as Kyle steered her out of the bar.

He led her towards the sand. "I prefer the beach to the road. A much better view."

"You read my mind." Dayna's smile broadened.

It was almost midnight and though the occasional boat taxied by they were largely alone.

Dayna kicked off her shoes and picked them up. As they strolled together, arm in arm, Kyle regaled her with stories of his Olympic triumph. Dayna listened eagerly as Kyle considered his good fortune.

He couldn't help his mind wandering to what might be beneath that cute sun dress. With any luck, he would be finding out soon.

"Have you ever swum across the Spit?" Dayna asked, pointing to the Broadwater that formed the channel. It was close enough to see the land on the other side.

"All the time," Kyle said. It was a point of pride for him. Back in the day, he used to do ten laps of it for his morning swim. These days, he spent more time in the heated pool. "But it can be a little cool in the winter."

"I don't know how you do it." Dayna shook her head.

"Oh, you'd be surprised. A little work on proper technique and stroke, and you'll be flying." He pointed to the buoy floating halfway across the water, marking the safest point of passage for the boats. "I could make it to that marker in a single breath."

Dayna's face screwed up in disbelief. "I'd drown before I got that far."

Kyle laughed. "I'm sure you've got more fight in you than that. Just kick like hell and you'll be there before you know it.

Dayna giggled. "Not me, but why don't we make this interesting?"

Kyle stopped dead. He could make out both the mischief and promise in those words.

"What did you have in mind?"

"Well, I'm not much of a swimmer," Dayna said, looking down at the sand, "but I'm very good at... other things. If you can make it to that buoy without needing to gasp for air, I'll show you what *I* can do with a single breath.

Kyle just about swallowed his tongue. Surely, he'd misheard her. He wasn't in a hurry to leap into the cold water, but with that sort of motivation, he would just about manage to walk on it.

Perhaps she just wanted to see if he still had it. Make sure he was who he said he was.

"So, you're saying, if I make it out there in one breath..." His voice trailed off.

Dayna sucked her bottom lip, vexing it with her teeth. "I'm very good with my mouth."

Kyle's eyes danced across those pillowy lips. He didn't doubt that for a moment.

"Done." He peeled off his shirt. Sure, he'd had a few drinks, but even on a bad day he could make it to the buoy.

Excitement fueled his pace as he kicked off his shoes. There was, of course, the chance she was toying with him. Perhaps she was trying to trick him into the water while she took off with his wallet. Given how many martinis she had downed, Kyle doubted she could run in a straight line. He would catch her before she reached the park beyond the sand.

Without Dayna noticing, he moved his wallet into his pants pocket and zipped the compartment shut. It was largely watertight, but that didn't matter much. Australian currency was plastic, and the water posed little threat to it.

She wouldn't be able to pinch his wallet if that was her plan. Kyle Cruz was many things, but an idiot wasn't one of them. He'd seen his share of scammers and thieves working the beaches over the years.

He wasn't nearly drunk enough to fall for that.

"You stay right there, missy," Kyle called. "I'll be back in a moment."

He raced down the beach and into the water. When he reached his knees, he took a deep breath and dove forward. Adrenaline flooded his system as he hit the cool water. A quick swim, and that hot little twenty-five-year-old was going to do wicked things to him. Kyle couldn't remember the last time he'd got quite this lucky.

He kicked hard, holding his breath as he powered across the bay. He kept his head down, wanting to be doubly sure he didn't blow the terms of the bet.

Normally, he could see underwater, but it was dark and his visibility barely stretched more than a few feet in front of him. Still, he knew where the buoy was. It would be bobbing out there, held in place by a chain stretching to an anchor on the ocean's floor. When his hand touched the outer shell, he surfaced and waved to Dayna.

"Made it," he shouted.

Dayna had her phone out, taking a picture or a video.

"Go, Kyle!" she called with a little wave.

Perhaps she was one of those eager groupies, the sort who followed athletes around in the hopes of seducing them. He had no intention of fending off her wiles.

He held onto the buoy with one arm while he caught his breath. He didn't want to arrive back at the beach panting and puffing. It sent the wrong message to his newest fan.

Seeing her standing on the shore reassured him that he hadn't misjudged the situation.

Better to get back to her before she rethought her decision. He pushed off the buoy and started the swim back to shore.

Something slammed into his stomach. Another object lacerated his chest, slamming him back toward the buoy.

Air blasted from his lungs as salt stung in the wounds.

Kyle flailed as he broke the surface, his head whipping about as he looked for whatever had hit him. It was difficult to see in the darkness.

Without warning, Kyle was yanked down into the water. His belt was pulled tight. He was sinking like a rock and hadn't even managed to catch a breath. Something large passed by him, shunting him again. It felt like a fish, but it was larger than anything he'd ever seen in the water.

Kyle floundered, reaching for his belt. Whatever had him was using it against him. He was running out of breath fast and the pressure was building in his ears. He was sinking deeper by the moment.

Thrashing violently, Kyle tried to fight his descent, but the creature holding him was simply too strong. It was as if a hand was dragging him down to a watery grave.

Something was moving nearby, but in the darkness, he couldn't make out what it was.

He prayed it wasn't a shark.

Reaching behind his back, he felt along his belt and his fingers brushed cold steel. The metal formed a loop, like a carabiner affixed to his belt, and dangling off it was a chain. Kyle reached for the loop. Something closed around his wrist. It was fine like fishing wire but as he struggled against it, something sharp pierced his flesh.

The more he fought, the deeper it bit, like hooks tearing at his flesh. His blood seeped into the water.

Kyle screamed, but in the darkness of the salty depths only a rush of bubbles came from his lips.

Hopefully, Dayna was raising the alarm, but with how far out he was, he knew he wasn't going to make it. He was already out of breath.

He looked up toward the surface and the spot of moonlight high above. He could make out a faint silhouette. It was too large to be a fish and was seemingly humanoid but for its tail.

Kyle's strength waned, but in the moonlight he would swear he was looking at a mermaid.

How many drinks did I have?

He ran out of breath and his vision swam. Unable to hold on any longer, he lost consciousness, saltwater pouring into his open mouth.

Self-pity o'clock.
Sunday April 23rd
2330hrs

My confidence in finding the Djinn waned by the minute. I sat at my desk in the office where I had been for most of the night. The untouched bottle of chardonnay sat on the edge of my desk. I had an empty glass at the ready, but it didn't feel right to indulge.

According to the papers, I'd closed the case. The Casper Killer was dead. The judge was safe, and the Gold Coast's latest serial killer would take no more lives. I should have been on cloud nine, but it was hard to celebrate when I had completely missed the mark.

I hadn't seen who was pulling the strings. The crime scenes were too clean, too well executed for an amateur with an axe to grind against his father's killers. TJ had just been the instrument.

The Djinn had been the one in control.

Why?

SIRENS AND SEA MONSTERS

That was what continued to elude me. What did she gain from his actions, and why toy with me?

I stared at the empty wine glass and considered cracking the bottle and pouring myself a glass. What could it hurt? I wasn't making much progress anyway.

I shook my head. Wine wasn't going to help matters.

Setting the glass aside I went looking for something to put some pep in my step. Leaving my office, I slipped into the small kitchenette out back.

Spying the coffee maker, I rubbed my hands together.

"Just what I need," I said.

Rummaging around in the cupboards above the sink, I located a sachet that I was pretty sure fit the machine and slid a mug under the spout.

Grabbing the milk from the fridge, I sniffed it to make sure it was still good and set it on the counter beside the coffee maker. A steaming hot cup of brew was just what the doctor ordered. I flicked the button to start it, but nothing happened.

"Oh, come on, you stupid machine. Work." I gave it a good hit just in case and, when it didn't start, I checked the cord, which wasn't plugged in.

I slid the plug back into the wall socket. The coffee maker whirred to life like R2D2 powering up. Lights flashed on the coffee maker, followed by a chime.

There were a dozen settings, and I'd never used the machine. It was a bribe to keep Glenda happy. I still hadn't mustered the courage to try and get her to make me a cup. Besides, swinging by Paradox for my coffee had given me plenty of excuses to chat with Courtney.

A whirring crunch broke my train of thought.

Faint wisps of smoke were rising from the coffee machine.

"Bad droid!" I shouted as I reached for the cord to rip it out of the wall, but flames billowed out of the machine, forcing me back. My heart raced as my late night coffee fix threatened to burn down my office. My rented office.

"Think, Darius, think." I grabbed the fire extinguisher from the end of the counter, pulled the pin, and attacked the infernal coffee maker with a blanket of thick white foam.

My coffee cup was blasted straight out of the machine, shattering as it hit the tiles. I ignored it in favor of the growing flames.

Foam smothered the rebellious machine, choking the smoke and flames until they sputtered out. I was left staring at the charred remains of a coffee maker and a two-litre bottle of now undrinkable milk.

I fought the temptation to hurl the useless machine through the window. That would just make more of a mess for me to clean. Instead, I yanked the cord out of the wall and then shoved the machine in the sink for good measure.

"Tea it is, I suppose," I muttered to myself as I boiled the kettle.

This I managed without incident, fortunately, as I had no other backup plans, and it was far too late to swing by Paradox. Finding a black tea bag, I threw it in a mug with a spoon of sugar, set it on a saucer, and headed for the door.

Glenda was not going to be thrilled about the coffee maker, but it was hardly my fault. The stupid machine had turned on me. Who needed AI to wipe out civilization when even a rogue coffee machine could start an inferno?

I eyed the smoldering mess in the sink. "Yes, you sit there and think about what you've done."

With tea in hand, I settled at my desk. Before me was a white blazer, a little black dress, and what had to be the most stunning and realistic red wig I'd ever seen. Not that I was a wig expert, but I'd seen it on a woman and not even realized it wasn't her real hair.

I liked to consider myself both observant and situationally aware, but perhaps I'd been distracted by her allure.

The outfit was all that remained of Mary Baker, also known as the Djinn.

Even now, I struggled to believe that she had so readily sucked me in.

She had sought me out, invited me to lunch, and interrogated me for the better part of an hour and a half. She'd been excellent company for a sociopath.

She'd done it in the hopes of learning what drove me.

I'd mistaken her intellectual interest in what made me tick, for interest of another sort.

Maybe I'd been listening to Carl for too long.

I'd been expecting to spend a rather enjoyable night with Mary and that bottle of chardonnay, celebrating the demise of the Casper Killer.

Instead, I was reading the same typed note, staring at Mary's intentionally discarded disguise, and asking myself how I had missed it.

I'd been over the outfit twice already. True to my expectations, there wasn't a single hair follicle or skin cell I could discern. I'd crawled all over it with a magnifying glass. The process had taken me hours, but I was confident there wasn't a single traceable element of Mary Baker left anywhere on them.

I picked up my tea and sipped it. Deep and earthy, the tea was just what I needed to fight off the fatigue clawing at my brain.

I reconsidered everything I knew about my latest case.

If it wasn't for Mary Baker bringing herself into my life, I'd likely be oblivious to the existence of my adversary.

That realization told me two things about Mary Baker, or the Djinn, or whoever the hell she was. She was both arrogant and dangerous. The Djinn was orchestrating murders across the Gold Coast. It was her guidance that had encouraged TJ to carry out his vendetta and had given him the understanding necessary to evade the authorities.

The crime scenes he'd left behind were as devoid of clues as this costume.

Four lives had been taken, and for what? Why was the Djinn even interested in the first place? What did she have to gain?

So many questions, and not nearly as many answers.

Her interference made no sense, but it had to be at the very core of the whole matter. If only she wasn't so good at covering her tracks.

TJ's last words had clarified her priorities: Five bodies, no prison. And he might have got away with it if Holly and I hadn't gotten to the judge before he did. At least one life had been saved. Unfortunately, the fifth body was TJ's.

Having a judge well disposed toward me couldn't hurt, but Mary had a lot going for her too. The sigil left on the door of the house I was going to meet her at meant that she was working with the cult of Beelzebub. The weird cultists had tried to sacrifice Cali and had attempted to kidnap my father.

It made no sense. According to their high priest, the Djinn had swapped the knife on him. But why the theatrics? What did she have to gain by antagonizing the people she'd tasked with kidnapping Cali Masters? And how had she known I would be there?

Unlike the host of other questions I'd been left with, these three bore potential.

Cali's mother was responsible for me taking the case. Had the Djinn put her onto me? I saw little other options for how she could be sure I would be there to stop the kidnapping.

The high priest's own words gave away their relationship. Clearly, he'd had dealings with the Djinn, and he'd felt betrayed by her. If I could find him, perhaps I could learn something of the mastermind behind this whole mess.

I tapped my keyboard and woke up my computer. Firing up my browser, I navigated my way to Cali Masters' social media profile. From there, it didn't take long to find the high priest. He wasn't exactly discreet. His entire page was an appeal to the baser nature of bored twenty-somethings in a search of a good time.

I stared at his profile picture, and the name beside it.

GraemeGraham Bilson.

Didn't exactly carry the same gravitas as the High Priest of Beelzebub, but I was going to need to talk to him all the same. I doubted Cali had any idea what she was getting into when she'd fallen in with them.

Leaning back in my chair, I stifled a yawn. At least the entire night hadn't been a waste. It wasn't the excitement I'd been hoping for, but I was making progress.

Mary Baker was the mastermind. She'd manipulated TJ, Cali's mother, Christine, plus Graeme and his cultists. Based on the conversation I'd had with her, she was clearly an expert manipulator and well versed in human psychology.

I was starting to form a picture of who she was. Even if I couldn't put a face to the Djinn, it was something to go on.

It was difficult to believe she had risked exposing herself at lunch. Was I really just sport to her?

Was this some strange test of intellect and wit. Did she fancy herself the Moriarty to my Holmes?

I laughed as I raised my tea. Holmes? Not on my best day. I was just a retired soldier trying to make a difference.

The Djinn was flexing on me. Not only had I not caught onto her game, but she had practically had to dob herself in. If she hadn't, I might have missed her existence entirely.

Picking up the wig off the table, I took another look at it. Perhaps I'd been too quick to dismiss the wig. After all, it was an excellent wig. Even I hadn't been able to tell it was fake. Perhaps I'd been focused on the wrong things. I'd been looking for clues on the wig. What if the wig itself was the clue?

My to-do list was growing rapidly. I was going to have to hunt down what was left of the cult, speak to Christine Masters, and go wig shopping.

I twirled it on my finger as I sipped my tea.

There was a rattle of bells as the front door opened. I bolted up in my chair, almost spilling my tea. I wasn't expecting anyone. Unless... I looked down at my watch and realized the time. It was 9 AM.

I'd spent the entire night dredging up what I knew of the Djinn and the Casper Killer case.

"Darius, are you in early?" Glenda, the iron maiden herself, called from the door.

"In here, Glenda," I called back, wondering how I was going to explain the coffee machine.

Glenda stuck her head in. Her glasses rested low on her nose to allow her to better judge me over the top of them.

"Not early, I see," Glenda raised an eyebrow as she spied the Chardonnay. "You've been here all night, haven't you?"

"It would appear that way," I replied. "Perhaps I ought to hire you for fieldwork, Glenda. Your keen sense of observation might come in useful."

"Smartarse." Glenda shook her head as she strode into the office. Her judgmental eyes swept from the wig in my hand to the clothes on my desk. "Someone's had a rough night."

She snatched up the bottle of Chardonnay. "A fine bottle. Clearly you shan't be needing any of this. I will take it in lieu of an apology for your cheekiness."

I shook my finger at her.

Glenda paused, staring me down.

I reached for the bottle. "I have plans for that one."

My plans had been to share it with Mary. Now, I wasn't going to touch it until she was in custody.

"Hold the phone if you can and wave off any interviews," I said. "I'm going to need a little rest before I head down to the station."

I'd promised Hart, or Olivia as she'd insisted yesterday, that I would meet her at the station and provide my statement. Given I'd been a suspect up until the end of the case, I thought it better to rest before I said anything that might be used against me in a court of law.

"Fine." Glenda pouted as she studied the women's clothes strewn inextricably over my desk.

"You know, Darius, when I said you needed a woman, this isn't what I had in mind. Though whatever you do in the comfort of your own office is up to you."

I glanced down at the wine and the complete ensemble. "Glenda, I'm not a cross-dresser. It's for a case."

She nodded slowly. "Of course it is, dear. You best get some rest after your big night. No judgement here, Darius."

"Glenda, I'm serious. They're clues."

Glenda backed slowly out of my office.

"Rather big ones. I'm not sure how I missed them," she whispered as she closed the door behind her.

Setting down the wine and the wig, I locked the door behind her. I didn't have the heart to tell her about the coffee machine. She would find it soon enough.

I stretched out on the carpet, bundled my jacket under my head, and tried to catch up on the sleep I'd missed. In my weary state, it came easy. I'd slept in far more hostile climates.

It was after 1300hrs when I finally woke. My muscles were a little stiff and my back protested the lack of a proper mattress, but all in all, I was feeling a little more human.

I waited until the phone rang and seized the opportunity. The second Glenda answered it, I made a break for the front door.

But the moment I left my office, she was onto me.

"Darius, what on earth did you do to my coffee machine?"

"Sorry, Glenda, can't talk," I said as I raced past her. "I'm heading down to the station. Hold my calls, please."

"Hold them? You'll be lucky if I don't go on strike," she called after me as I breezed through the front door.

"I'll deal with it later," I called back, and then added in a whisper, "If those two idiots Gibson and Hart don't arrest me first."

Statements & Serial Killers. Monday, April 24th 1330hrs

THE HOMICIDE DIVISION RAN out of the Southport Police Station, a specialist division of the Queensland police service. These overworked detectives serviced a considerable caseload spread across a diverse geographic region.

Their cases could be anywhere from Ashmore to Coolangatta. Bodies might show up anywhere from the beaches to the mountainous hinterland. Like me, one day they might be traipsing through a national park; another they might be roaming the concrete and glass jungle of Surfers Paradise.

The Gold Coast was the party and tourist capital of the state. The crimes they worked ranged from organised to impassioned. The Gold Coast was Queensland's sin city, and these detectives had their work cut out for them.

They could use any help they could get. At least that was my estimation. There were far too few of them for the case load they were assigned.

It was one of the reasons I couldn't work out why Gibson and Hart had it in for me. I wasn't on the payroll, but I was another set of willing hands. Maybe it was the media attention? It did complicate matters, but people defaulted to believing a Paranormal Investigator must be a con artist. The positive press coverage gave me credibility and kept me in a job.

Maybe, if I played my cards right, I could win over the detectives. I had some runs on the board now. First the Crypt Killers, and now the Casper Killer. I was quickly forming something of a reputation for making the lives of the local police easier. If only I could get them to see it that way.

I wasn't excited at the prospect of spending time with Hart and Gibson. After all, they'd rather recently been trying to arrest me for murders I hadn't committed. But I'd promised Hart I would come in and give my statement. I figured it would serve me better if she didn't have to chase me down to get it.

This was my way of extending the hand of friendship and cooperation. That and not throwing them under the bus with the reporters gathered at the judge's residence yesterday.

It would have been easy to air my grievance with them and have it run as the headline story on the seven o'clock news. I could see it in my mind's eye.

Police chase paranormal investigator while he does their job for them.

It would have made me tremendously unpopular. I hoped they appreciated the gesture.

Leaving the tank parked in the street in front of the station, I made my way up the stairs and into the station lobby.

A middle-aged sandy-haired constable stopped me at the front desk. "What can I do for you today?"

She was curt, and from the faded, sun-bleached navy-blue uniform, she wasn't accustomed to spending much time indoors.

"Darius Kane, here to see Detective Hart." I gave her a smile.

"One moment." She raised a finger and then picked up the phone with her other hand.

Balancing it there with her shoulder, she dialed an extension to summon Hart from the bowels of the department.

When she was done, she pointed to a row of chairs in the lobby. "You can wait there. She'll be right down."

"Thank you." I headed for the seats, but my butt had barely grazed the worn leather when Olivia Hart strode down the stairs and into the lobby.

"Darius Kane, I was beginning to think you were going to stand me up."

"What man in their right mind would do that?" I replied.

Her piercing blue eyes, blonde hair worn high, and striking pantsuit made me want to stare and I had to fight not to. I wasn't one of the detective's fan boys, but I didn't have any trouble understanding what they saw in her.

I also got the impression she enjoyed commanding the attention of others, but I was confident anyone who strayed too near to that particular fire got burnt.

"You certainly took your time though." She glanced down at her watch. Then, in one sweeping appraisal, she took in my rumpled slacks and dress shirt, the product of sleeping on my office floor. I still hadn't been home to change. I'd been too focused on the Djinn to bother.

"You're looking a little worse for wear. Long night?" Hart asked. Her tone was absent the usual blend of suspicion and condescension I'd grown accustomed to. If I didn't know better, I might have thought she cared.

"You know me, detective. Evil never sleeps and neither do I."

"No night off for the hero that stopped the Casper Killer?" She put a hand on her hip. "You need a new boss."

She was trying to butter me up, but I wasn't falling for it.

"What can I say? He's a bit of an ass," I replied as I rose from the seat. "Gibson not joining us?"

"He's upstairs preparing the room. Come with me."

She beckoned me to follow her up the stairs, but I hesitated.

"The room, you said." I paused long enough to draw her in. "Not a cell then?"

I let my lips peak up into a smile so she knew I was kidding.

"Ha, ha, ha, Darius. We're past that. Come on, I don't have all day."

I bounded up the stairs after her, passing two detectives coming down on their way out. The smaller of them recognized me and turned to his partner. Loudly and off key, he started humming the Ghostbusters theme song.

It wasn't the first dig I'd endured, and I doubted it would be the last. But if I was going to be compared to Peter, Ray, Egon, or Winston I would be damned if the patron saints of paranormal activity were going to be insulted by it.

As he mangled the final bars, I called from the landing after him, "Come on, detective, if you are going to lay it on, you best learn the tune. Three out of ten for the melody, but a seven for persistence. Anyone who can run a joke to its completion in spite of an obvious dearth of musical talent deserves at least that much."

"Smartarse," the detective called as we rounded the landing and continued climbing.

So much for making friends.

"Did you have to antagonise him?" Hart asked.

"You know what they say, detective. When you love what you do, you'll never work a day in your life."

"And our holding cells are the most affordable housing on the Gold Coast. Something can be both true, and inconvenient."

She wasn't wrong. I'd let my ego get the better of me. "Respect is a two-way street, Detective Hart. I'm not in the habit of letting people walk all over me."

"It's Olivia," she replied. "No need to be so formal. I told you yesterday."

"So you did, Olivia," I replied. "First name basis. Better watch out. People are going to think you like me."

Olivia paused in front of an open office. Her smile had an edge to it. "Let's not get ahead of ourselves."

My ego deflated like a burst balloon. Probably for the better. It had a habit of getting me into trouble.

Inside the office, Detective Gibson was setting up some recording equipment on the table.

Entering the room, I extended my hand. "Detective Gibson, good to see you again."

"Hello Darius." He eyed my hand.

"Is everything okay, detective?"

Gibson cocked his head to the side. "No *I told you so*? No mocking us for suspecting you of being the killer?"

I looked back at his partner. "Olivia, here, has kindly informed me we're turning over a new leaf. I've also been told that being an unrepentant smart arse will only slow the healing process."

Gibson swapped glances with Olivia and then motioned at the seat. "By all means, let us heal."

I took the offered seat, as Olivia sat down beside her partner.

Gibson walked me through the usual preamble and proceeded to take my statement.

I started at the beginning, our meeting at Mooney's workshop. I left out that his widow hadn't yet engaged me. I was confident the detectives were well aware of that fact, but I wasn't about to confess to breaking and entering.

I shared the information I'd gathered on the various murders and how I had pieced together clues from each of the scenes that led me to the conclusion that the killer had to be tied to Mooney's original negligence. No other motive linked all the victims together.

Where the detectives had looked at Victoria's condition and TJ's apparent death and accepted the seeming reality that neither was in a condition to carry out such a plot, I'd been forced to dig a little deeper.

It was either that or accept the notion that a ghost really was murdering these people.

Sharing the details of my visit to the nursing home, I explained how I deduced from the birthday cards that TJ was indeed still alive and well. Aided by Victoria's connections at Births, Deaths, and Marriages, he'd falsified his death and bought himself enough time to carry out his killing spree.

"We shall have to follow up with her," Gibson said. "It's aiding and abetting, of course. Unfortunately, there is nothing here that would constitute evidence in a case against her, but we can try."

Hart tapped the table. "I imagine she's trashed those cards, but we'll look into her connections regardless."

"She was certainly complicit," I replied. "You're right, though. I have no actual evidence she helped him plan the murders, but she definitely falsified his records. She said as much when I antagonised her."

"Something of a talent," Olivia interjected.

"What can I say? I'm good at winning friends and influencing people," I replied. "But surely if you delve a little deeper into it, you'll find out how and where the records were manipulated. That might give you what you need."

They both looked at me impassively, and I backpedaled.

"Not trying to tell you how to do your job, just some ideas. But as it's not paranormal activity, I'll leave that one in the hands of the professionals."

Gibson nodded, and I carried on. I shared how Holly and I rushed to the judge's residence on suspicion that TJ might have smuggled himself into her car at the country club. I explained that Mooney's entire murder was a trial run. It was the only way to get past the judge's security without raising any alarms. He knew he only had one shot at such a high-profile target.

"I suspect if you do any digging, you will discover TJ landed a job as a valet at the country club under an assumed identity."

"We already have." Gibson set his pen on the table. "And as far as we're concerned, the judge is safe, the killer has been stopped in his tracks, and the matter is concluded. Is there anything else you'd like to add?"

I shook my head. I had intentionally left out Benjamin Marino and his visit to the garage. It was clear he wasn't responsible for Mooney's death and while he was clearly angling for the purchase of the workshop, I had nothing on him. He could benefit from Mooney's death without being the cause of it.

In the absence of any evidence, I had no desire to antagonise the Gold Coast's kingpin. I'd done enough of that when I'd threatened to set him on fire.

"I must ask, Darius," Olivia said, "why did you go to Holly Draper and not us with this information?"

"Hang on." I leaned back in my chair. "We did call you detectives, while we were en route to the judge's house."

"We ran the timestamp of that call." Gibson stroked his chin. "You had to have known for at least twenty minutes before you picked up the phone."

So they had done their due diligence. At least they were thorough.

"Look, detectives, you were trying to arrest and implicate me. Providing you with information leading to the apprehension of the killer from unverifiable sources was just as likely to encourage you that I was somehow involved."

The room was silent. Perhaps we hadn't rounded the corner as readily as I had thought.

I rested my palms on the table. "Now you have the judge's testimony and irrefutable evidence that I was only acting in the interest of my client and the general public. I'd like nothing more than to conclude the matter and continue my work unimpeded by the good detectives of the Queensland Police Service. I've worked two cases now, one with the cooperation of the department and one without. I much prefer the former."

"Well," Gibson said, pressing stop on the recording, "you're certainly endearing yourself to the public and the judiciary. We see no reason why we can't coexist."

"Where doing so won't compromise an ongoing investigation," Olivia added fixing me with a knowing look.

That was a broad disclaimer, but it would have to do.

"Of course, and I have no intention of hauling criminals in off the street," I replied. "That's not my job. When I find them, I'll merely try to detain them until the real heroes show up."

"I knew we could work things out," Olivia answered with a smile that almost seemed genuine. She was looking to bolster her reputation and anything I could do to facilitate that was certainly winning her over.

But I planned to keep my eyes wide open. I wasn't convinced that she had so swiftly changed her stripes, though perhaps she had come to terms with the notion she could profit from working with, as opposed to against, me.

Holly's thoughts on Olivia seemed to be in that vein. She'd called the detective a career climber.

Perhaps Olivia just meant to leverage my notoriety for her own ends. If that was the case, I was confident I could channel it. If she was playing some other game, and trying to entrap me, it made her doubly dangerous though. I would have to watch my step.

"Well, if that's all, detectives, I must be about my day. The phone hasn't stopped ringing since yesterday, and I have a number of cases that demand my attention."

It was a fib, a minor one, but nothing they would concern themselves with. The phone certainly was ringing and the emails were piling in, but I had no interest in taking new cases.

The Djinn was the sole target of my focus, and I intended to use my day to do a little research on her namesake. It had to mean something.

"There is just one more matter," Olivia called, leaning forward in her chair to stop me before I could rise.

"And what's that?" I tried not to let my concern show. I'd left details out of my narration. I didn't want the police pursuing the Djinn until I knew more.

"Those lunatics at the church who tried to kidnap your father," Olivia said. "We just wanted to let you know that we are on it."

"On it?" I asked. "But that wasn't a homicide. No need to trouble yourselves with those crazies."

I was trying to get them to drop the cultist's case. If the Djinn was seeking to protect her identity, the High Priest was a loose end. One I didn't want lingering in police custody. I had questions for him.

"When someone tries to kidnap one of our citizens, particularly the father of the Gold Coast's favourite paranormal detective, the Queensland Police Service doesn't just sit on its hands." Olivia laid it on thick.

I didn't want anyone fighting me for Graeme. I should have been thrilled they were throwing their weight around to ensure my family's safety, but the police taking Graeme into custody before I could get to him threatened my chance to question him properly.

He had to know something about the Djinn, like where she operated from, and how to contact her. He certainly knew far more than I currently did.

"You don't have to do that." I managed a smile. "They are just some weirdos I inherited from another case. A college girl fell in with the cult and I got her out. They took it poorly. But in the end, no one got hurt."

Except Graeme. I was pretty sure I'd broken his nose. I was downplaying events in the hope the department would let it wallow in their low priority case pile.

After all, my father was home, safe and well. He was probably trying to put up the patio right now, and I was confident his lack of DIY skills posed the greater threat to his health.

"We've done some digging, and two kidnappings in a week certainly makes them a priority." Olivia burst my bubble. "While we haven't got any other confirmed criminal activity, we're working closely with missing persons and other specialists to apprehend them. An all-points bulletin went out for Graeme Bilson this morning. We'll let you know when we get this nutcase off the streets."

I was going to have to find him before they did because I doubted they would let me question him once he was in their custody.

"Well, I appreciate that." I did my best to sound sincere, in spite of the fact it was hindering my plans. "If there's anything I can do to help, you just let me know."

"We'll keep you informed, Darius," Olivia said. "In the meantime, maybe go home and get some rest. You look a little worn out."

I rose to my feet. "That, detective, is an excellent idea."

Olivia opened the door for me, and I flashed her a parting smile before heading down the stairs.

In the tank, I headed not for home, but for Cavill Avenue: the heart of Surfers' nightlife and home to the Paranormal Palace.

If anyone had a bead on the Djinn, it would be Esmerelda. The only question was, what would it cost me?

Captains & Con Artists.
Monday, April 24th
1415hrs.

LEAVING THE TANK PARKED in the narrow laneway that ran parallel to Cavill Avenue, I slipped through a quiet alley and into the open-air shopping strip. If I wanted a true expert in the paranormal, I was going to need to stop by her palace.

I spent half of last night googling the Djinn. I'd trawled through dozens of websites dealing with the mythical creatures, the origins of their particular mythology along with any popular folklore.

I didn't for one minute believe that I was dealing with a capricious spirit. After all, I'd spoken to Mary Baker, eaten lunch with her, and felt her skin against mine. She was flesh and blood. But I'd learned long ago there was power in a name. And if Mary Baker was choosing to identify herself as the Djinn, it gave at least a little insight into how she perceived herself.

She was also several steps ahead of me. I needed to do some opposition research. Unfortunately, like much of the Internet, content was only as good as those who posted and moderated it. In my experience, when it came to the paranormal, they all paled in comparison to the fountain of knowledge that was Esmerelda.

Esmerelda was the owner of the Paranormal Palace, a purveyor of fortunes, and as gifted a saleswoman as had ever existed on the sandy shores of the Gold Coast. At least, that was how I saw it. My opinion certainly didn't stop a host of clients beating their way to her door in the name of obtaining a reading.

She also bought and sold all manner of relics and antiquities. I couldn't fault her for making a living off the paranormal. I certainly was. We just worked at different ends of the spectrum. Esmerelda sought to confirm her clients' superstitions; I worked to debunk them.

It was an unlikely sort of alliance, but one that had helped me in the past.

I might doubt how she came by her information, but there was no denying the fact that she was an exceptionally useful source of knowledge and gossip.

I started down the concrete stairs that led to the Paranormal Palace. They'd been worn smooth and polished by the steady traffic over the decades. The mall here was older than I was, but every now and then, the owners gave it a fresh lick of paint to keep the tourists coming back.

As I descended into her lair, I considered how I might make my inquiry. Esmerelda had given me crucial insight into James Mooney's death that had ultimately led me to TJ.

Without her, I might have taken weeks to come to the same conclusion. She might have believed there was a serial killing specter on the loose, but her information helped all the same.

Perhaps she had heard something of the sociopath identifying herself as the Djinn.

When I pushed open the door to the Paranormal Palace, a flood of cheers drowned out the usual chimes that marked my entrance.

Moving aside the gauzy curtain I stepped into the store. Rows of paranormal paraphernalia were organized neatly onto shelves, though how anyone found anything in here was beyond me.

The store stocked everything from crystal balls to potion making ingredients. One could find vampire hunting supplies, silver trinkets to deal with werewolves, and a host of iron talismans meant to deter the fae. It was a celebration of superstition, and apparently quite a lucrative one.

Today, though, there seemed to be some sort of speaker presenting at the back of the store. The speaker's attire reminded me of an English captain several centuries at odds with the society we were now living in. His worn and tattered red coat was faded, its epaulets hanging by frayed stitches. Beneath it he wore a simple linen shirt and trousers, and he carried an old whaling harpoon.

A series of chairs were arranged in a semicircle before him. Fifteen eager listeners had been crammed into the relatively tiny corner of the store, a mix of bored pensioners and impressionable youngsters.

The captain, I labelled him mentally, leaned forward, his foot resting on an old sea trunk that had seen better days. He was a grizzled sort of soul, his dark brown beard giving way to grey. The wild wiry strands were bundled together and held in place by a series of metal rings.

He brandished the harpoon above his head as he regaled his audience.

I approached cautiously, not on account of the spear but for fear that I might somehow get dragged into his little bit of theater.

"I spied the great beast," the captain said, his voice deep and bordering on a growl. "It was out beyond the reef and retreating to deeper waters, its prey ensnared in its slimy tendrils."

The captain raised one hand as if pointing to the horizon. "He made for the safety of his lair, but I took off after him, the only soul with enough courage to save that young lass."

The crowd hung on to his every word.

"You'll not take her, Kraketogar, and you'll plague these waters no more. Swift the creature was, sure, but Captain Cronkwhile's ship be quicker still. Twin engines, you see."

Captain Cronkwhile paused, waiting for the eager nods of assent from his captive audience. "I bore down on the tentacled beast, and when the kraken realized it couldn't shake me, it turned."

He slammed his foot on the floor and waved the spear aloft.

The audience recoiled.

"Up came its slimy tendrils, snaking around my boat. The sheer weight of the beast slowed us to a crawl as he began to drag me down into the depths. Armed with my trustee harpoon, I had to make a choice—abandon ship or, like Ahab, go after the beast that had so eluded me."

He drew a deep breath. "I spotted his head, lurking just beneath the water. Running along the prow, I dove head long into the water, my harpoon aimed for one of its massive leering eyes. My aim was true. In one sure motion, I plunged it through the creature's eye and into its brain."

The crowd sat on tenterhooks. Clearly, I'd interrupted story time at the Paranormal Palace. Whatever method actor Esmerelda had paid was enjoying his own performance. The audience, too. This beat bingo day at the local retirement village.

"I slew the beast, its slimy tentacles releasing my vessel as the weight of its sinking carcass threatened to drag us all beneath the waves. I ripped my spear from its ruined eye socket, rescued the poor lass, and swam back to my boat. Together, we watched as Kraketogar vanished into the depths, never to rise again."

Along with any evidence. *Very convenient.*

"And that was the last the people of Byron Bay ever saw of it. Fortunately, I had the presence of mind to preserve some of the beast's blood, and today, you have a chance to purchase your very own copy of Monsters of the Deep, signed by myself, Captain Cronkwhile, with ink distilled from the essence of Kraketogar himself. There are only ten available, so if you want one, you best speak to my assistant, Walter, before you leave."

The captain pointed to a wiry man with sandy blond hair sitting apart from the others. He had a small portable table beside him on which were stacked leather-bound volumes of the captain's tome and an EFTPOS machine at the ready.

"But be quick," the captain added, "because once these truly collectible antiques are sold out, there will never be their like again."

The crowd clapped as the captain set down his spear and rested his hands on his hips. He looked awfully proud of himself.

I ignored his generous offer and headed to the counter where Esmerelda was waiting, a smile gracing those pillowy lips of hers.

"Where did you find that menace to society?" I asked, keeping my voice quiet enough it wouldn't carry.

Esmerelda recoiled. "Menace? Don't tell me you don't recognize Captain Cronkwhile, the most renowned oceanic mythographer of our time? His documentation on creatures of the deep is without equal. He just happened to be touring the country and chose my establishment for his presentation. It's been very good for business.

"Oh, I don't doubt that," I said. "He's certainly very good."

Esmerelda raised an eyebrow as she noted my sarcasm, but she didn't let it diminish her good spirits.

"I must thank you, Darius. Your mention of the Palace in the press conference at the judge's house was simply superb. The phone has been ringing off the hook all morning. I'm booked for the next month straight."

I returned the smile. "I'm nothing if not a man of my word, Esmerelda. Your information on Mooney was spot on. It was a ghost from his past seeking revenge, only he was far more living than dead, at least at the time."

The memory of wrestling with TJ for control of the gun caused my smile to fade. The whole affair seemed like a waste of a talented young life. I couldn't help but wonder what he might have accomplished if he'd set his mind to other pursuits.

"Lucky thing for that judge," Esmerelda replied. "Just in the nick of time. You have a talent for cutting things close."

"Better late than never," I replied, resting a hand on the counter between us.

"Don't tell me you've come to collect payment," Esmerelda said. "I was only joking about the mischief we might get up to together."

The colour rose in my cheeks. "Ah, no, that's not why I'm here."

My brain and mouth seemed to struggle to get themselves in sync. In spite of being two decades my senior, or at least that was my best guess, Esmerelda's playful flirting still managed to knock me off balance. I could never tell if she was serious or not.

No matter the case, I had no intention of taking her up on her distracting suggestions. Personally, I was looking for someone a little closer to my age.

"Such a shame," Esmerelda replied, running her finger down my chest. "I'm sure we'd make some wonderful memories together."

I straightened up, taking my chest out of reach as I tried to let her down gently. "I've never been in the habit of mixing business and pleasure."

Esmerelda sighed. "I suppose you're right, Darius, but if you're not here for a dalliance, what brings you to the Paranormal Palace today? If it's not the good captain, perhaps you need something else? His book could certainly come in useful in your line of work, though."

"I have enough works of fiction in my life already." I chuckled. "I'll leave those for the die-hard fans."

"Don't be so dismissive. One of these days, you're going to come face-to-face with a creature of the supernatural world and you're going to be found wanting for lack of preparation. It worries me."

"That makes two of us," I replied, not entirely joking.

I'd met plenty of two legged monsters in my lifetime, and I hadn't been prepared for any of them either.

"I've come with a very specific question," I said, trying to steer Esmerelda back to the matter of the Djinn. "One that is suited for your particular expertise."

Esmerelda perked up, her eyes sparkling as she sensed the opportunity to do business.

With her interest piqued, I tapped the counter. "Tell me, what do you know about the Djinn?"

Esmerelda's face twisted like she'd sucked a lemon. "Don't you name malicious spirits in my store."

"Why not?" I asked.

"They are dangerous creatures, Darius. Spirits that are not to be trifled with."

"What makes you say that?" I pressed. I needed more than that if I was going to catch Mary Baker.

"In times of old, the people looked to the Djinn for protection. They were seen as benevolent, helpful creatures, but as belief and culture shifted, their worship was seen as idolatry and any believers persecuted. Even their own people largely abandoned them. Now the Djinn roam the lands trading mischief for favors as they seek new disciples. Those who aren't careful can easily be ensnared in their wiles. In extreme cases, they might even possess your body and carry out heinous acts in your name. They destroy lives and reputations."

Well, that sounded entirely unpleasant.

"Have you heard of any being present here on the coast?" I asked.

"No, and I wouldn't entertain them here in my store. Not for a minute. Wiley, vicious, hurtful creatures. Why do you ask?"

"Someone or something is operating on the Gold Coast who refers to themselves as the Djinn. I merely wanted to know if you'd heard of them."

"No," Esmerelda replied, "but they sound like trouble to me.

Not nearly as helpful as I'd hoped, but something she'd said did stand out. If the Djinn was trying to gather acolytes, it might explain why she had coached TJ on committing his grisly murders, or why she'd guided the high priest of Beelzebub toward his human sacrifice. It was possible she was operating under the same broad parameters as the Djinn in mythology: selling mischief and granting wishes of revenge. I figured it was best to maintain the metaphor while talking to Esmerelda.

"I suspect one might be in town. If you hear anything, please let me know. And if you do make enquiries, be discreet."

"Discreet? I don't know that I'd dare invite the wrath of those creatures by inquiring after them. You ought to avoid them too. Take a different case. That would be my recommendation."

"What dangerous creatures might ye be talking about?" a gruff voice interjected. I turned to find Captain Cronkwhile approaching with all the confidence of a man who had no business joining our conversation but was determined to, nonetheless.

"Never you mind," I replied, not wanting to involve a stranger in my hunt. The last thing I needed was the clumsy captain bumbling after the Djinn.

"The Djinn," Esmerelda volunteered from behind the counter. "Can you imagine being reckless enough to pursue one?"

"Dangerous game, stranger. You can't spear a spirit and the creature will soon have you under her sway. Best keep something on your body with the name of God written on it. Only protection against the Djinn."

"Sound advice," Esmerelda said. "I have just the thing."

She reached beneath the counter and pulled out a crucifix on a gold chain.

"I'll consider that," I replied, hoping that agreeing with the captain would be the quickest course of ejecting him from the conversation. I didn't know him, and I certainly didn't trust him.

He persisted anyway.

"Captain Cronkwhile at your service." He stretched forth his hand. "And you are?"

I took his hand. "Darius Kane, Paranormal Investigator."

"A hunter by another title," the captain replied, shaking my hand. "As long as you're not competing for my prey, we'll get along fine."

"Prey?" I asked. "What exactly are you hunting?"

"Sirens and sea monsters, mostly," He said. "Have you not heard? They are right here under your very nose. Mermaids spotted in the bay, other shadowy creatures of the deep coming and going. This town is turning into a melting pot, and I mean to put a stop to it before lives are lost. Captain Cronkwhile does not leave innocent people exposed to these denizens of the deep."

"You're hunting mermaids?" I paused. In my mind's eye, I couldn't help but picture him chasing a red wig wearing cosplayer down the esplanade. "Like Ariel?"

"If only." The captain nudged me with his elbow. "No, the true creatures of the deep have sharp teeth, mangy hair, and a scaled tail. If you see one in the water, you best be out of it. Whatever you do, don't be lured deeper into the depths by their siren song."

I shook my head. Clearly, he was crackers, but it wouldn't endear me to Esmerelda if I offended her star speaker, so I nodded and thanked him for the advice.

"Esmerelda, always a pleasure to see you," I said. "If you hear anything on that other matter, be sure to let me know."

"Before you go." The captain placed a hand on my shoulder. "Are you sure I can't interest you in my book? If you are operating here on the coast, you'll no doubt be encountering all manner of sea creatures. The book could be of tremendous assistance. I'll even give you a discount. Call it a professional courtesy."

I entertained his pitch. "And how much might that be?"

"For a fellow adventurer, I'd do it for a hundred cash." He paused. "And an offer to split the bounty fifty-fifty if you ever find a beast worthy of both our attention."

He was an enterprising con artist.

"Let me think about it," I said. "I'll get back to you."

I headed for the door before I could be sold anything else. As I climbed the stairs, I thought of Esmerelda's words and the offer of the crucifix.

Could it be possible that a malicious spirit had possessed Mary Baker? Was some other power compelling her to commit these heinous acts? Or was that just the mind of a man who'd enjoyed lunch and was hoping there was some other explanation?

My mind lingered on that meal as I slipped through the open-air shopping plaza and into the alley where I'd left the tank.

I was so focused on the distracting memory of Mary Baker, I didn't see the meaty fist until it thundered into my cheek.

Kissing Concrete.
Monday, April 24th
1510hrs

IT WASN'T THE FIRST time I'd tasted the porous pâté of grit and grime that made up the pavement of the Gold Coast, and I sincerely doubted it would be the last.

Still, experience didn't make it any more enjoyable.

I saw stars, plenty of them, as my world whirled about me. I closed my eyes and rubbed my smarting jaw.

I opened my eyes to a pair of hulking legs on either side of my head. Even as my vision cleared my brain started stringing together a plan.

My attacker was bigger than I was, but I knew how to deal with brutes. Compromising any tender joint that bore his considerable weight would ensure he went down just as hard as I had. But first I needed to brace for the inevitable follow up. A kick to the ribs would be customary for a beatdown, but it never came.

My attacker was seemingly content with his opening gambit.

I reached out with one arm, but the giant backed away.

Pivoting, I used my momentum to rollover and push myself to my knees. I shoved myself off the concrete and got a good look at my attacker.

Attackers.

Three of them.

And faces that were familiar to me. Ones that I'd been hoping not to see again any time soon. The last time I'd laid eyes on them had been in James Mooney's garage.

I rubbed my jaw as I looked into the eyes of Benjamin Marino and his two rent-a-thugs. Brushing myself off, I cracked my neck and looked at the thug that struck me for explanation.

"I owed you that, for the garage," he said, a note of giddy triumph in his voice. "Now we're even."

"Even?" I repeated. "Blindside a man like that and you'll be lucky if you're not taking your meals through a sippy cup for the rest of your life."

"You think you're pretty tough, don't you?" The big bruiser chuckled. "Might want to get some ice for that jaw. It's gonna swell real nice."

I'd survived Hell Week in the SAS. It included a panoply of pain inflicted by the most sadistic bastards who'd ever worn the uniform. If a single punch in the face was enough to take me out of action, I'd be a disgrace to my regiment.

I considered my position while doing my best to suppress the urge to perform a much-needed lobotomy on the thug who'd slugged me.

There was a lot that differentiated me from the two bozos Marino carted everywhere as his hired muscle. They were big, brawny, and struggling to share a brain cell between them. I was smaller, perhaps, but where they looked dangerous, at least to someone with less training, I *was* dangerous. The military had made sure of that.

However, beating them senseless would see me back at the police station, this time in cuffs, so I held off.

"What do you want, Marino? I have places to be. Besides, I thought I was clear yesterday."

I'd threatened the kingpin in no uncertain terms. The fact he'd circled back meant he was either petty, proud, or stupid. Or perhaps he hadn't taken me seriously.

Marino scoffed. "Thanks for fitting me into your busy schedule."

I was overdue at my parents and this distraction was only making me later. I balled my hands into fists, as I readied for round two.

"Darius," Marino began, "yesterday you made a number of poorly conceived accusations against me, calling into question my reputation and character."

"A fine upstanding citizen like yourself," I muttered through my swelling lip. "Why would I ever do a thing like that?"

"My thoughts exactly." Marino ignored my sarcasm. "You made some assertions about Mr. Mooney's unfortunate demise. I do note that you didn't repeat any of those for the news stations yesterday. That was prudent on your part. But I wanted to come here to clarify matters. Ensure we understand each other."

"You could have sent a text," I replied. "The number is on the website."

"Then I wouldn't have been able to enjoy your apology in person." Marino shrugged. "I also find it's much easier to see eye-to-eye when you are standing face-to-face."

I tried not to let my jaw droop open; every motion smarted. Marino had to be kidding. If he thought I was going to apologize, he had another thing coming.

"If you're wanting that, you'll be here all day." I looked down as I ran my hand through my hair while using the motion to check behind me. "I certainly won't."

"You called me a murderer." Marino set his hands on his hips. "You impugned my reputation."

"Oh, please." I had to struggle not to choke on the words. "Don't play the innocent victim with me. So Mooney wasn't you. That doesn't make you a saint. Mooney dying while you wanted his property, it's not a big leap to make. I'm sure I wasn't the only one who thought it."

"Most people had the good sense to keep it to themselves," Marino replied. "You should learn from their wisdom."

"Jumping me in an alley isn't likely to change my opinion."

Marino looked at his thugs. "You know I could have these two rough you up. It'd be your word against ours. Even the Gold Coast's favourite freak wouldn't be able to win that courtroom over."

"You could try," I said, holding his stare, "but my patience is already worn out. If Beavis here throws that punch, I'm going to rip off his arm and beat you all to death with it."

"Are you quite finished?" Marino ground his teeth.

"No. I told you if you come after me again, I will tear down everything you have ever built. Your business, your property, your fledgling criminal empire. I am not to be trifled with."

"Neither am I, Darius. Let this serve as a reminder." Marino's voice rose. "You'll stay away from me and my interests, and you'll keep my name out of the press. If you do, we'll never have to speak again. But if I find you sniffing around my affairs, then we are going to have an even less pleasant conversation than we did today. Do you understand me?"

I took my time. I didn't want him to think I was intimidated by him. He'd also placed me in something of a moral quandary. I was almost certain the kingpin committed crimes on a daily basis. Maybe not Mooney, but his empire was certainly built on the blood and suffering of others. I couldn't exactly give him my word when I was almost certain to cross paths with him again.

"I'll do my best to leave you alone, Marino, but you need to stay well out of my way. Do that and we have a deal."

Marino puffed out his chest, straining at his suit coat. It wasn't what he'd asked for, but it was all he was getting.

It was possible that he was considering forcing the issue, but I was on my feet and already deciding which of his thuggish guards I would use as a human shield in the event he tried to draw that pistol I knew he was carrying without a permit.

"Let him go, boys. I'm sure Darius here has to pick up Scooby and the gang."

The thugs looked at each other, missing the reference entirely.

Where had he found those idiots? Did they not have a TV when they were kids? Or were they born in the gym and had never left it?

The thugs parted and I strode past them, down the alley and into the laneway where I'd parked the tank.

I glanced over my shoulder twice to make sure they weren't following. On reaching the tank, I checked my car for tampering. I doubted Marino's thugs had the knowledge to plant an explosive, but I was sure cutting some brake cables was a core skill on their CV.

An abundance of caution was in order, but I found nothing. Climbing up into the car, I fired up the engine and headed for my parents. The patio was going to be up by the time I got there, but I could bring a few refreshments for the boys, reward them for saving my dad from having a heart attack or nailing himself to a support beam.

Besides, speaking of Scooby Doo, I still needed to pick up Max, my own puppy partner. No doubt my parents would have spoiled him rotten, but I missed the little guy and was keen to catch up on a much-needed walk.

Making my way across town, I swung by the bottle-o and grabbed a slab for the boys, a liquid bribe to apologise for my tardiness and ensure they didn't hold it against me.

Then it was a quick jaunt into suburbia as I made a beeline for my parents' house.

As I drove, my mind played back the details of the last few days. The cult of Beelzebub were on the run, and now they had the police chasing them. At least it meant my family should be safe. Despite that, maybe I would see if Carl could crash on the couch at my parents while I ran the cult down. Just in case.

I was the last to arrive at my parents' house. I'd told them two o'clock, hoping the heat of the day would be passing, but still give us enough time to get the framework up before dinner.

It was pushing past four pm and I imagined most of the work had already been done. Still, better late than never. I grabbed a loaded toolbelt from the tank and strapped it around my waist.

I didn't bother with the front door; I just headed straight down the side yard. I'd barely made it through the gate when Max charged up to the fence.

"Hey, there little guy. How are you doing?"

Max shuffled excitedly side to side, barely able to contain himself as his tiny tail wagged furiously.

I scooped him up before continuing my journey around the house.

The patio frame was already up and in place, the supports bolted into the concrete and secured to the trusses that had nearly crushed Dad the other day.

While my father had the carpentry skills of a domestically challenged alpaca, Sonny, Carl, and Doug were a lot more practical. Carl had been a carpenter before he'd enlisted, and had returned to his trade when we'd gotten out. No doubt Carl had directed efforts and averted disaster.

"Look who's just in time to eat," Carl called from his place atop a ladder.

"That's about right," Sonny chimed in. "Ask us to come help and you show up in time for the barbecue."

"What else can we expect from Queensland's foremost paranormal detective?" Carl's voice was a perfect imitation of the news presenter on Channel 9. They were the only station that had criticized my work on the crypt killer's case.

"You know what they say about too many cooks spoiling the broth," I replied with a grin. "Besides, you guys look like you've got this well in hand. Maybe I'll come back in an hour to help turn the sausages?"

"Cheeky bugger," Doug called. "Get over here and lend us a hand with this sheet."

He was trying to wrestle a sheet of corrugated iron into place on the roof. His eyes played over my jaw, and he paused. "Oi, Darius. What happened to your face?"

I could feel the bruise forming already.

"Minor disagreement with a door," I replied, not wanting to bring up Marino and dampen the mood. "I figured you lot would be done already. How far off are we?"

"The nerve on him," Carl huffed. "We've been down a set of hands. I hope you at least brought some beverages to atone for your tardiness."

"There's a carton in the car, boys. Payment for a job well done."

Carl grinned as he tightened the fitting he was working on. "Then all is forgiven. It's the little things that let us know you care."

Setting Max down, I got to work. With the four of us in place, construction moved even faster.

Carl sidled up beside me. "Most doors don't have four knuckles. Who'd you offend to get that shiner?"

"Ruffled a few feathers on the Mooney case. Nothing I can't handle."

"You're getting old, Darius." Carl put his arm around my shoulders. "A few feathers, you say? There was a time it would have taken an angry mob to land a blow like that on you."

He wasn't wrong, but I liked to think it was because I was distracted by the Djinn, not simply getting old and slow.

"Cowards jumped me when I came around the corner. This was the only one they got in." I didn't bother to add that it was the only punch they'd thrown. It seemed like an unnecessary detail.

"Good," Carl said. "So nothing to worry about then?"

"I don't think so," I replied. "But if you haven't got any plans, would you mind crashing here for a few nights? Just in case? I need someone to watch out for them while I run something down."

Carl held my gaze. "You'd tell me if you needed help, wouldn't you?"

I clapped him on the back. "Of course, buddy. Just worried about those kidnappers from the church yesterday. Police are on the prowl, but they haven't scooped them all up yet. Shouldn't take long, a day or two perhaps."

"You got it, mate. I could use a home-cooked meal or two, anyway."

My father fired up the BBQ, which was probably the safest place for him, and the rest of us worked to fit the last few sheets on the roof.

When the patio was finally done, I did a quick once around to ensure the supports were firmly fastened. Dad wouldn't want it to fall down with the first stiff south-easterly that blew through the place.

Max played around my feet as I did my final inspection of the patio my father had talked about putting in for the better part of my lifetime.

Carl went to grab a fresh beer from the cooler, and Doug piled onions onto the BBQ to help my dad.

I was heading back to the tank to deposit the tools when Sonny stepped in front of me.

"Darius," he began. There was an awkwardness in his tone. His shoulders were slouched, and he was staring down at his feet. It was an unusual look on the big Samoan. I hadn't seen him this dejected since he'd borrowed his mother's car without asking and gotten a hiding for it in the tenth grade.

"What's wrong, mate? You don't seem yourself."

Sonny didn't meet my gaze. "I, uh, was wondering if you could look into something for me?"

Sonny wasn't in the habit of asking for favors. In fact, he'd helped me on two cases and never asked for a thing in return.

"Of course I can. What's bothering you?"

The creases in his brow deepened.

"I know it's not your normal sort of case, mate. But I think I'm in serious trouble."

Case by Case. Monday, April 24th 1810hrs

I WASN'T YOUR STOCK standard private investigator for a reason.

Namely, I didn't want to spend all my days chasing cheating husbands and children that had run away from home.

It wasn't that I didn't like to help, but that market was a little crowded and I didn't like price wars. Invariably, you end up working for little more than minimum wage until you earn a reputation.

When you're a paranormal detective, there is a whole lot less competition. Largely because most people who would be your competition aren't willing to endure the scrutiny of the public to help those struggling with paranormal problems.

That said, I could see the weight resting on my friend's shoulders. Sonny was family to me, and I wasn't about to leave him swinging in the breeze.

"Tell me what's going on, buddy. How can I help?"

"Well, it's about my daughter, Leilani."

My mind raced with possibilities. A sixteen-year-old girl could get herself into all kinds of mischief on the Gold Coast.

"What trouble is she in?" I asked, careful not to raise my voice. If Sonny had cornered me on my own, he didn't want the others to know what was going on.

"None at all," Sonny replied, "You know her mother. She is not the sort to tolerate any foolishness. Leilani is actually doing really well, killing it in school and on a co-curricular front."

"Okay…" I couldn't see the problem.

"Leilani has always been a really talented swimmer. At first, we didn't realise how good she was, but with the school's encouragement, we've been trying to get her ready for professional competition."

"She's that good?" I asked before kicking myself for not knowing more about my friend's children.

"She is, and getting better every day, but her mother and I can only help so much. We figured she could be even better with a little training and some refinement on her technique."

"So, you went looking for a trainer?" I asked, suspecting that was where the trouble lay.

Sonny nodded. "Leilani was really keen to pursue it professionally. So we checked out a bunch of coaches. There were a lot of choices, but we wanted the best, so we settled on Kyle Cruz. He was an Olympian himself, and he runs a high-profile swim school here on the coast. We figured he was our best chance, given he already works with the national teams. So we put in an application."

The name rang a bell. In the back of my mind, I felt like I'd heard something about him on the news recently but couldn't put my finger on it.

"Kyle Cruz, Olympian. I'm with you. Did she get in?"

Sonny ran a big hand through his thick mop of hair.

"We interviewed, went through the application process, and everything was going well. They gave us the fee schedule and I almost passed out."

"That much, huh?"

Sonny nodded. "It was considerable. But my wife and I thought she deserved every chance to pursue her dream. So we emptied our savings and we gave it to them to cover the next two years' coaching. There was a discount if we paid upfront."

"How much are we talking?" I asked, bracing for the bad news.

"Twenty-five thousand." Sonny's voice was little more than a whisper.

My eyes just about rolled out of their sockets. I could start to see where the stress was coming from.

"And now you've had a chance to think about it, you want out?" I asked.

"It's not that," Sonny replied. "When we started the process, everything was above board. But since then, there has been a lot about him in the press. Some sort of court case. At first, they said the claims were just nonsense. My wife and I were starting to reconsider and when we reached out to the school this week, they said we'd have to talk to Kyle direct."

I wasn't seeing the problem. Sonny had his own orbit. Most people sitting across the table from him would likely give the friendly giant whatever he asked for. I doubted Kyle would be able to scare him out of a refund.

"And how did that go?"

"It didn't." Sonny looked crestfallen. "We were texting back and forth to organise a time, but he never showed up for the meeting. It was yesterday and now we can't reach him. His phone has gone dead, and his office is telling us they don't know where he is."

Well, that certainly complicated matters. "And you think he's taken the money and run?"

"That's what we were thinking," Sonny replied. "And we really can't afford that, Darius. Not with things being the way they are. If Leilani isn't going to be coached, we need it back to help her buy her first car, man. I don't suppose you could help us track him down?"

If Sonny were any old client off the street, I would have thought twice. In anything but the slowest of weeks, a con artist coach wouldn't have rated a mention. But for Sonny, there was no question in my mind.

"Of course, man. I'll start asking some questions, see what I can find out."

Sonny's sagging shoulders perked up a little, and he managed to smile. "If you need an extra set of hands, don't hesitate to ask."

"It's the least I can do," I replied. And I meant it.

Even with his life savings swinging in the breeze, Sonny had still showed up to help erect a patio. That was the kind of friend he was. I would run down his wayward coach if it was the last thing I did.

My week was getting fuller by the moment. I'd been hoping to go after the Djinn, but I needed to look into Sonny's problems now as well. Not to mention, somewhere out there, Graeme Bilson was on the run, and every minute the police got a little closer to him. I was going to have to make him a priority, but I had no idea where to go next.

"I'll start looking tomorrow and let you know what I find."

Sonny gripped his ginger beer. "Thanks, man, I really appreciate it. Lucille will too."

"Happy wife, happy life," I answered, not that I really had any experience on that front.

"Ain't that the truth," Sonny replied. "I wouldn't want to be Kyle Cruz if she catches up to him. She's just about ready to burst a blood vessel."

"Well, see that she holds her horses just a little while longer. It's only been a day. There might be a perfectly reasonable explanation as to why he hasn't answered the phone."

"And if there isn't?"

"Then he could be dangerous, which is all the more reason for her to leave him to us."

"What are *we* going to do?"

I imagined Sonny had a few thoughts on that front but was being good enough to follow my lead.

"Well, we run him down, find the weasel, and squeeze him until your cash falls out."

"You can do that?" Sonny asked.

"Not legally," I replied, "but we'll encourage him vociferously."

Sonny took a deep breath. "Don't get yourself in any strife."

We parted ways and on my way to the car I texted Holly Draper. Perhaps she would be able to turn up something on the missing cultist.

A missing swim coach was a distraction I could ill afford, but until I could find a lead on Graeme, I wasn't making any progress on that front. I may as well devote my attention to ensuring my friends weren't taken advantage of.

If I couldn't find Bilson, I was going to have to get down into the weeds and try to run down Mary Baker's costume, or perhaps look into the car TJ used to smuggle himself into Mooney's garage. If I was right, it was possible Mary Baker had been the driver.

It wasn't much, but it was something.

I put away my tools, locked the tank, and made my way to the back yard. The boys were restoring the outdoor dining setting while my dad was carrying a tray laden with steaks, sausages, and onions.

My mother emerged from the house with a bowl of potato salad in one hand, and a garden salad in the other. When it came to entertaining, even if it was just me and my mates, she did not know how to take it easy.

She set the salads down and made a show of examining the patio.

"Look at all this shade," she gushed. I told your father he could do it. Never doubted him for a minute."

I couldn't help but laugh. It was my mother's concern that had got me involved in the first place. That and seeing Dad handle a circular saw and knowing it was an ambulance visit waiting to happen.

I sat down at one end of the table as everybody else claimed their seats.

Mom offered grace, and then it was on, everybody heaping a scrumptious portion of the fresh BBQ onto their plates. I took the first sausage, cut it up into smaller pieces, and slipped it down into Max's bowl at my feet.

"Who is a good boy?" I said as I ruffled his coat.

Max tucked in, brushing against my hand from time to time to ensure I didn't slack in my duties.

Looking down the table made me grateful. Not everyone would be willing to spend their public holiday putting up a patio, but they'd done it without complaint and largely without me.

You couldn't find three guys like Carl, Sonny, and Doug. At a glance they looked as if they couldn't have less in common. Carl, the handsome womanizing ex-serviceman who liked to surf. Sonny, the friendly giant who was equally happy crushing you like a bug on the rugby field, as he was singing in church on a Sunday. And Doug, who looked like a runt next to the three of us, but what he lacked in stature he made up for in loyalty and spirit. Doug and I had been friends since school, and there was nothing he wouldn't do for his mates.

I cut into my steak, dipped a piece in the BBQ sauce, and popped it into my mouth. It was just what I needed after the day I'd had.

I chased it with another bite and then headed to the kitchen to fix myself a rum and coke. As I set my glass on the counter and opened the cupboard, looking for Dad's stash of Bundaberg rum, my mobile started ringing.

Hoping it was Holly, I reached for my phone.

No such luck. I didn't recognize the number and it wasn't stored in my contacts. I set the phone on the kitchen bench. If it was important, they would call back.

STOKES,STEVEHIGGS

I placed a handful of ice cubes in the glass then filled about a third of the glass with rum and topped up the rest with coke.

The phone rang again. Same number.

They were certainly persistent.

My gut told me the call was likely to interrupt a perfectly good dinner.

I weighed my choices. The Casper Killer would bring all sorts of attention, perhaps it would be a new case. A paying one.

I was already busy with the Djinn and now Sonny's con artist coach, but someone had to actually pay me if I wanted to keep the lights on.

Ignoring my gut, I answered the call.

"Darius Kane, Blue Moon Investigations. How can I help?"

"Oh, Darius," a deep voice played down the line. "Geoff Consella, from Consella, Santini, and Black. How are you?"

The name wasn't familiar to me. As far as I could tell, I'd never met him before in my life, though the way he rattled off names made me feel like I ought to have. Consella, Santini, and Black. That sounded like an accounting practice or a law firm, if ever I'd heard of one.

"Hi Geoff, what can I do for you?"

"I was looking to hire you for a case." Geoff paused, the first hint of uncertainty creeping in. "I, uh, wasn't sure of the protocol, so I thought it would be best to call you directly."

"I'm just sitting down for dinner, Geoff. Any chance I could give you a call later to discuss it?"

62

Geoff's breathing filtered down the phone line as he considered the question for what felt like an eternity. "I'd rather we discussed it in person. Any chance I could prevail on you to swing by for a chat?"

House calls weren't particularly uncommon in my line of work. Often, the house was the root cause of the paranormal phenomenon perplexing my clients.

"Sure thing. I can come by in the morning and we can discuss it," I replied, picking up my rum and coke.

"No," Geoff answered sharply. "I mean, it's quite time sensitive, Darius. I was hoping I could prevail on you to come by this evening. Now, even. You mentioned you were about to sit down for dinner. I could have my chef whip up something for us both."

Private chefs were not common in these parts and suggested Geoff was doing pretty well for himself. Still, I wasn't about to walk out on dinner with my friends and family.

"I can't. I have obligations here. Tomorrow is the best I can do."

"I'll triple your rate," Geoff replied. "If you come by tonight. Otherwise, I'll have to call someone else. Don't make me settle for second best, Darius."

As far as I knew, I was the only game in town. I wasn't sure if he was bluffing but triple my going rate would certainly help keep the lights on.

"Where abouts are you?" I asked, glancing down at my watch.

"Sovereign Island," he answered. "I can text you the address."

Sovereign Island. Well, he could certainly afford my rate. I wasn't in the habit of taking advantage of folks, but something told me Geoff wasn't looking for his next dollar.

"Send it through. I'll be there at eight-thirty," I answered. "That really is the best I can do."

"I'll take it," Geoff answered. "See you then."

I hung up the phone and headed back to the dinner table. After missing out on most of the work, I knew there was no way I could skip out on dinner. Mr. Consella was just going to need to wait a few hours.

I looked at the mountain of food in front of me. I was going to need to go a little easy if I planned to eat with Geoff as well. As I took a sip from my rum and coke, I couldn't help but wonder what was so urgent he was willing to triple my rate just to speak to me tonight?

Second Dinners are for Winners. Monday, April 24th 2010hrs

Sovereign Island was one of the ritzier suburbs on the Gold Coast where anything with a view of the water was expensive enough you would need to sell your firstborn just to consider it.

But there was a difference in class between those properties that could actually see the ocean or the Broadwater, which were as desirable as they were expensive, and those that were on the canal.

Developers had long since realized that if they diverted water from the natural rivers and watercourses to create more canals, it equaled more expensive waterfront property for them to sell.

Sovereign Island was one such canal-created estate. As I drove through the streets, I admired the expensive real estate on either side of the road, each of them with their own private piece of waterfront. Living here spoke volumes to the net worth of my next potential employer.

Ultimately, it was the main reason I'd taken the appointment. Though I was busy trying to work out the identity of the Djinn, I couldn't afford to knock back paying work. Particularly not with a client that had this sort of cash.

I reached the address and parked out front. It was a massive property, all rendered stone and tinted glass. My tank looked out of place in a suburb filled with Porsches and Ferraris.

I parked in the driveway of the expansive two-story house. The whole property had been finished in white render and blue accents that gave off a Mediterranean vibe.

"I could suffer through living here." I chuckled, just a little envious.

Jumping out of the tank, I fastened a leash to Max's harness and set him down.

"On your best behavior, please."

Max wagged his tail as if to say that much was obvious and fell in behind me as I headed for the door. He sniffed the path, then made his way along the edge of the garden, a scent catching his nose before he joined me at the door.

The property's entryway was a three-meter-high wall of tinted glass, stretching from floor to ceiling. With the tint, I couldn't make out any of the house's interior. Doubtless they could see out, but I couldn't see in.

The doorbell had a camera built into it. I pressed the button and waited.

"Hello?" A gruff voice filtered through the speaker; I recognized Geoff's voice from his call.

"Geoff, it's Darius Kane."

"Ah Darius, I'll be right there."

The massive glass door swung inward courtesy of a large, motorized hinge. In the doorway stood a man in dress pants, a long sleeve shirt, and expensive brown wingtip dress shoes. They were of the sort that looked hand-stitched, a lost art these days, and expensive when you could find it.

Geoff was perhaps five feet, four inches tall. Not really what I'd expected from the deep gruff voice on the phone. He wore suspenders and had a freshly shaved head with a thick red beard that was neatly cropped several inches below his chin. He was impeccably groomed, but the day's tie had been discarded somewhere along the way.

"Mr. Kane, lovely to meet you. Thank you for coming on such short notice."

I shook his hand and examined the red mustache beneath his nose. There was no residue there. A promising sign.

Cocaine usage was particularly prevalent in the legal profession. Men with money working in a high stress environment tended to indulge and that was the vice of choice. At least it had been when I was at university. The law school at my university had been famous for the devil's dandruff.

If Geoff was seeing paranormal phenomena, my first concern was whether or not he was indulging in the potent powder that might produce a degraded mental state.

"It's my pleasure, Geoff. You seemed quite beside yourself on the phone. How can I be of service?"

"Not here in the hall." Geoff waved me into the house. "Come, I have dinner on the table. Let us talk over a meal."

I entered the home.

"Who's this?" Geoff asked, fixing Max with a look that settled somewhere between interest and skepticism.

"This is my partner, Max. A Beagle's nose has more than forty times the scent receptors of a human. You wouldn't believe how often it comes in helpful."

"Very good," Geoff replied. "I'll take all the help I can get."

He led the way down the hall. It was tiled with porcelain and buffed so bright I suspected if the lights weren't so dim, I would be able to see my reflection in them. We passed a number of rooms, including a bathroom and guest room, before entering a large kitchen and dining area. The dining area opened through a set of bifold doors onto a patio with a spectacular view of the Broadwater. An expensive boat was moored at a private pier.

I wondered when he had the time to take it out. Working to maintain this sort of lifestyle had to be all-consuming.

Geoff pointed to the glass dining table. "Pull up a seat, Darius. The chef is just plating up now."

I'd gone easy at the BBQ in preparation, but I was still going to need to pace myself. I pulled out a chair and slid into it, settling Max down on the floor beside me. In the kitchen, a young chef, perhaps in his late twenties, prepared a pair of rib eye steaks, before setting them onto two plates.

Beside the steaks was a gentle heap of mashed potatoes, an array of baby carrots, and squash.

Geoff slid into the seat opposite me, and the chef carried the two plates to the table.

"What would you like to drink, Darius?" Geoff asked.

I wasn't used to being wined and dined, but with my propensity to work nights, I figured stocking up would come in handy. I'd gone light on at the BBQ just in case, and that was looking to be a good call.

"Just juice for me, thanks. Apple, if you've got it."

"Make that two apple juices, Barry. Break out the good stuff from Stanthorpe, would you?"

The chef re-emerged moments later with a pair of glasses brimming with a dark reddish amber juice. Stanthorpe was known for its produce, and I'd had the good fortune of drinking some freshly pressed apple juice from there on a camping trip when I was a kid. It had been delicious.

He set them down, and Geoff gestured to the plate. "By all means, Darius. Dig in."

Barry hovered by the table as I picked up my knife and fork. I was a little hesitant to eat before the host. Not that I thought Geoff was trying to poison me, I just didn't want to convey the image of a starving PI desperate for his next job.

"Shall I fetch something for your partner, sir?" Barry asked as I was deciding where to start.

I looked down at Max, who'd already gorged himself at the BBQ. "What do you think, Max? Still hungry, buddy?"

Max let out a single bark.

"He's a big fan of sausages, if you have any."

"Have any sausages." Barry chuckled. "Please, what sort of kitchen do you think I run? I believe I have some pork and honey back there somewhere. Perfect blend of sweet and savory for our friend."

"That would be splendid."

Barry fired up the pan and in no time, the smell of sausages wafted from the kitchen.

I cut into my steak, a perfect medium well done, and looked across the table. "You mentioned there was a matter you wanted me to investigate?"

I held the knife and fork ready to eat, but I was still waiting on the host. Geoff plucked up his own utensils, and sliced a strip off the edge of the eye fillet. Pushing it through the sauce, a mushroom gravy by the look of it, he popped it in his mouth.

Geoff clearly wasn't the sort to be hurried along.

I slid one of the baby carrots through the mashed potato and devoured it while I waited for him to answer.

Geoff chewed loudly, staring down at the table between us. He seemed to be struggling to find the right words. An unusual conundrum for a lawyer.

"Darius, you're a man with a growing reputation for finding the truth of things."

"Well, that's being a little more polite than most put it," I replied, cutting into my steak. I wanted to challenge him a little, get a bit of a feel for the man. "Most people tend to call me a charlatan or a con artist. At least until they need me."

"I'm a lawyer, Darius. I've been called all that and worse. It doesn't change the truth of the matter. You have a knack for getting to the bottom of unusual phenomena."

I nodded. "I've had a number of high-profile cases recently. Most of my clients have unusual problems and are looking for someone who is willing to give them the time of day and the benefit of the doubt, so that they can be solved."

"Precisely." Geoff slapped the table with one hand. "An open mind, that's what I liked about you on that interview on the weekend. Everyone else thought that Draper woman was mad, ghosts and killers and the like. But you got to the bottom of it and saved Judge Saunders in the process. It was the judge who recommended you to me."

"Really? You know the judge?"

"Occupational hazard," Geoff replied. "I'm a criminal defense attorney, Darius."

That explained the lavish lifestyle. Criminals, certainly those who operated at the more successful end of the spectrum, tended to pay well to avoid the consequences of their *alleged* actions.

"And exactly what did the judge think I could do for you?" I enquired.

If Geoff was used to dealing with criminals on a daily basis I couldn't help but wonder what it would take to unsettle him.

Barry popped a dish down in front of Max. There were two sausages that had been carefully cut into narrow slices.

Max dug into his second dinner, and I nodded my thanks, still waiting for his boss to share what was on his mind.

"Well, Darius, I saw something the other night. I haven't been able to get it out of my mind and I need you to look into it for me."

"That's all rather vague," I answered with a smile. "You're going to have to give me more than that, Geoff. What are we talking? Ghost? Sasquatch? "

Geoff took a long sip of his juice. He didn't present as the sort to subscribe to paranormal problems. But then again, most folks didn't run around with their beliefs tattooed on their forehead. I'd met one or two actual tinfoil-hat-wearing loonies, but Geoff struck me as someone with full control of his faculties.

Perhaps that was why he was so bothered. Having seen something that challenged his worldview, he needed me to disprove it. As I spooned a dollop of mashed potato into my mouth, I savored it.

"It's the truffle oil." Geoff gestured with his knife. "Really elevates the dish."

I was lucky if I got the time to mash potatoes when I cooked. I certainly didn't have those kinds of condiments around the house. It explained why my potatoes tasted like sadness, and these tasted like they had been basted with MSG and heroin.

I scooped up another spoonful of the heavenly goodness. Whether I took the job or not, I was going to be well fed.

"I'm just going to come out and say it, Darius. No need to judge me. Everyone else already has."

"I don't judge my clients," I replied. "Not my job. I fix problems, not make them worse."

Geoff set down his utensils and folded his arms, resting them on the glass tabletop.

"The other night I was working late in the office. It was just after midnight. I'd gotten up from the desk and was looking down at the river, like I often do. I spotted a shape moving up the river. At first, I thought it was a dolphin on account of the tail fins. But when she surfaced, I realized it was a woman, with a tail. A mermaid, Darius. Full head of brackish red hair and everything."

I did my best to keep my expression neutral. I wasn't sure what I was expecting, but that wasn't it. Geoff didn't seem to be the sort to believe in fairy tale creatures.

In fact, his legal mind should have defaulted to rationalisation. For him to have gone to the effort to drag me over for this conversation, he had to be serious.

"You haven't laughed in my face like everyone else," Geoff mused out loud. "I suppose that's a good start."

"I'm not in the habit of mocking my clients," I replied, slicing open a squash. Not my favourite vegetable but whatever seasoning Barry had used made them smell enticing. "Tell me more. I assume you got more than a passing glance at the creature?"

"I saw her clear as I'm looking at you right now. An honest to goodness mermaid."

"If you don't mind me asking, what did it look like?"

Geoff was the second person to mention mermaids to me today. This couldn't be a coincidence.

"Bright red hair, pale skin. She rested in the water but when she saw me watching her, she dived back under the surface. I got a parting glance of that great big scaly tail, and she was gone."

As far as I could tell, he certainly believed his story was true. Still, I needed to filter out other possibilities.

"I don't want to upset you," I began. "But you wouldn't have been indulging in anything at the office, would you? A late drink, or perhaps something stronger?"

"Totally sober," Geoff replied. "Have been for years. I know what it sounds like, but I know what I saw. It wasn't a fish or a dolphin or some kind of shark. She looked like a very human woman, but for the massive greenish gray tail propelling her through the water."

I thought back to my emails. There had been someone else talking about a mermaid sighting. In the hubbub with the cult of Beelzebub, I had ignored it. Now I had a second potential witness.

I had never chased a mermaid before and frankly, I wasn't sure where to begin. I imagined that was going to depend on what Geoff wanted from me.

"What would you like me to do about it, Geoff? It doesn't seem like the mermaid caused you any problems. Perhaps we wait and see if it returns?"

I didn't want to knock back a paying job, and clearly Geoff had the cash to pay. But I wasn't sure what he was expecting me to do for him. Proving a magical creature's existence wasn't going to be easy, and I could be at it for weeks or months with nothing to show for it.

I could see Geoff getting tired of that fast, and tired lawyers grow litigious.

Besides, I still had to look into the missing swimming coach and chase down the Djinn. I wasn't entirely convinced I could do anything for Geoff.

The ocean was a large place and while my position on the paranormal was well established, I couldn't definitively speak as to what did or did not exist in its depths. I was a little curious, but it could very well turn into a wild goose chase.

"I want you to find me evidence of the creature's existence," Geoff replied. "I made the mistake of telling others what I saw. My partners at work, other colleagues. They all think I'm crazy."

That didn't particularly surprise me. I'd garnered that reaction from plenty of folks.

"They think I'm having a nervous breakdown. Look at me, Darius." Geoff pointed to himself. "Do I appear to be anything other than a man of sound mind?"

I found myself nodding. "If you're a loony tune, you certainly have me fooled."

"Can you help me?" he asked. "If the partners at the office think I am nuts, they are going to put me on leave. It will be the end of my career. People don't hire insane defense attorneys."

I hadn't really challenged him yet, and if I was going to work for Geoff, I wanted to know how he reacted when he didn't get his way. It was all well and good to wine and dine me when he wanted something, but what could I expect if I couldn't find his mermaid?

It was entirely likely that I could spend weeks chasing his mermaid and find nothing.

I wanted to get a bit of a taste for what I might be in store for when nothing showed up.

"No, they usually hire shrewd and devious bastards with an excellent understanding of the law and the loopholes available to reduce one's likelihood of ending up in one of our state's finer penal facilities."

Geoff's lips creased upward into a grin. "I'll take that as a compliment."

Of course he would. Lawyers were great at seeing things the way they wanted to.

"You want me to root around in the bay, find evidence of a mermaid. Mind you, no definitive evidence has been turned up in human history. Sightings, certainly, but never anything that can be corroborated with hard evidence. This could be a wild goose chase, Geoff."

"I know what I saw," he said. "The river and Broadwater aren't that big, and others have seen things too. I'm not crazy, and I need you to prove it."

What would it hurt to look around? Particularly, if I was doing so on Geoff's time.

I shrugged. "As long as you understand that I charge by the hour, whether we find your mermaid or not."

"You provide me with a report of what you've done, and I'll pay you regardless. I'm not a no win, no fee lawyer and I don't expect you to work for free, Mr. Kane."

I leaned back in my chair. "In that case, I'll start tomorrow. Could you provide me with the address of your office? I'm going to need to start there."

"I'll send you through the location of our office, along with the GPS coordinates of the place I believe I saw the creature. Like I said, it was just after midnight. So you might want to search at night."

"Naturally." I wasn't really expecting a mermaid sighting to have taken place in the broad light of day. If it did, there would have been thousands of witnesses. The Broadwater was the most trafficked piece of ocean on the east coast of Queensland.

"I'll send you through my contract," I replied. "It's hourly plus disbursements. Nothing you wouldn't have seen the last time your firm hired a private investigator."

"That's the second time you've mentioned your rate." Geoff replied. "Does it look like I'm hard up for a dollar, Mr. Kane? Let me put your mind at ease. If you find the mermaid, I'll pay your disbursements, your hourly rate, and a finder's fee of ten thousand dollars. Will that help raise the priority of my case?"

Ten thousand dollars would go a long way to establishing my new business. It would also help me fund my search for the Djinn.

"To the very top of the list," I replied, confident that was what he wanted to hear.

"That's more like it," he said. "Then we have a deal."

We finished the delicious meal and a baked cheesecake for dessert. The entire affair had me convinced I ought to work the case if for no other reason than to come by and provide regular updates. Barry was a treasure, and a wizard in the kitchen.

When I was done, I rose from my seat.

"I appreciate your time, Geoff. You send those details and the signed contract, and I'll get to work. If she's out there, I'll find her."

"You'll let me know the moment you have something?"

"Absolutely," I replied. "I hate to dine and dash, but I still have a few matters to see to this evening."

"The number I gave you is my private mobile." Geoff stood up. "Please don't contact me at the office on this matter. They record everything."

Of course they do. Because when you're representing a bundle of crooks, you need a record to protect yourself.

"On your mobile, only," I replied. "Understood."

Geoff walked Max and me back to the door and saw us out.

I lifted Max into his seat before pulling myself up into mine. As Geoff shut the front door, I stared at the steering wheel.

"Darius, do you realise what this means?" I muttered. "You're actually going to have to hunt a mermaid."

Or whatever it is Geoff had seen and thought was a mermaid.

I didn't have the faintest clue where I was going to begin, other than doing laps of the Broadwater after midnight and hoping for something. I was going to have to dig up the old email and find out what the other witness had seen.

I fired up the engine and pulled out onto the street. As I crossed the bridge out of Sovereign Island, I looked out at the dark waters of the Nerang River that became the Broadwater and wondered if a mermaid could really be in there.

A shiver ran down my spine as I realized that those depths could hide all manner of dangers.

What waited for me in the dark waters?

Welcome guest or troublesome pest? Tuesday, April 25th O635hrs.

I NEVER DID LIKE being woken by the doorbell. The last time it happened, the good detectives of the homicide department were at my door. The fact Max wasn't going ballistic likely meant it wasn't Detective Hart.

I clambered from the bed and pulled a set of jeans over my boxers. Snatching a t-shirt off the pile of clean laundry, I pulled it over my head on the way to the door.

Max stood at the front window, his front paws up on the sill, his tail wagging as he peered through it.

I took a quick look through the peephole.

Holly Draper.

Her unannounced arrival on my doorstep filled me with mixed feelings. When you are in the military, seldom was the presence of reporters a good thing. We'd either been babysitting them under the most trying of circumstances so that the folks at home understood the reality of the conflict we were fighting, or we were extracting those who had carelessly gotten themselves into trouble pursuing a headline story in an unstable region. Neither had particularly endeared the profession to me. The scandals they generally hunted for only made a difficult job even harder. If people were acting unethically, they ought to be held accountable, but seldom did reporters seem to consider the consequences of what they published. At least, that was how it had seemed to a grunt like me.

Holly, however, seemed to be a cut above the pack. She had been instrumental in helping to catch the Casper Killer. And while that story had no doubt furthered her career, her timely intervention had helped us save the life of a sitting judge.

There was also the fact the story she wrote was quite flattering to me and my fledgling business. I made the mistake of opening my inbox during my all-nighter at the office and found hundreds of emails, everything from ghouls to werewolves and bigfoot sightings. The story had broken at prime time and business, or at least potential business, was flooding in. I would have my pick of cases for weeks to come.

Holly Draper rang the doorbell again.

"Darius," she called. "I know you're in there. I've already called the office."

I looked down at my crumpled T-shirt and jeans. There wasn't anything between Holly and me, but I was hardly putting my best foot forward.

As my mother had so aptly pointed out, Holly was rather attractive. A little young, perhaps, but she was bright and relentless. Both traits I admired, like that mattered. She would be out of my league on a good day, and today we weren't even in the same solar system.

I unlocked the door and pulled it open, leaving the screen door between us.

"Hey Holly, what can I do for you?" I asked, trying not to squint at the early morning sun blazing behind her.

Holly looked me up and down. "Good morning, Princess. What on earth happened to you?"

I looked down at my watch. It was barely after six-thirty, and she was judging me.

"It's a long story," I replied as I pushed open the screen door. "Come on in. Sorry about the mess."

Holly stepped over a pile of recycling I'd been meaning to take out to the wheelie bin. "You're a busy man, Darius. Who has the time to worry about housekeeping when you're catching killers?"

"I was talking about me," I chuckled, looking around the house. "It never gets much better than this."

"Don't sweat it," Holly replied. "You should see mine. I barely set foot in it but to sleep. It looks like a bomb hit it."

I very much doubted that, but it was kind of her to say.

Max circled around her feet until Holly gave in and stooped down to pat him.

"Hey there." Holly scratched him behind the ears as she looked up at me. "I'm sure a little raucous celebration was in order, but you look like hell."

"Believe it or not, no alcohol was involved in this particular disaster." I gestured down at my disheveled state. "It happened all on its own. I know what you're thinking. I'm a man of many talents."

Holly gave me the sort of look mothers give their adult children who still live at home a decade after they should have moved out. "Not even one drink?"

I let out a sigh. "Okay, so maybe there was a rum and coke, but believe it or not, the rest of this is natural talent."

"That's some talent." Holly laughed.

Max nudged her hand. She'd been remiss in her duties and needed reminding.

"Who is this adorable little fellow?" Holly asked as she resumed patting him. My partner shuffled happily as he wagged his tail in approval.

"This is Max, an otherwise excellent judge of character," I replied, eyeing my puppy partner. "Traitor."

Max danced giddily. Here she was making fun of me, and Max was selling me out for an ear scratch.

"Don't worry about him, Max." Holly grinned. "He's just grumpy he woke up on the wrong side of the bed. He'll come around."

I tried to shake myself out of my sleep-induced stupor.

"So the story went well then?" I asked.

"Splendidly. Thanks for that, by the way. My editor has been singing my praises all weekend."

I sat down at the table. "That's good news. You've certainly earned it."

Holly scooped Max up and sat down opposite me. "That's kind of you to say, but I'm still surprised you didn't sell me out to curry favor with the cops. That Detective Hart is not my biggest fan."

"Well, that's not my problem." I shrugged. "I told you I'd do it, and I'm a man of my word."

"I'm discovering that." Holly's lips settled into a smile. "It's a refreshing change."

I tried not to linger too long on those inviting lips.

Don't get distracted, Darius.

I raised my gaze back to her eyes. "Holly, I don't want this to come out wrong, but why are you here?"

"A gal can't just come by and thank you for getting her out of the doghouse with her editor?"

My stomach rumbled loudly. I might have had two dinners, but I was already getting peckish.

"The Casper Killer story sent the paper's ratings through the roof, and we've seen more traffic than we have in months. So I just wanted to say, thank you."

"You're welcome," I answered.

Her gratitude was a welcome change of pace from most of the people I had worked with since starting my little agency. The customers were grateful, but authorities and the media treated me with a healthy dose of skepticism. I couldn't blame them. Most of them thought I was bilking people out of their hard-earned cash when all I really wanted to do was solve their problems, paranormal or otherwise.

"You didn't have to come all the way over here. A text would have sufficed. Unless you have a bacon and egg muffin in that handbag of yours, then you'd be my hero.

Holly's smile got a little wider.

It was one of those cocky grins when someone knows something you don't. I was still waking up and clearly well behind the eight-ball.

Holly ran a hand through her hair, pushing it back over her shoulder. "I don't, sorry. But I've always been a big believer in the notion that actions speak louder than words. You helped me with the Casper Killer. I want to help you."

My mind raced. What was she talking about. Then it hit me. In the excitement of my new case, I totally forgot that I'd sent out a text looking for help tracking down Graeme Bilson.

The police hadn't found him, and they'd had a whole department on it.

"Help me?" I answered. "You've been making fun of me since you came through the door."

"You asked for that," Holly replied, "by answering the door like a zombie. But what if I were to tell you I'd spent most of the last night tracking the movements of the cult of Beelzebub, in particular their high priest, Graeme Bilson?"

"No." I leaned forward in my chair. I'd only sent that text last night. How could she have possibly found anything in that time? She was clearly far better at concealing an all-nighter than I was.

Not only had Graeme threatened my family's health, he was also the only person I knew of who had had dealings with the Djinn. If she was behind the kidnapping of Cali Masters, then he had to have some means of communicating with her.

It was the only lead I had in this whole mess.

"Why didn't you start with that?" I replied, getting to my feet. Blow breakfast; if she had a bead on Graeme, I was ready to hunt him down. "Where is he? Let's go!"

"Easy, tiger," she replied. "No one likes a man who's in that much of a hurry to get there."

The innuendo made me blush, and Holly's smile only broadened. "Oh Darius, you're adorable. I'll stop teasing you, I promise."

"Tease me as much as you like, as long as you do it while we're moving. The police are hunting him, Holly. If they find him before we do..."

My voice faded as I realized I hadn't told Holly why we were hunting him, and I wasn't sure that I wanted to.

"Well, let's just say Detective Hart is unlikely to give you any credit, or me any access to ask some questions I have. They have already raided his house, visited his parent's place, and canvassed known associates. Everything's come up empty and they still have a lot of manpower hunting for him."

"Well, that's embarrassing for them, isn't it?" Holly laughed. "Only took me a few hours. I'll be sure to let them know when we find him."

I might have been trying to turn over a new leaf with the good detectives of the Queensland Police Service but if leaving them out of the loop meant getting access to Graeme first, I would risk their ire.

"So how did you find him when they couldn't?" I asked, hoping to learn a trick or two to help me in future cases.

Holly pulled out her phone, flicked through a few screens with one finger, and slid it across the table to me. "Graeme posted this on his social media three years ago."

On the screen were pictures of our ignoble high priest, in considerably better shape than I'd last seen him, standing in a rain forest and smiling. He was posing for a picture beside a massive hardwood tree.

"I'm not sure how this helps us," I replied, studying the picture for an identifiable marker.

"This is Lamington National Park," Holly replied with a grin. "I recognize the spot. I hike that trail at least once a month."

Holly enjoyed the outdoors? Something we had in common.

Focus, Darius.

"And what, you think he's hiding there in the mountains?"

"Almost certainly." Holly tapped the table. "He's posted dozens of pictures there but none in recent years. Clearly, he spent some time in the park and anyone who has spent enough time there knows about the Shagin' Cabin."

"The Shagin' cabin?" I raised one eyebrow. I'd walked the trail at least a handful of times over the years. I'd never come across a cabin.

Holly's brow furrowed. "You've never heard of it? It was all over the news when I was a kid. The mayor was carrying on an affair with his secretary. He couldn't very well rent a hotel room in town. Everyone would know. So he purchased a dilapidated old cabin up in the mountains. It cost him almost nothing, but he got it tidied up, and he and his assistant would stop in when they were out on the road and enjoy a little afternoon delight. The cabin borders on the national park. One day, some hikers stumbled onto the cabin. The mayor was caught, his wife was furious, and they've been fighting ever since. The cabin's still in dispute and so hikers that use the trail a lot know they can squat there for shelter if they get caught in a storm."

"And you think he's holed up there?" I could see why the police hadn't found him. A dilapidated shack in someone else's name—it was perfect.

Holly nodded. "It's the only place I can think of. The police have already run down all the other obvious bolt holes. With the right supplies, he could squat for weeks, laying low while this blows over."

"Or he could be planning his next move," I said. "He's already tried to kidnap my father once. I won't be certain we're out of the woods until he's been caught."

"I guess I should have brought a McMuffin with me," Holly laughed as I looked for my boots. "Are we taking my car or yours?"

She drove a lovely red convertible and a trip through the hills of the Gold Coast hinterland seemed like a refreshingly charming way to spend the day.

But if we were hiking in the wilderness and dealing with unsavory characters, the equipment I was carrying in the tank could come in handy.

"Why don't we take mine this time around? I have a few tricks that might come in useful if the situation turns hairy."

Holly raised an eyebrow. "You think he'll put up a fight?"

I filled Max's bowl with some extra biscuits. Much as he might like to come along, most national parks were dog-free zones. The spoilsports.

"Well, given he was willing to sacrifice an innocent woman in the name of his bizarre cult and he tried to kidnap my father, I'm not ruling anything out. If he is in that cabin, he'll have had time to prepare for visitors."

"Good thing I'm bringing my own muscle then." Holly patted my chest, the warmth of her hand sending a wave of temptation through me. "Your car it is. I don't mind being chauffeured around."

Holly set Max down and we snuck out the door while he was distracted with breakfast.

I strode up to the tank's passenger door and opened it. "Your chariot awaits."

Holly climbed up into the car and looked down at me. There was a glint in her eyes that warned me of the impending mischief.

"You know if this whole investigator thing doesn't work out, you have a promising future with Uber."

"If you're going to keep being such a smart arse, you can walk." I shut the door before she could give me any more sass. I rounded the car and climbed up into the driver's seat. "If you walk quickly, you might just get there by tomorrow, but you'll have certainly missed your story."

I was joking, of course. I would never make a lady walk, but she'd been ribbing me since she'd shown up on my doorstep and I wasn't going to let her take me for an easy target.

Holly extended her hand. "Truce?"

"I'm prepared to accept your surrender, yes."

"Not on your life." Holly chuckled. "Don't say I didn't give you a chance."

I backed out of the driveway. Max was at the window, staring at me like he'd been betrayed.

I waved. "I'll make it up to you later, buddy."

We pulled out into the busy Gold Coast traffic and chatted away as we headed out of town. A quick detour for a much-needed McMuffin and we were off to the hinterland.

My phone rang, the in-car system picking it up to display 'Mum' on the car's screen. I answered it on hands-free, mindful of the risk of Mum embarrassing me.

"Hi Mum, how are you?"

"Oh Darius, you answered. I was just about to leave you a message."

It said something about my pattern for answering the phone that people who called never expected to get me.

It wasn't my fault. I couldn't particularly answer it when I was staking someone out, or in a compromising situation. On top of that, I often worked nights and slept during the day when most normal people were out and about.

"Just in the car heading into the hinterland. What can I do for you?"

"You left so quickly last night, I didn't get a chance to ask how you were doing. Are you okay?"

Always the concerned mum. I probably hadn't helped matters by showing up with my face beat in.

"Yeah, Mum, things are good. Starting to settle into a nice little rhythm with the agency."

"Glad to hear it." My mother didn't quite sound convinced. She paused, a little too long.

I reached for the console, ready to end the call. I was confident that anything that came after such obvious reluctance was bound to embarrass me.

"I meant to tell you last night. I saw you on the news the other night, dear. You're getting famous."

"Thanks, Mum. That's not why I'm doing it, but it doesn't hurt. Getting lots of calls for new work." I eased the car onto Nerang Murwillumbah road.

"Speaking of calls…Wasn't that the young woman who called by the house? Holly something or other."

Holly grinned in the passenger seat, and I held a finger to my lips.

"Don't you dare," I mouthed to her.

If my mother for a minute thought the two of us were together on some sort of date, she would book the wedding chapel. She had Pastor Nick on speed dial, and I would never escape her infernal plotting for grandchildren.

Not to mention the inevitable embarrassment with Holly.

"Holly Draper, Mum. Yes, that was her."

"She seems lovely, dear. Perhaps you ought to invite her over again. Tea, perhaps or something lighter."

"Mum," I warned.

"Anything really, dear. It doesn't need to be formal, but you're not getting any younger, Darius."

"Goodbye, Mum."

"Darius, don't you—"

I hit the button before she could finish the sentence. If I didn't hear the threat, she couldn't hold it against me. Or at least, that was what I was hoping.

We were still a ways out from the trail we planned to take, and I wasn't ready for my mother to make the balance of this trip with Holly incredibly awkward.

"She seems lovely," Holly said, breaking the silence that had settled over the car. "You really ought to go a little easier on her."

"I love my mum to death," I replied, "but she has less concern with what my time-line for a family might be and is wholly driven by her desire to have grandchildren underfoot to fill her days. It'll happen when it happens—if it happens."

I didn't add that with my luck with women, it seemed less likely by the day. That felt like a little too much honesty for this particular trip.

"Not looking to have a family then?" Holly asked.

I shot her a sideways glance. "Why? Are you offering?"

Holly's big brown eyes went wide.

"I, ah..." She went looking for an answer but couldn't find one.

"I'll have to remember that one." I chuckled as I changed gears. "I do believe that's the first time I've ever seen you speechless."

Holly folded her arms. "I thought we had a truce."

"Oh, we did but you broke it when you sided with my mother. But I'll make you a deal. I'll answer the question if you do."

Holly looked out the window. We were climbing through the hinterlands, the roads were tight winding affairs that clung to the hillside. Out the window, rolling greenery stretched out into the distance as it fell toward the coast.

"I mean it could happen one day," Holly said, and I was pretty sure she was talking about kids, rather than me. "At the moment I'm kinda focused on my career. It's just been so hard to get traction at the newspaper. Even now, it feels like my editors find reasons not to print my pieces. If they didn't generate such a buzz, I doubt I'd have got out of the gossip column."

"That sucks. You seem to have a natural talent for it."

It wasn't idle flattery. I'd read her piece on the Casper Killer. It was the headline that had drawn me in, but it was the quality of the narrative that had kept me interested. She had an excellent way of communicating with her readers. One that spoke to a long and productive future with the written word.

"Thank you. I agonize over those stories. My bosses still believe it's our job to tell people what to think. In this day and age, I think we need to do a better job of telling the story, let the facts speak for themselves. If we have done our job right, people will develop an informed opinion rather than have it jammed down their throat. Needless to say, that's not company policy."

"You've done a great job of changing the topic," I replied, easing out of the tight bend.

"Patience. I'm getting there." Holly settled back into her seat. "I guess it's hard to consider starting a family when I'm just starting to get ahead. I don't want to give my bosses any excuses they could use to pigeonhole me. What about you?"

I knew what was holding me back, but I didn't really want to come across as needy or desperate.

"I've just never found the right person. I figure kids deserve every shot at the same thing I had growing up. Happy house, parents that cared about each other. It's just not that easy to find, you know?"

I regretted the question as soon as I asked it. I doubted Holly had any issues finding men who wanted to be around her.

"Oh, come on," Holly replied, her face serious. "Girls I know would stab me in the back with a nail file to find an eligible bachelor like you."

"Well, I've never met them," I replied. "Though in fairness, I wasn't looking that hard. I joined the military and being deployed is hardly conducive to a long-term relationship. By the time I got home and got discharged, I had some work to do on me, first."

"Hard to adapt to life after service?" Holly asked.

I'd expected a light-hearted drive through the country. Instead, we'd arrived at children and PTSD. I wasn't quite ready to talk about the latter.

"Let's just say there's a lot of reasons I work nights," I replied. "This gig suits me pretty well. I really wasn't expecting it to take off like it has, but I've been so busy taking cases, I haven't had much of a dating life."

I also managed to omit the fact that the last time I'd tried to ask a barista out, I'd ended up on a platonic date with her overprotective male friend.

"Alright." Holly fixed me with a look that made me feel a little like I was being interviewed. "So you're not anti-kids, you're just taking your time."

I nodded. "I'd like to find someone who thinks for themselves, enjoys a good adventure, and doesn't mind that I spend my nights chasing ghosts and ghouls and werewolves. I don't want to be told to settle down and get a real job. This one keeps me grounded, and it helps people. That matters to me."

"Why compromise on what matters most?" Holly agreed.

We made idle chitchat the rest of the way up into the mountains. I knew the hinterland and national park pretty well, though Holly had me beat. She had picked Graeme's favorite trail from a photo. That took more than a passing familiarity with the national park.

A myriad of roads and walking trails crisscrossed the range. We didn't want to take the road leading to the old cabin. If he was there, Graeme was certainly watching it for any sign of pursuit and would leg it if he saw us coming.

The two of us simply couldn't cover that much ground. There were a thousand places to hide in the national park and surrounding property. If he had suitable supplies or bushcraft we might never find him.

I steered the tank around a wide sweeping bend. On the left-hand side of the road there was no shoulder, just a steep descent filled with trees and thick foliage. On the right-hand side was a steep rocky slope heading up the hill. It wasn't until we rounded the corner that I discovered the sedan coming the other way.

It was straddling the center line and headed right at us.

Cutting Corners.
Tuesday, April 25th
O840hrs

THEIR CARELESS DRIVING LEFT us with nowhere to go. The teenage driver in the sedan, panicked like a deer in headlights. His girlfriend screamed. With the steel bull bar built onto the front of the tank, a front-on collision would be far worse for them than for us.

The teenager started to correct and stomped on the brakes, but half-way through the corner as they were, they started skidding out of control.

"Darius!" Holly's voice was high and panicked.

I didn't answer.

I swung left, taking the tank out of the inevitable head on collision. The sedan shot past us, missing my side of the tank by mere inches.

The second my left side wheels were off the road, the uneven traction caused the tank to slip sideways. The extra weight in the back only accentuated the problem.

Holly gripped her door with one hand, and the center console with the other. I knew better than to step on the brakes with the vehicle's wheels on different surfaces.

Instead, I pulled on the handbrake, engaging just the rear wheels. They locked up on the softer grass and sod and set us in a sliding drift around the corner.

The rear left-hand side of the tank struck a tree. I stepped on the accelerator, and the tank launched back up and onto the road.

I righted the tank and pulled back into our lane, my heart racing.

Holly's knuckles were white, but apart from her warning shout, she'd not said a word.

I looked over my shoulder. The sedan had carried right on down the road. They hadn't bothered stopping, probably because the teenage driver had soiled himself and didn't want to be caught.

No doubt my tank's rear panel had taken a beating, but I couldn't stop to check it out – there wasn't enough room on these windy roads to do so safely.

"Well, that was exciting," Holly said, her voice a little shaky. "How on earth did you manage that?"

"Defensive driving course," I answered.

"I've done one too. They didn't cover that."

I laughed. "Mine was with the SAS. They do things differently in The Regiment. Though I must confess, the last time I had to do that I was in a G-wagon in the desert. Sorry, I'm a little rusty."

"Sorry?" Holly's jaw drooped. "Those kids are lucky it was you driving. You saved both their lives. Ours, too."

The attention made me feel a little awkward. We were getting close to the cabin, so I shifted the focus off me.

"How do you want to tackle the approach? If he's in there, Graeme will have eyes on the road."

"I've been thinking about that," Holly replied. "If we head straight to Lamington National Park, hike the trail across, and cut through the scrub, it's probably our best bet of sneaking up on him."

It was a good plan. With the amount of time Holly spent out here, I was happy to lean on her navigation expertise.

We pulled into the national park and found a space. According to Holly, the trail would take us within a few hundred meters of the cabin. It was pretty dense scrub but that would work in our favor.

I pulled on a camouflage jacket I kept in the back seat and made my way to the large tool compartments fitted into the tray of the tank. Rummaging through the surveillance trunk, I grabbed a bodycam and strapped it to my chest.

"What's that for?" Holly peeked over my shoulder.

"Evidence." I closed the container and locked it. "I'm not the law, and when we find him, we're gonna want all the evidence we can get. I don't want conflicting testimony at court."

"I can collaborate your story," she said. "There are two of us, and I've got your back."

"And I appreciate that. But I've learned a little preparation can make life a whole lot easier."

Holly had planned for the hike, and was wearing a practical set of hiking shoes, long pants, and a T-shirt under a jacket. It was the sort she could tie around her waist if the weather got a little warm.

I stood by the tank and considered my choices. Buried deep in the equipment chest in the tray was a rifle. It was registered, but carrying a firearm in public was the sort of act you could be arrested for.

That said, there weren't a lot of cars about and we wouldn't be on the trail all that long. My gut was telling me I might need the gun. There was every chance Graeme could be armed.

On the other hand, the police were on Graeme's tail. And if the police caught us armed, in the middle of a national park, I would be in for a world of trouble. The police might not love a paranormal investigator in their backyard, but they would certainly be opposed to a vigilante. It would be impossible to argue my way out of that. So I left the gun and instead settled for a small backpack with a few essential tools, all of which could double as a weapon if the need arose.

I was a trained operator. The high priest would need a gun just to level the odds.

Don't get cocky, Darius. I heard my instructor's voice in my mind. *That's what gets you killed.*

He was right. There was no telling what waited for us at the top of the mountain.

"Are you ready?" I asked as I buckled the pack on.

"Born ready," Holly said, turning toward the trail. "Are you ready to spoil his day?"

"Let's do it," I replied, hoping against hope that we caught him off guard. Otherwise, he was in an elevated and secluded position. If our would-be priest had armed himself, we could be walking right into his kill box.

I considered calling the cops, but there was no chance I was leaving this to the authorities. I needed information and as far as I was concerned the high priest had offered his last sacrifice.

Holly set the pace, and I fell in behind her. I was a little taller, so while she navigated the trail, I kept an eye out, just in case we happened upon Graeme or any of his cronies out on the trail.

Lamington National Park. It was a name that always made me hungry. I couldn't help but wish I had a packet of the delicious desserts in my bag – snacks made everything better.

As we picked our way up the trail, I mentally added them to my shopping list. I doubted this would be the last case I worked in these mountains and some sponge dipped in chocolate dipped in coconut was both energy and deliciousness waiting to happen.

We made good time hiking. The old cabin was on private property with obvious sight lines of the road. Perhaps that was why the mayor liked it. If his wife ever thought to check on him, he could see her coming with plenty of time to sneak his mistress out the back door. It was a spot of brilliance on Holly's part to even consider Graeme might be there.

The more we hiked, the more convinced I became that we were on the right track. Graeme was an outdoorsman, the national park offered him a host of options for his isolation. If we caught him napping, we might just get the drop on him, particularly coming at him over the top of a ridge as we planned. We would have the advantage of height and visibility. That was the good part, but between now and there lay a fairly grueling hike. Or at least it felt that way with my less than stellar sleep of recent days.

"Just for once," Holly said, "I'd love it if the subject of my story was reclining on a beach in the Bahamas and not forcing me to sweat it out on a mountain, or hiding in an alleyway, or ambushing someone outside of Parliament."

"Then maybe you ought to cover more financial crimes," I replied. "Those are the sort of crooks who have Bahamas money and are very good at fleeing to pretty non-extradition countries."

"Yeah, but they are boring as hell," she replied. "Who wants to chase dodgy accountants and insider traders?"

Certainly not me, that was for sure. I would rather chase ghosts and werewolves any day.

We hiked straight up the hillside, deviating off the beaten path to follow a fire break to the top of the ridge. Before we crested it, I held out my hand to stop Holly.

"What's wrong?" she asked.

"If you're right, the cabin is going to be just over this ridge. And with the fire break eliminating most of the tree cover, if he happens to be looking in this direction, we're going to be silhouetted against the sky. Not exactly where we'd like to be."

"What are you suggesting?"

"Let's slip back down the line a little, cross the open ground, and double back into the forest. More work, I know, but better chance of throwing him the surprise party he deserves."

"You did a lot of this in your previous life, didn't you?" Holly set off down the edge of the firebreak.

"Yep, but it was a lot easier back then," I muttered. It wasn't exactly true, not in every sense. But in terms of the outcome, it was simpler.

"What do you mean?" Holly glanced back over her shoulder.

"Back then I carried an M4A1 carbine, and the sorts of places and people we were sent looking for didn't need to be detained. I'd feel a lot better about this if I was armed. He certainly might be."

"I couldn't find one registered to him." Holly paused before breaking cover. "I had a friend run the check for me, just in case."

"Let's hope they're right," I replied as I caught up with her. We slipped back into the trees together.

Holly had to have friends on the force too. It made sense. The quality of her information was always top-notch. Who it was and why they were so freely giving it to her was another matter.

If I had to guess, there was some eager young impressionable constable with a crush on the journalist. I couldn't blame him. She was easy to look at and surprisingly pleasant company when she wasn't grilling or embarrassing me.

"Still better safe than sorry," I said. "Keep as many trees between you and the cabin as you can. If he starts shooting, we get to cover and call the police."

"And give them Graeme? Not likely," she said. "I want my story."

"It's that or storm a building held by an armed and desperate fugitive. I want answers, but not badly enough to die for. That's when you call the ones in the bullet-proof vests."

Holly looked unconvinced.

As we neared the top of the ridge, I took the lead. If someone was going to get shot, I didn't want it to be her.

We made our way through the trees, moving slowly to prevent unwanted noises. I was a trained woodsman and avoided dead fall as a habit. Holly did pretty well too, but from time to time, she still managed to find a mound of dried leaves, all of which crunched and broke underfoot. The dry weather made for an excellent alarm system.

We stalked down the ridge. I slipped between two impressive eucalyptus trees and paused. Holly bumped into me from behind.

"Oi," Holly whispered, "why did you stop?"

"Because of that." I pointed past the towering trees koalas favored.

Holly leaned forward.

I stooped down and placed my finger almost on the slender piece of fishing line strung through the trees. It was just above the ankle, designed to catch someone's foot as they passed through. I followed the line to where it raced up the trunk of a tree and around a series of silver bells.

"A cheap but effective alarm system," I whispered.

A dozen more strings formed a loose perimeter. Examining them, I noted the line was fresh and the bells still had a sheen that gave away the fact that they had only recently been installed. Anything out in the weather here on the Gold Coast tended to rust or corrode.

"Somebody's here," I replied, "and they don't want any unannounced visitors."

We stepped carefully over each of the tripwires and stalked closer to the cabin. It was less than fifty meters away. We circled around until we were approaching from its southern face. There were no windows on that side, and it made for the best avenue of assault, equally distant from the front and back doors. If we were detected and he made a break for it, we would see him.

I rested my back against the log wall and listened for movement inside.

Nothing.

Inching around the building, I wondered where he was. At this time of the morning, he should be up and about, but not a sound came from the cabin.

I maneuvered around to the front of the cabin until I reached a window. I peered through it. A pack rested on an old wooden rocking chair just inside the front room.

A fresh pile of canned goods on the kitchen bench and an old cast-iron skillet, with traces of a meal sat on the stove.

Holly's guess was looking right on the money. But, I reminded myself, we could just be surprising a hiker or a squatter. The log cabin had a second room I couldn't see into. I peered down the other side of the cabin. Its windows were closed, the curtains drawn. Reaching the front door, I tried the handle.

With the slightest of squeaks, the door opened. It wasn't even locked.

My heart beat loudly in my ears as I held my breath. The old mechanism wouldn't have taken more than a minute or two to pick, which was no doubt how they had got in.

The door swung open, and I crept inside followed closely by Holly. The interior remained still. Getting a closer look at the stove, I changed my assessment of the situation.

It wasn't breakfast; it was last night's dinner, and it was cold Campbell's soup. Not nearly the glamorous spread I'd enjoyed being wined and dined by Geoff.

The supply of cans on the bench conveyed the impression that someone intended to be here a long time.

I motioned for Holly to stay put, and then made my way toward the bedroom door. I was careful to test each plank to ensure it wouldn't move or squeak too badly.

The bedroom door was unlocked. Twisting the knob slowly, I pushed the door open. My heart felt like it would explode from anticipation.

I halted in the doorway. Graeme Bilson, the high priest of Beelzebub, lay on the mattress.

Only, he was dead.

Hired Guns. Tuesday, April 25th 0923hrs

HOLLY GASPED, AND I nearly jumped out of my skin

"I thought I said to wait outside?" I hissed.

"Not now, Darius." She gripped my arm. I doubted it was her first body, but it's not something you can easily get used to.

The small back room of the cabin was only about four meters wide, and most of the space was occupied by the bed.

The body of Graeme Bilson, the high priest of Beelzebub, rested with his back against the wall.

Graeme had been shot, two in the torso, one in the head. The Mozambique Drill, as it had first been known, was a close quarter shooting technique ruthlessly efficient in ensuring a target didn't live long enough to carry out any intended violence.

Graeme appeared to be unarmed, which meant whoever had done this wasn't protecting themselves. They were ensuring Graeme didn't survive to talk.

The Djinn. It had to be.

Blood stained the front of his shirt and trousers and ran down into the bed all around him. Some of it still looked a little damp, but much as I wanted to examine it to see what I could learn, I wasn't going to touch the body in what was no doubt going to become an active crime scene.

"We're not the first to find him."

I groaned. Another lead to the Djinn had run dry.

"But who would have done this?" Holly asked. "It's barbaric."

I knew the answer to that, and if I was going to keep dragging Holly deeper into the case, she ought to know what we were up against.

"The Djinn," I said, moving around the bed to take a closer look at the corpse.

"The what?" Holly's voice was a little strained. She was trying to hide the effect the body was having on her, and she was failing.

"It's the name she goes by." I leaned over Graeme to check his wounds. They couldn't be more than an hour or two old. We were late, but not by much.

We hadn't passed anyone on our way in, which meant the shooter must have used the more direct road and driveway to access the cabin.

Which likely meant Graeme had been expecting them, not running from them. Had he been meeting with the Djinn here?

"What do you mean *she*? Who is she?" Holly's questions came thick and fast. "You knew someone else was looking for him?"

Her voice shifted from shock to irritation.

"Not knew, suspected," I replied, stepping back and leaning against the cabin wall to gather my thoughts. "And I only just became aware of her myself."

"You're going to have to give me more than that, Darius. I thought we were coming to interrogate a kidnapper, but that's another body."

I didn't know what to say. The Djinn was dangerous, and Holly sniffing around looking for her could well get her killed.

"I can, but you have to promise you won't print a word of it until we capture her."

Holly looked at me and then at the body. It was almost as if she could smell the story.

"You know me, Holly. I'm not trying to rob you of a story. I'm trying to save your life. This man is dead because he was the only link that could connect me to her. She is covering her tracks, and she is good at it."

"And you're not going to tell me?" Holly's hands went to her hips, as she did her best to avoid looking at Graeme.

"Not unless you swear that you will keep it to yourself until the right time."

Holly found my gaze and held it, fire smoldering in her eyes. She was not happy at the notion of smothering a story.

"I'm not telling you to keep it to yourself forever. Just until we catch her, then the story is yours. I promise, just like the Casper Killer."

I hoped our track record would be enough to win her over. Publishing everything we found about the Djinn would only broadcast our progress. She was clearly adept enough at evading us without giving her any other advantage.

"Okay," Holly relented. "We better call this in and then you need to tell me everything."

I nodded, and she took out her phone.

While Holly alerted the police, I scanned the room again for any sign of a clue that might help us.

When I didn't find anything, I headed for the bedroom door, intending to search the rest of the cabin. As I passed through the doorway, into the main area of the cabin, a shadow fell across the room.

Based on the angle, someone was standing by the window, the morning sun blazing brightly behind them. The shadow's arm raised.

I snuck a glance as I threw myself forward, behind the cover afforded by the kitchenette.

The glass shattered as the first shot struck the door jam well behind me. I rolled across the timber floor and slammed into the weathered kitchen cabinets.

Holly screamed from the bedroom.

The second and third shots were closer, smacking into the kitchen counter. Splintered shards of timber shot out of the countertop as I hunkered down beneath it.

"Darius!" Holly screamed.

"Stay put," I shouted back. There were no windows in the bedroom. So if the killer wanted Holly, he was going to need to come through the cabin and get past me to get to her.

My heart pounded, my ears ringing from the shots as adrenaline coursed through me. I'd been operating on the assumption the assassin had fled the scene. After all, they killed Graeme Bilson to stop us from getting any information that might lead back to the Djinn. Why would they linger?

I'd been working on the premise that the Djinn was trying to clean up after herself. It hadn't dawned on me that she might simply lay a trap and wait for me to wander into it. If she wanted me dead, why toy with me at all? She could have killed me when I showed up to our 'date' the other night.

What was she playing at?

More shots thudded into the timber all around me. Fortunately, it was too thick for a small caliber handgun to penetrate.

My bag was on the other side of the cabin, across almost four meters of open ground. There was no way I would reach it without catching a bullet in the back for my troubles. The cabinetry I was leaning against housed one of the only storage areas in the entire cabin.

Whatever cooking utensils the mayor had stored in his love shack ought to be there, if none of the squatting hikers had looted them.

I pried open the cupboard beneath the sink and peered inside. A few old pots and a small tool tray rested inside. Most of the tools were old and rusty: an ancient claw hammer whose head rattled loosely as I picked it up, and a chisel with a rusty blade.

Still, they were better than nothing, and the window wasn't that far away.

I tucked the chisel into my belt at the small of my back and grabbed the hammer.

It wasn't going to beat the pistol at range, but there was a reason most military training regimes considered a hammer one of the most deadly close quarter weapons. Unlike a knife, a hammer was quite difficult to block in unarmed combat. Its focused, targeted impact shattered bones and cracked skulls.

An amateur with a hammer was dangerous. A trained soldier? Well, if I got within arm's reach, our assassin would be in for a world of hurt.

Not that I wanted to kill him. If this assassin was working for the Djinn, I had questions and I needed answers. The way the assassin kept firing, he had to be close to changing his magazine. That would be my best chance of not catching a bullet.

Reaching above the counter, I grabbed a can of baked beans. I drew back as two shots punched through the other tins. Soup ran out of one of the punctured cans and dripped down the front of the cabinet, right onto me.

Cold chicken soup. It could be worse.

The pistol clicked on an empty chamber. I rose from behind the bench, a can of baked beans in one hand, the hammer in the other.

I hurled the can right at the cracked window. The pane had more holes in it than the plot of a daytime soap opera, and I was shocked it hadn't already broken. The can of baked beans fixed that, smashing through the glass to send a shower of shards at the assassin. The can slammed into the assassin's head.

With a grunt of pain, the assassin turned the gun on me. They were acting on instinct and hadn't processed the fact it was empty yet.

Bursting through the window frame, my bulk sending the remaining shards of glass in all directions, I found myself face to face with a six-foot tall, broad-shouldered man in a balaclava. In his hand was a small lightweight black pistol.

I swung the hammer. The pistol flew from his grasp.

The assassin startled when his pistol struck the floor of the cabin. He turned and bolted in the opposite direction from the cabin. I tore out of the cabin, heading after him.

As I ran, I called over my shoulder. "The gun's down, Holly. Don't touch it. It's evidence."

I leapt off the porch and onto the rocky ground. The assassin was fast and had a head start. I'm not much of a sprinter; I'm just a bit too heavy to move fast and it was never a skill I felt I needed to pursue. The army wanted me to be able to strap fifty pounds to my back and run at a steady pace for hours. That I could do. The sprinting thing? Not so much.

Based on the direction he was heading and the fact we hadn't passed him on the way in meant he had parked somewhere off the driveway or the main road.

I sucked in a deep breath. Ahead of me the assassin barreled down the hill, parallel to the driveway.

The rocky trail sloped downhill. If I could distract him, he might just slip. Drawing back, I hurled the hammer at him, but he was farther away now, almost twenty meters, and the hammer was not particularly well balanced. It sailed clear over his right shoulder. The assassin didn't even break his stride.

As we ran through the scrub, I called after him. "We've got your gun. How long do you think it will take the police to ID you?"

It was an empty threat. The weapon was likely unregistered but that wasn't the point. I was just trying to throw him off his game. If I could distract him long enough for him to twist his ankle, it might make the difference.

The assassin didn't even turn to acknowledge my presence. He just continued his mad dash down the hillside. If he wasn't careful, he would fall hard enough to snap his damned neck.

I stuck with him, not wanting to let him out of my sight.

Up ahead, a log lay in our path. The assassin vaulted it, one gloved hand on the log as he went over. Risky. The added momentum could cause him to lose his footing.

Rather than leap over it, I stepped up onto the log. Only it was rotten. My boot crumbled through the rotten timber, and shot out from under me.

My glove protected my hand from the worst of it, but I hit a patch of loose rocks and went down hard. My backside kissed the rocky ground hard enough to bruise my tail bone, and I was rewarded with a nice run of gravel rash up my arm.

A little dust cloud rose around me. I forced myself to my feet and kept running. I had lost a good thirty meters on him and wasn't making any of it up now.

He was getting closer to the road with every moment and ducked behind a thick stand of trees, vanishing from sight for the first time since we left the cabin. He could be running, or he could be lying in wait to spring an ambush. I drew the chisel and held it ready for anything. But as I rounded the stand of trees, I wasn't face-to face with a killer.

Instead, I was staring at the tailpipe of a white Toyota Camry as the engine fired up. The spinning wheels sprayed gravel everywhere when he punched the gas.

I hurled the chisel after him. It flew through the rear window, shattering it.

My eyes went to the number plate.

Unfortunately, the plume of dust and the stand of trees stopped me from getting a good look at the last few digits. I groaned audibly as the assassin shot off down the hill.

I reached for my phone. I needed to call this murder in. If I was quick enough, perhaps the police could pick him up.

Lifting it from my pocket, I found the screen was completely shattered.

I had landed on it when I fell.

"Double damn," I grumbled as I tried to bring up a keypad to dial 000.

No luck. The screen wasn't even registering my touch. I fought the urge to hurl the phone as hard as I could. By the time I got back up the hill to Holly, the assassin would be miles away.

When it came to the Djinn, nothing was going my way.

Well, that wasn't entirely true. I was alive. That counted for plenty, but it was hard to see the glass as half-full when I was further from my foe than I'd ever been.

I hadn't been able to ID the attacker, but I knew with certainty that he was not Mary Baker.

The woman I'd met for lunch was slender and toned. She'd worn shoulder pads to bulk out her jacket. This attacker was more of a mountain than a man. Either someone else had wanted Graeme Bilson dead, or Mary hired out the hit.

Trudging back up the rocky slope, I was forced to confront a third possibility.

Perhaps Mary Baker wasn't the Djinn at all. Why risk a face-to-face meeting when she could have just as easily confused and distracted me by sending someone else in her place? The more I thought about it, the more I realized it was entirely possible.

Perhaps Mary was just another minion working for the shadowy mastermind known as the Djinn.

If that was true, I was even further behind than I thought.

My shoulders heaved as I recovered my breath. I'd been so close, if I hadn't lost my footing, I might have managed to catch him at his car. The assassin was no amateur. I might not have been as fit as I once was, but anyone who could run that distance over uneven ground down a steep gradient was no run-of-the-mill civilian.

I made my way back up to the cabin, my grazed arm smarting, my pride a little hurt. It could have been worse. I could have caught a bullet.

I was going to need to be more wary in my pursuit of the Djinn.

A shiver ran down my spine. If I'd caught a bullet here, it might have been the end. Bleeding out in a remote cabin, almost an hour from emergency responders; that would have been a real problem.

"It's just me," I called as I approached the cabin. Pushing open the door, I found Holly holding a frying pan ready like a baseball bat.

"Whoa, easy, tiger." I raised my hand in case she swung out of instinct or fear.

"Is he...?" Holly's hands trembled.

"He's gone," I replied. "He got to his car before I could reach him. Didn't even catch the number plate."

"Any idea who he was?" Holly set down the pan on the bench.

"No clue, but he knew what he was doing. Definitely ex-military or someone with police training."

"What makes you say that?" Holly asked as she made her way over to me.

"Shooting pattern is reminiscent of either institution a decade or two ago. Not current best practice, though. So if I had to guess, he's probably late thirties, early forties, and fit as hell. He outran me, and I'm fit."

"What happened to your arm?" She inspected the gravel rash.

"Log gave out and I went down," I said.

"Ah, well, at least we're both alive. And we've got his gun. That's something."

I bent over the weapon but didn't pick it up. "Not as valuable as you'd think. Someone has welded the serial number. Highly illegal, but quite untraceable. Unless we can find who is selling them and squeeze them for information."

"Still something," Holly replied, cheerily. "I've worked with less."

She was right. I needed to stop feeling sorry for myself and start looking at what we were working with.

"The police are going to be here soon," I said. "Probably best if we have a look around before they do. I imagine they aren't going to be fans of us crawling all over their crime scene."

"Right." Holly checked her watch. "We've only a few minutes. I'll start out here. Why don't you take the back room?"

"There's a spare set of gloves in the backpack. Probably best use those, just in case."

Holly headed for the backpack, and I made my way back into the bedroom. I'd seen more than my fair share of bodies, so Graeme's presence didn't prevent me from doing what needed to be done.

Unfortunately, Graeme's body yielded no further clues. The cause of death was apparent and while it gave me a little insight into the expertise of the killer we were dealing with, it didn't tell me anything about Graeme's relationship with the Djinn.

I checked through the bedding and beneath the bed, taking great care not to move the body. I was hunting for anything Graeme might have dropped but found only some cracked macadamia nut shells and a mentos wrapper.

Heading back into the cabin proper, I continued hunting. Holly was searching Graeme's bag, a move the police wouldn't approve of, but in the current circumstances, there was little choice. We needed something.

"Check this out." Holly waved a small pamphlet. "Doesn't seem like the sort of scene for a cult leader."

I took it, noting the all too familiar chapel on the front. It was a pamphlet for the Trinity Lutheran Church. The pamphlet was worn and creased like it had been folded and jammed in a pocket.

"It's where they tried to kidnap my dad," I replied. "They hit during bingo night. Fortunately, I was there to help."

"Good thing too," Holly replied. "So not a lead then."

"Nothing new, I'm afraid."

On the other hand, it did indicate that whoever had planned the attack had been there before. How else would they have picked up the leaflet? Just how much research had the Djinn done on me? I hadn't been to church in months. Had she been looking into my family? And why? What had I done to her?

Sirens drew me back to the present and I jammed the pamphlet into my backpack.

"Let's wait for them out front," I said. "At least give them the illusion we haven't been ransacking their crime scene."

Throwing my pack over one shoulder, I headed out front, Holly right beside me. Time to face the music. After all, we had a body, a murder weapon, and an absentee killer.

We would be lucky if we didn't spend lunch in cuffs.

Disappearing Dollarydoos. Tuesday, April 25th 1630hrs.

SIX HOURS.

That was how long it took our friends at the Queensland Police Service to determine we weren't murderers. I didn't blame them. They were only doing their job. If anything, their thorough approach to the whole affair was reassuring.

They'd been pretty skeptical, but most murderers don't leave their weapon, call the police, and loiter at the scene after carrying out the dirty deed.

After giving our statements, and walking them through the whole ambush twice, including another trip down the hill to where the killer's car had been parked, we were free to go.

Albeit with the admonition not to leave town.

On the ride back, Holly interrogated me on the Djinn. I shared what little I knew, cautioning her not to broadcast her own investigations.

As far as I was aware, the Djinn had killed everyone else who crossed her path. Why she was toying with me, I didn't know. But I didn't want Holly paying the price for it.

I brought her back to my place so she could pick up her car. After she left, I showered and changed, then scooped up Max and headed out to make good on my promise to Sonny.

Starting my research, it wasn't particularly difficult to find the swim school where Sonny and Lucille had enrolled Leilani. Kyle Cruz was anything but modest about his achievements, and within all of thirty seconds on the Internet, I had half a dozen news articles and an address to start with.

I could have called, but if Kyle was skulking around his swim school, hiding from parents, I didn't want to warn him that I was coming.

Perusing the Olympian's social media profiles gave me a pretty good idea of what I was dealing with. He'd won Olympic gold in his early adulthood and backed it up with a handful of other international titles. At the end of his considerable swimming career, he'd taken the most obvious path available to him, coaching.

It was a natural progression for most athletes, though certainly not all had what it took to teach others what they could do themselves. A quick look through the reviews told me that his courses seemed to deliver. Which meant it wasn't a straight up con. The school had been in business for years, so he probably wasn't in the habit of charging exorbitant fees and ghosting people. News of that sort of thievery spread fast.

If he was cheating Lucille and Sonny, it didn't appear to be his normal MO. There were dozens of glowing reviews, including video testimonials of athletes that he'd helped prepare for the Commonwealth and Olympic games. By all accounts, Kyle Cruz appeared to run a successful swim school.

Of course, I'd also found the reports dealing with the court case Sonny mentioned. Kaley Winters, one of his students, had accused him of sexual harassment. I could see why it spooked Sonny. A father was never going to risk exposing his child to that.

To give him the benefit of the doubt, the Bulletin's weekend section announced that Cruz was acquitted last week. Nevertheless, I found the timing and his subsequent disappearance more than a little suspicious.

However, apart from those allegations, the more I searched, the more evidence I gathered that Kyle was in fact a successful coach, albeit an expensive one.

Which made his sudden ghosting of my friends all the more unusual. Was the fact that he'd disappeared right after they had paid him coincidence? Or was it related to the court acquittal? Or had Kyle decided to take that money, along with other recent enrollments, and make a run for it?

Two possible motives so far. Who knew what else lurked beneath the waters?

Armed with information, I headed to the swim school to see what I could make of the whole mess. Perhaps there'd been a misunderstanding. Or maybe Lucille had lost her temper and scared him into hiding. Whatever the case might be, I was confident my best shot of finding the truth was by stopping by in person.

The swim school ran out of a small commercial office located near the Gold Coast Aquatic Center in Broadbeach which had hosted the Commonwealth Games and a host of other international aquatic events since.

I timed my visit to be approaching closing time on purpose. It tended to motivate staff to answer my questions in the hope they might get out of the office a little sooner. Never doubt the willingness of an employee to tell you whatever you want to know at five to five so that they can roll out the door for TGI Friday or evening drinks at the local pub. It was a useful trick that always served me well.

Setting Max up in the tank with his doggy drink bottle, the windows cracked and the center tray full of dog biscuits, I headed inside. It was cool enough at this hour; he wouldn't be in any danger of overheating.

I pushed open the hinged glass door and found myself in a small lobby with a receptionist's desk. Behind it, several doors led to offices, and between them was a wall covered in pictures of swimmers holding up their accolades.

A young woman in her early twenties manned the desk. She was dressed in a white polo shirt and wore her hair loose at the shoulder.

She greeted me with a smile. "Hello, can I help you?"

"Hello." I made my way to the counter. "I was hoping to meet with Kyle. Is he around?"

She broke eye contact, looking down at her keyboard. "I, uh, I'm afraid he's not in today. Can I take a message?"

Her manner didn't do anything to convince me all was well at the school.

"That's okay. I'd much rather talk to him in person." I leaned on one elbow on the raised counter. "Any idea when he will be in?"

She shook her head. "I'm afraid I don't know."

She didn't even check her calendar, which meant one of two options: either Kyle had instructed her to hold all appointments, or she genuinely didn't know when her boss would be in.

I tried another investigative tactic to discern which I was dealing with here. When interviewing someone dishonest, I often found that making them repeat their story would reveal inconsistencies.

"What days is Kyle usually in?"

The receptionist winced. "He's usually in to meet new students and conduct entry interviews on Tuesdays and Fridays."

"But not today," I asked, knowing very well it was Tuesday. It had been a long day, but not so long that I'd forgotten that.

"No, I'm afraid I haven't seen him today at all."

I nodded, in spite of the fact she hadn't really provided much of an explanation. "Oh, is he unwell?"

"I think so," she replied. "Truth be told, we haven't seen him since last Thursday."

That didn't bode well for anyone.

"When was the last time you spoke with him?" I pressed. Perhaps he had called in to explain his absence.

"On Friday, right before court, but I haven't heard from him since."

I leaned on the counter and gave her my least intimidating smile. "Is that unusual, or does it happen often?"

One might expect a staff member to be a little alarmed when her boss didn't show up to work and had been incommunicado for days. Unless, of course, Kyle had a habit of going off the reservation.

The receptionist opened her mouth but before she could answer me, one of the office doors opened and a man of average height and appearance emerged. He wore dress pants, a white shirt that was open at the collar, and a set of glasses pushed high on his nose. He couldn't have been more than twenty-seven or twenty-eight and looked like every accountant I'd ever met.

The receptionist gave me the nervous look of someone who'd already said too much.

"Brandi?" the man said. "How are those enrollments coming?"

She glanced down at the screen. "Uh...I was just preparing the class lists when..."

Brandi looked up to me, realizing she didn't even have my name.

"Darius Kane," I said, cursing his ill-timed appearance. I felt like we were just getting to the crux of the matter.

Brandi nodded. "Of course, Mr. Kane. I was just working through them when he arrived looking for Kyle. I was just explaining—"

The newcomer raised a finger to cut her off. "That's okay, Brandi. I'll take it from here."

He gestured to me. "Mr Kane, why don't you come with me?"

I stepped around the counter and followed him into his office. A row of filing cabinets filled one wall, and a laptop on a desk rested on the opposite side of the room. Several photos adorned the walls. One boasted him and Kyle standing in front of the Aquatic Center together. Another was of him graduating from college, and a third showed him standing on the beach with a sandy haired woman a few years younger than himself. They had their hands intertwined together. In the other, they raised matching martini glasses. She was a little mousy for my tastes, but the two of them looked happy.

A pair of faded leather seats stood in front of the desk, and I leaned on the back of them.

"I appreciate you making time for me when I don't have an appointment," I began as he rounded his desk and sat down. "But I was looking for Kyle. Who might you be?"

"I'm Lawrence, his business manager." He pointed to the seat opposite him. "It's not any trouble at all, but tell me, why is a private investigator of your reputation looking for my coach?"

Coach, not boss. I figured Kyle owned the place. Maybe Lawrence was his partner.

When I didn't answer, he pressed on. "Do you know something I don't?"

That was a little more defensive than I'd expected, and his reaction to my name, while not as bad as some, indicated he was aware of who I was. He'd chosen not to have a crack at my profession and called me a private investigator rather than something less polite, so either he preferred to avoid conflict, or he was trying to butter me up to stay on my good side. The question was why?

"I can tell you what I know if you'll tell me how long he's been missing for."

Lawrence leaned back and folded his arms. "What makes you think he's missing?"

I rested my head on my hand, keeping my eyes on Lawrence. There was something a little off about him. I just couldn't put my finger on what it was.

"He hasn't been in since Friday. Brandi out there hasn't seen or heard from him, and you, Lawrence, are acting a little skittish. Care to explain why your boss is missing and you haven't filed a missing persons report? What are you hiding?"

"Whoa there." Lawrence raised both hands to stop me. He kept them both above the desk which was where I preferred them when I was interviewing con-artists and crooks. If this was a sham operation, Kyle's business manager would almost certainly be in on it.

"It's not like that," Lawrence replied. "First off, I'm his partner. And second, I'm sure there's nothing to be alarmed about. Kyle has gone missing before. This isn't the first time."

I leaned over the desk. I was larger than Lawrence and my proximity caused him to back away. I was close enough I could reach over the desk and grab him if I was so inclined. I let him squirm.

"This isn't the first time he's gone AWOL?"

Lawrence shook his head. "Kyle likes to drink. Everyone knows that. He won his case on Friday and spent the weekend celebrating. Hard. I expected to hear from him yesterday to deal with some business issues, but he skipped our meeting. I just assumed he was on a bender. It's unusual, but he always shows up by Wednesday classes. There's nothing to be alarmed about."

"What happened when you called him?"

Lawrence scratched at the nape of his neck. "His phone is dead. I went by his apartment last night just to check on him. He wasn't there."

How did he know Kyle wasn't home unless he got inside?

"You have a key?" I asked.

"Of course." Lawrence dismissed the question like it wasn't a big deal. Perhaps they were friends as well as business partners. "I've run more than a few errands for him over the years. He figured it was more convenient if I could come and go when he needed me to."

Still, my gut was telling me something was amiss. Kyle was the cash cow, the coach that drew all the high-paying parents. If I were Lawrence, I would be worried about being able to afford my mortgage every time Kyle went on a bender. One bout of drunken stupidity could be the end of their business. Frankly, Lawrence

S.C. STOKES, STEVE HIGGS

was lucky Kyle had been acquitted. That case could have put a real damper on their little school.

"Kyle isn't at home, he's certainly not here, and still, you're not worried?" Their laissez-faire attitude had me a little concerned.

"Look, Darius. If you knew Kyle, you wouldn't be nearly this worried. He probably found some rich widow with a fetish for swimmers and is holed up in her pool house sipping margaritas and reliving his glory days. Like I said, it wouldn't be the first time."

Maybe it wasn't the problem Sonny and Lucille thought it was. Maybe they had just been unlucky enough to be dealing with him right before his latest bout of revelry. By the sound of it, there was every chance he would simply surface when he was thrown out of whatever cabana he was hiding in.

"Can I ask why you're looking for him?" Lawrence asked. "Don't you normally take, uh, different cases?"

It was the question I'd been waiting for. Still, I wanted him to work for it.

"I take whatever comes through the door," I replied with a shrug.

"Well, if we didn't hire you, who did?" Lawrence asked, stroking his chin.

There was no avoiding the question.

"Look, Lawrence, I'm going to level with you. My friends recently enrolled their daughter in your swim school. They paid their tuition, but this court case gave them some concerns. They asked to meet with Kyle."

Before I had even finished the sentence, he held up his hand. "Look, in the media's eyes, you're guilty until proven innocent, but that case was thrown out last week and our reputation has been damaged irreparably. Once Kyle has finished his little bender, we will be countersuing that little liar for damages and libel. Someone needs to teach her a lesson."

That was a whole lot more aggressive than I'd expected. I'd touched the wrong nerve, clearly.

"Look, I'm not saying anything about the allegations, simply that the case had concerned my friends who were looking for reassurances. Kyle skipped their meeting. They haven't been able to reach him. They won't know about his celebratory proclivities and are understandably concerned about the considerable fees they have paid in advance."

"I see." The furrow in Lawrence's brow relaxed. "You'll have to excuse me. I've been pestered by reporters and media for months. I'm just here trying to run a business and make a living."

"I get it," I replied. "Didn't mean to salt the wound. Just looking out for my friends."

"Your friends..." Lawrence glanced down at his laptop. "That wouldn't happen to be Lucille, and her husband, what's his name?"

"Sonny." The fact he wasn't certain who I was referring to, confirmed they weren't the only parents who might have voiced concerns.

"Lucille has called me twice this week already. I can understand their concern given the circumstances, but, Mr. Kane, that which I've said to you, I've shared in confidence. Kyle might like to drink, but he is an excellent coach. One whose swimmers win. He's innocent of all charges, and as soon as he is back, I'll organize for him to meet with your friends. They will be reassured that this is the place for their daughter's success and all will be well. There is no need to panic. Just give us a day or two and Kyle will be right as rain and ready to go."

"You seem pretty confident you'll find him," I mused out loud. "Do you have some way of tracking him?"

Lawrence raised an eyebrow. "Like an airtag for philanderers? I wish. Short of searching every pool house, cabana, and penthouse suite on the Gold Coast, we're both out of luck."

I didn't have that sort of time to spare. It must have shown on my face, because as Lawrence rose from his chair, he said, "Look, Darius, I'm sure he'll show up at the pool at ten AM tomorrow morning for classes. We've got nothing to worry about."

"And if he doesn't?" I rose to my feet.

"Then, Darius, we might need your help finding him. But in the meantime, stand down, relax, and reassure your friends that they're in good hands. The school's reputation speaks for itself and if they genuinely want to cancel their daughter's enrollment, we'll be happy to process a full refund."

Lawrence's face tensed like a doctor delivering a bad diagnosis. "But I have to caution you against that."

"Why's that?" I held my ground. I'd been waiting for the catch. Nothing in life was this easy.

Lawrence jammed his hand in his pocket. "On news of the acquittal, registrations for next season have surged. If Lucille cancels her daughter's place, even temporarily, someone else will take it. There are simply too many other parents willing to pay to have their children taught by the best. It's nothing personal, but it could be years before she'd be considered again."

"I'll keep that in mind." I turned for the door, but paused when my hand touched it. "Class is at ten o'clock tomorrow?"

"Exactly, Darius. Mark my words. Kyle Cruz will be there in his board shorts and polo, training our county's next gold medalists."

"I'm relieved to hear that," I replied, looking for any hint of deception. "I'm sure Sonny and Lucille will be too."

Lawrence was nervous but under the circumstances, I could hardly blame him.

"Like I said, not my first rodeo." He paused before asking "Is there a number I can reach you at if I do need your help?"

I drew out my business card and placed it on the desk. "You can call that number night or day. If anything comes up, just let me know."

"You'll be the first one I call." He ushered me out of the office.

In the lobby, I couldn't help but feel the need to press him, just in case. The last thing I wanted was to have to waste another trip.

"You seem a little nervous, Lawrence. Is everything alright?"

"Like you said, he's missing." Lawrence groaned. "Without Kyle, I'm a business manager without my star talent. I can't teach those classes and there isn't anyone willing to pay *me* twenty-five thousand a season for lessons. If he doesn't turn up, I'm out of a job. I need Kyle to get off his backside and get back to work."

The line was delivered well. Either he'd been here before, or he'd been practicing.

"I appreciate your time, Lawrence. I won't take any more of it. If you need me, give me a call. I'll happily track down your boss for you."

The lobby was empty, Brandi having long since abandoned her post. Lawrence walked me right to the front door.

"That girl, the one from the court case..."

Kaley Winters," Lawrence said.

"That's the one." I turned to face him. "You haven't heard anything from her since Friday, when the case settled?"

"Not a word," Lawrence replied. "I expected them to call looking for the balance of their fees back. With the case settling, they have to be short of money, but still no call."

That was interesting. Not that I suspected they would have a leg to stand on.

"No worries, Lawrence." I offered my hand for him to shake. "You knew Kyle well. Where did he like to drink?"

"The Watering Hole," Lawrence answered without reservations. "Kinda lame old school joint out on the Spit, but Kyle loved it. Always drank there."

The Spit was a decent drive, and this was the Gold Coast. Bars and pubs stood on every street. "Why out there? Why not something closer?"

Lawrence shrugged. "It's popular with swimmers and surfers. People recognize him and there are lots of photos and Olympic memorabilia on the wall. He finds it a little easier to seek company there."

Kyle was a womaniser and an alcoholic. I was starting to see why Lawrence wasn't particularly surprised at his partner's apparent bender.

"Appreciate your help, Lawrence. You have a great night."

I stepped out onto the street. The sun was vanishing over the mountains and the Gold Coast was coming to life for the night. As I made my way to the tank, I ran through the case in my mind.

There was a chance that everything was just as Lawrence had asserted, but his nervousness made me uncomfortable. So instead of dropping the case like he'd suggested, I decided to check out The Watering Hole.

If Kyle was a regular there, they might have seen him Friday night. Or perhaps they hadn't, and their relationship wasn't as peachy as Lawrence would have me believe.

Either way, I was going to find our missing coach and ensure he spent some quality time with Sonny and Lucille.

Just as long as someone else hadn't got to him first.

The Spit. Tuesday, April 25th 2140hrs

WATCHING THE DARK WAVES lapping at the sand, I had to think there were certainly worse places in the world to conduct a stakeout.

I'd parked the tank at the Spit. The rounded promontory was the perfect place to start my mermaid investigation. To my east lay the Pacific Ocean. At this latitude, unless you landed on a remote island, you would hit nothing until you reached South America. It was a truly mind-boggling expanse of water. Who was to say what could be found in those depths?

It was one of the reasons I'd taken Geoff's case. At least it would be interesting.

Out to my west, the sea filtered around the headland and formed the Broadwater. One could see from the Spit to the mainland across the channel, but it was still deep enough for considerable water traffic to pass through.

Anything coming or going from the Broadwater would have to pass straight by me.

The Spit had the bonus of being conveniently located near The Watering Hole, the bar where Kyle enjoyed drinking. This way, I could potentially kill two birds with one stone. I would spend a few hours looking into my rich lawyer's aquatic issues, and perhaps when things quietened down a little, or I needed refreshment, I could pop over to the bar and see if anyone remembered Kyle.

Reaching across the center console, I petted Max. He was on his rear paws on the passenger seat trying to peer out his window which was a little easier than trying to see over the dash. He was an inquisitive young beagle. It was one of many things that had endeared him to me.

He had the same natural curiosity I had.

"Sorry, buddy, maybe I should have bought you a bigger cushion."

Max pushed back against my hand, content to sit in the car for the time being, but I knew there was a clock on his patience.

Max was at the beach and would not settle for anything less than a walk along it. I pulled out the tray on the dashboard and hoped the small mountain of dog biscuits I stashed there would keep him distracted a little while longer.

Max tucked in, accepting the bribe with a string of lapping and crunching.

While he did, I stared through the windshield at the water. Geoff Consella certainly didn't strike me as a crazy man. Nor did he strike me as a user. The fact that he swore he'd seen a mermaid, enough to damage his own reputation, gave me pause. The ocean was a big place, and we were discovering previously unknown species every year.

There was always a chance that one of them explained what Geoff had seen from his office late that night.

Though what a mermaid would be doing swimming up the Broadwater was beyond me. With plenty of boat traffic, and an abundance of people, swimming in the Broadwater wasn't particularly discreet. Of all the water in the area, the Broadwater had to be the most likely place for harm to come to the creature.

Add to Geoff's testimony the fact that others like Captain Cronkwhile had seen it or believed it was there and it became credible that something might be in the Broadwater.

I wondered who had spoken to the captain. It might be worth hearing from them also. Perhaps with a few accounts I could triangulate the creature's location.

Rolling waves lapped across the Broadwater, driven by wind and tide. Not the best weather for boating but still the occasional vessel taxied in or out of the canals. Nothing remotely resembling a mermaid, though.

I put my chair back a little and set my feet up on the dash. I ruffled Max's coat and considered my options for tracking the Djinn. Graeme Bilson wasn't leading me to her, so my leads were waning.

I had only her intentionally discarded disguise and potentially the car dropped at Mooney's garage. It was likely the Djinn had been the one to deposit TJ there. I didn't see them risking involving someone else in such a sensitive element of their plot.

I'd been through the car, twice now, but I hadn't been thinking of who might have been driving.

Perhaps there was a stray hair, or some indication as to where the car might have come from. It was possible TJ owned it, in which case its registration might lead me back to wherever he had been working from when he planned the murders. That could be a valuable source of information gathering. Or perhaps the car was stolen, and footage of the heist had caught the Djinn without a carefully prepared disguise.

Both possibilities were a long shot, but they were better than nothing.

As I thought through everything I knew about the Djinn and TJ, I realized I had completely overlooked someone: TJ's confidant, Victoria. Given her advanced years, I'd written off her involvement after she'd given away the Casper Killer's identity.

But she had definitely known what TJ was up to. There was a chance she knew something about the Djinn too. Perhaps she was the Djinn herself, though that seemed unlikely. Unless my theory about Mary Baker being a pawn was right, or Victoria was both an Oscar-winning actress and had the best hair and makeup department on the face of the planet.

Still, I couldn't dismiss it. If she was wily enough to falsify government records, who knew what else she had a hand in. There was more to her than met the eye, and there was every chance that Mary Baker might not be the mastermind behind the whole matter. Sure, she identified herself as the Djinn in her note, but if you were baiting a paranormal investigator, would you really show up to lunch, reveal yourself to him, and then antagonise him?

That was a dangerous thought. The more I pondered on it, the more I realized until I learned more, I was better off questioning everything.

What was the Djinn's motivation? Why was she toying with me? How had I earned her attention? I was a retired soldier who'd worked two paranormal cases, the Crypt Killers and the Casper Killer. Sure, both had garnered media attention, but beyond that I couldn't see a motive.

Why was the Djinn willing to see Cali Masters kidnapped by the cultists? Clearly, she didn't want her dead. Otherwise, why swap out the knife? The kidnapping seemed like a little piece of theater intended to draw me in. But to draw me in without risking Cali's life? The Djinn clearly wasn't opposed to dropping bodies; Graeme Bilson demonstrated that. Was the Djinn somehow attached to Cali Winters?

She'd also coached TJ until he'd been an expert at murdering people, she'd even managed to keep him ahead of the police for a time.

How had Cali's mother even known to call me? I hadn't asked. Now it seemed like a glaring oversight.

What if Cali or her mother were the Djinn? It was an absurd thought, but one I couldn't entirely dismiss.

"Darius, you're being paranoid," I muttered. Still, the thought made me uneasy, and I was going to need to follow up on it in due course. I would need an excuse to call in and see them.

I considered my closed cases, the Crypt Killers and the Casper Killer. I had stumbled onto both of them. The two cases were dissimilar in most respects.

The Crypt Killers were a gang of drug dealers operating out of a cemetery, using the fact the general public wouldn't want to be there at night to conceal their existence.

The Casper Killer was a murderous son out for revenge.

What did the Djinn get out of helping TJ? If I could work that out perhaps I could better identify her.

"Five bodies, no jail." That was what TJ had said with his dying breath. The killings were TJ's revenge, but had the Djinn also benefited from his actions? I made a note to speak to Tommy about it. Perhaps we could narrow the net of potential suspects by seeing who else might benefit from their demise.

After all, the victims had been a mechanic, a prominent financier, a criminal attorney, and a sitting judge. It was a pretty broad spectrum set of targets and potential motives, but it was something. If I operated on the assumption that the Djinn had an agenda that involved their deaths and was trying to keep me busy and distracted while they carried out their plans, it accounted for most of what I'd experienced.

It was a good theory as far as working ones went, and it would have to do. We'd been in the car for well over an hour and Max was pawing at the window in the hope of going outside.

"You're right, boy. There's little chance we will catch a mermaid sitting in the car. Let's go for a walk."

Max barked his agreement, and I fastened the leash on his collar. When I set him on the ground, he took off toward the Broadwater. I let the leash play out. At this hour, there weren't many people around to bother. I fell into step behind him, locking the car with the remote and tucking the keys in my pocket. We stepped down onto the sand, Max sauntering along behind me for a moment before dragging me down onto the firm wet stuff closest to the water.

"I don't suppose you can smell a mermaid from here, can you, Max?"

I was only kidding, but beagles do have an exceptional sense of smell. If Max did run into one, he would be able to stalk it, at least in shallow water.

Contrary to Hollywood movies, shallow water doesn't conceal one's scent, rather it adheres to it. Making tracking prey along a river or stream far easier than you'd believe. Of course, the Broadwater was too deep for that, but there was no harm in a little wishful thinking.

Max just wagged his tail as he dragged me to the water's edge. It was late, and the beach was deserted. We wandered along in no particular rush.

We passed Kyle's favourite pub, music filtering out the open doors and over the sand. I made a note to stop in on the way back, but continued down the beach scanning for any signs of life in the water as we went.

Geoff's office was still a good kilometer or two farther down, but it couldn't hurt to be thorough in my sweep of the bay.

A cool breeze blew the salty air off the water, and I savored the smell. There was no place quite like home.

The farther I walked, the more convinced I became that we were looking for a potentially imaginary needle in an enormous haystack. While we might come up empty, at least Max and I were getting some quality exercise.

We were getting close to SeaWorld, one of the Gold Coast's popular tourist parks, when my thoughts were drowned out by two loud engines tearing up the Broadwater. I raised my gaze to find a boat heading toward the open ocean. It was well above the speed limit, its lightweight hull slapping against the water as it went, a jet-black powerboat with a massive pair of red engines on the back. Not exactly a stealthy vessel.

I couldn't help but recognize the figure clinging to its wheel.

"You have to be kidding me," I muttered.

Max's gaze followed the boat as the familiar frayed epaulets of Captain Cronkwhile sped past us, his trusty whaling spear resting in a holder at the back of the vessel.

His boat was in far better condition than his outfit. Perhaps he was selling more books than I thought.

"That lunatic is going to get himself arrested by the water police." I shook my head as he vanished into the distance.

There weren't that many police on the water at this time of night though. Any that were on shift were likely to be chasing narcotics rather than narcissistic sea captains with a need for speed. Drugs were the real crime here on the Gold Coast.

As the captain vanished, I chuckled. I might have dismissed him at the Paranormal Palace, but here we were, both chasing mermaids. I wasn't going to tell him that, but it did make me wonder if Geoff was responsible for the captain's presence here on the coast. Had he hired us both to increase his chances of clearing his name?

I wouldn't put it past him, but competing with others could complicate matters.

Having him follow me around would only slow me down, and I didn't want him harpooning some poor cosplayer in a scaled tail and a wig.

Which, if I was being honest, I thought was the most likely scenario. Both for the captain's involvement, and in explaining what Geoff had seen in the water late that night.

With the captain gone, we continued down the beach, Max padding along and dragging me behind him. This was the longest walk he'd had in days, and my little partner was pleased as punch.

As we neared SeaWorld, he stopped, lifted his head, and barked twice, his signal for having found something of interest that was out of reach.

"What's that?" I asked as I scanned the water.

Max stared straight out at the water, not across the bay, but back toward the Spit, as if something were lurking in the Broadwater.

The waves were choppy, and I studied them, looking for the object of Max's interest. As the waves rolled, I thought I saw a shape break through the spray. It was a passing flash, something gray with a sheen to it. Then it was gone as the next wave passed over it.

At this distance, it was impossible to tell in the moonlight exactly what it was. But something was moving through the Broadwater. And it was just beneath the surface. I'd seen it break.

I gulped. The time was just after eleven pm. This was the same time Geoff had spotted his aquatic visitor.

Could it really be a mermaid?

Surely not. It could certainly be a shark. Plenty of those in the Broadwater.

It could also be a dolphin. I couldn't be sure until I got a better look. Some of the beaches were netted, but the Broadwater wasn't.

As the waves rolled over the Broadwater, I caught a glimpse of it again, just a flash of a silver-gray tail as it vanished beneath the water.

The shape was heading toward us and the canals. The shape would vanish momentarily and appear again between the waves in fleeting glimpses.

A dolphin made sense. It would have had to come up for air, but they also tended to play, whereas whatever this creature was had the tendency to dive beneath the waves, staying just out of view of observers who might be watching.

I needed to take a closer look at whatever it was, but it was approaching fast. I didn't relish the prospect of a swim at this hour, yet I didn't see that I had any other choice.

I kicked off my boots and ripped off my shirt. The weather wasn't particularly cold, but a midnight swim posed other dangers. Still, it was my best chance at finding out what the creature was.

In the S.A.S. I'd done my fair share of night dives. I wished I'd brought my diving knife with me. At least that would give me something to protect myself with if I needed it.

I hadn't been planning on a swim, but perhaps that was shortsighted on my part. I was looking for a mermaid, after all.

"Stay here, boy." I patted Max on the head. He was a pretty reliable partner and unless a pretty female beagle strolled past, unlikely at this hour, I could trust him to watch my clothes and wallet. There wasn't much cash in it. I bundled my things in a small heap out of reach of the tide and raced down to the water's edge.

The water was cool, but I took three steps into the surf and dove in. I was a confident swimmer. It was one of the core requirements of service in the SAS.

On any day ending in a 'Y' I could swim back and forth across the Broadwater without a worry. At night, I thought twice about it.

With swift strokes, I made my way out into the bay, setting an intercept path with the shape cutting through the waves. I scanned the water around me as best I could. If a shark found me, my day was going to get interesting real fast.

When you considered the amount of people swimming in the ocean every minute of every day around the world, or even just here in Australia where most of the country's population lived within 100 km of the beach, shark attacks were an infinitesimally small chance of occurrence.

But small wasn't zero.

I'd trained in far worse conditions though. Anything short of a great white shark wasn't going to trouble me. I swam out into the middle of the Broadwater treading water where I hoped the creature would pass by. Fifty meters out, there was a flash of silver before it dove. This time, it didn't resurface.

"Oh no," I grumbled.

The creature had gone deep and was coming right for me, but at this rate it would be kissing the bottom of the bay before it reached me. The deeper it went, the more impossible it got to track.

My heart beat faster, both from the exertion and the adrenaline of the unknown.

Taking a deep breath, I dove after the creature. The pressure built in my ears as I went. There was no chance I was letting the creature get past me.

Visibility diminished rapidly the deeper I went, and the current tried to pull me out of position. The Broadwater cared little about my search for the strange silver tail.

The tail hadn't been shaped like a shark's, or a dolphin's for that matter. It was broader than I'd ever witnessed and tapered at both ends.

I dove deeper, searching for Geoff's mermaid, kicking for all I was worth and wishing I had my flippers. The silence in the water was unsettling, nothing but the steady pulse of my heart, the only indication of any life down here. I held my breath as long as I could, searching in every direction and finding nothing.

Something clipped me, spinning me around in the water.

Before I could react, it tightened around my wrist. It had a vicelike grip as it yanked me downward. I tried to look behind me, but in the darkness, I could barely make out the shape that had me by the wrist.

I kicked at it, but it sliced through my foot.

My heart raced as we got deeper and deeper. It was going to drown me.

Blood drained from the wound in my foot, and I still hadn't even got a proper look at what I was dealing with. Still, I couldn't follow it to the bottom of the bay. I was running out of air. Focusing on the cold grip it had on me, I pressed my hand against the joint of its thumb. That particular digit wasn't meant to move more than a few degrees laterally.

Down, down, down we went. Darkness enveloped us both.

I forced the thumb with everything I had, leaning into it until I felt it snap with a satisfying crack.

The grip opened, and I was free.

As the creature descended onward, I kicked for the surface, my lungs burning with every stroke. My foot was weak and sore, the salt stinging the open wound, but I kept heading upward.

I looked down at the grey tail already vanishing into the distance. I stopped my ascent, questioning if I should give chase, but it was too fast, and my lungs burned with the need to draw breath.

With a few more kicks I broke the surface to draw a mammoth gasp of air. It had never tasted so good.

Looking around, I searched for the creature, but it was nowhere to be seen.

Whatever it was, it had attacked me.

Damn near drowned me.

I was in no shape to go after it, not unarmed with a ruined foot. Maybe the Captain had it right with a whaling spear.

With shaky strokes, I made my way back to shore, checking around me to ensure the creature hadn't returned. But I didn't see so much as a glimpse of it.

On reaching the shore, I dragged myself up the sand. The saltwater smarted in my wound, but I gritted my teeth and tried to ignore it.

Max barked when he saw my current state.

Sitting down beside him, I took inventory of my wound. There was a deep gash in the side of my foot like the creature had tried to shear through it. It needed to be bandaged at the very least. Fortunately, I had a first aid kit in the tank. What was more disconcerting than the wound was that the creature hadn't even been exerting itself as it had tried to drown me.

"Good job, Darius," I muttered as I picked up my boots and shirt and started hobbling back to the car. "Mermaid, one. Darius, Zero."

Still, I'd expected to find nothing, so in my somewhat twisted logic, the night was going better than anticipated.

Drowning Disappointment. Wednesday, April 26th 0030hrs.

EMBARRASSED, BLEEDING, AND FRUSTRATED, I limped back to my tank.

I was still trying to process what had happened to me. In the darkness of the Broadwater, I'd seen little, and what I did see failed to make sense. I could have sworn something with a tail was swimming toward me, but whatever hit me sliced through my foot like it was nothing.

Remembering the cold feel of the creature's grip, I couldn't help but think it felt more like steel than scales. The clean cut lent itself to the same hypothesis, but in the murky depths of the saltwater, it was impossible to say.

If it was a mermaid, it was as terrifying as anything I'd ever encountered. Fighting for my life, I'd done little more than break its finger. Even if I had hurt it, the creature had been able to go to depth and leave me behind.

Who was I kidding? Thinking I'd hurt the creature was being a little flexible with the truth, akin to a boxer claiming a win after blocking his opponent's blow with his lower lip.

I was beat up and bloody, and the beast hadn't cared in the slightest.

How had it known to dive? Had it seen me making my way into the water? If it had, its eyesight was better than mine. I hadn't even seen its head.

At least I'd found something. Not that I had anything to show Geoff for my troubles. At least I knew there was something in the Broadwater. What it was I had not the first clue. I would need to be better equipped next time.

I hobbled up to the tank and popped Max's leash over the mirror. Sitting on the passenger seat, I pulled out the first-aid kit from the dashboard. The breeze made the air more than a little chilly, but I needed to deal with one problem at a time.

Bleeding beat out the cold by a fair margin.

After flushing the wound clean, I took a closer look. It was deep, the sort that would ordinarily require stitches. I wasn't particularly feeling in the mood to sit in the ER at Gold Coast University Hospital, so I pulled a tube of medical glue out of the kit, applied it liberally to the wound, and squeezed it shut.

Let me tell you, that stuff is a man's best friend, more than once I'd helped Sonny or his sons patch themselves up after backyard rugby went a little too far. It was the sort of thing they didn't sell in stores. Probably because of the overwhelming temptation to use it to stop teenagers from talking back.

Content that the glue would hold, I bandaged my whole foot with gauze. Not my cleanest work, but it would do.

Reaching into the back seat, I grabbed a spare towel and dried myself, or at least as much as I could manage without actually changing my clothes. I was wet, cold, sore, and not much in the mood for anything but sleep, and I still had one stop I needed to make.

Ignoring the fact I looked like a hobo after losing a fight with a wombat, I eased my shoes back on.

My left foot smarted as the shoe pressed against my wound, but I'd had worse, and I couldn't rightly walk into the bar barefoot and bleeding. It was not the sort of image that conveyed professionalism.

"More like an idiot who went for a skinny dip," I muttered as I pulled on my shirt. I had no idea if Kyle Cruz had even been here, but Lawrence seemed to think so. Which made it as good a place as any to continue my investigation.

I hobbled to the bar, Max's leash in hand. It was after midnight and the place still had patrons. It wasn't your classic Aussie pub, loaded with eighteen-year-olds getting absolutely smashed while flailing about to impress whatever women were unfortunate enough to be loitering at twenty to one in the morning.

This one had a slightly older crowd, residents of the coast, surfers, and golden oldies out for a drink and a bit of live music. I walked past an old-time jukebox that was quiet in favor of a guitarist strumming away in the opposite corner. About a dozen patrons lingered at the bar or booths, drinking their night away.

Frankly, I was a little surprised anyone was here at this hour on a weeknight, but the pub certainly seemed to have a loyal following.

Max and I made our way up to the counter. One glance at the man behind the bar told me he could handle himself. He was squat and muscled, and the only hair on his head was a well-kept beard. He glanced down at Max and frowned.

I hadn't seen any signs about pets, and given the Spit was a pretty common dog beach, I'd made the assumption it would be fine to bring Max inside. Perhaps I'd been wrong.

"What can I get for you?" the barkeep asked. There was an air of skepticism in his voice as if he were wondering if I'd already had too much and was simply trying to get me to talk to confirm it.

"Rum and coke," I replied calmly. "Plenty of ice, please."

The barkeep reached beneath the bar and fetched a tall glass. He scooped it full of ice, and worked the taps with an efficiency that told me he knew what he was doing.

He came back with a glass filled to the brim. He didn't spill a drop.

I handed him a twenty. He wandered to the cash register, slid the bill into the till, and produced my change. When he returned, I waved him off and told him to keep it.

He nodded, the slightest hint of a smile forming on his lips.

Perhaps that would atone for my partner's presence.

He slipped the note and coins into the tip jar and lingered. "Awfully generous of you."

Perhaps he just wasn't a dog person. Whatever the case, he hadn't run me out or told me to chain up Max outside.

I sat and listened to the guitarist, a surfer in board shorts and a worn out singlet, strumming away on an old acoustic guitar. It was quite pleasant. Any other day, I would be in danger of having a good time.

I waited for the bar keeper to serve the other patrons and have both the time and inclination to talk. Not that he looked like a particularly chatty sort, but I certainly didn't want to try plying him for information while he had his hands full.

Finishing the rum and coke, I considered ordering a second, but given I'd already made a fool of myself once tonight, I held off. I needed to be clearheaded. When the music came to a lull, the barman leaned on the bar in front of me.

"Haven't seen you in here before." It was more of a statement than a question.

"My first time," I replied, trying to match his manner. "I was just wandering along the beach with my partner when we heard the music and thought it sounded like a good place to take a load off."

"Normally, I'd ask him to stay outside," the barkeep said, "but as long as you clean up after him, and he behaves, he should be right to finish out the night in here."

"It's very accommodating of you," I said, leaving a pause, hoping he would introduce himself."

"Phillip. And you are?"

"Darius." I eyed my empty glass, still weighing my options.

"You want another one of those?" I shook my head. "It's late and I still need to drive. Maybe just a Coke this time round."

"Fair enough," Philip replied and fetched the drink. I handed him another bill and when he returned with the change, I nodded to the tip jar once more.

Philip deposited it in the jar and leaned on one palm on the counter. "Police or armed forces?"

I raised an eyebrow. "What makes you think I am either?"

He chuckled. "The way you walk, the steady but consistent habit you have of checking your surroundings for potential dangers. You're trying to look relaxed but you're pretty alert for after midnight, which means your actions are habits rather than conscious effort on your part. That along with the way you carry yourself and your seeming lack of concern at wandering the Broadwater alone and late at night. You're one or the other. So which is it?"

He was more perceptive than I'd expected.

"Armed Forces. Retired. Two deployments."

"Thank you for your service," Philip replied and from his tone, I could tell he meant it. Perhaps he had friends in the service.

I nodded. I never knew what else to say to that. Recognition made me a little uncomfortable.

"Well, Darius, anytime you need a drink, you just come on down. We'd love to have you."

Philip was just about to leave, and given I'd sated his curiosity, I might not hear from him unless I ordered another drink, and I was running out of cash. I'd greased the tip jar liberally and hoped it would pay off.

"Philip, Could I ask you something?"

He took the dishtowel off his shoulder and wiped down the counter. "Me, first."

I shrugged. "By all means."

"You weren't idly wandering the Broadwater when you stumbled upon my bar, were you?"

"What makes you say that?"

Philip sighed, but his body tensed in readiness. "There is a defined difference between a man wandering in after midnight looking to drown his sorrows, and a man with a mission. You're the latter. You planning on causing any trouble?"

"None whatsoever," I replied, a little bothered that was his first concern.

"Then what can I do for you?" he asked, though he didn't relax one iota.

"I'm looking for a man and was told he often drinks here. He's not in tonight, but I was wondering if you've seen him?"

"This man got a name?" Philip tossed the cloth back over his shoulder.

"Kyle Cruz, an ex-Olympian. He runs a high-end swim school near here."

Philip nodded. "I know Kyle, but I'm not in the habit of gossiping about my clients or giving their whereabouts to strangers who have just walked in the door."

"Not a problem at all, Philip. I was just wondering if you've seen him recently, because no one else has seen him since Friday and when I spoke to his business partner, he suggested Kyle often came here to drink. Did you see him Friday night? Or any night since?"

"I saw him Sunday night but haven't seen him since."

I straightened up. "He was here?"

"Sure was, and he was celebrating pretty hard. Bought at least one round for the bar. Apparently, his court case was dismissed. Tried to get himself proper drunk too."

"You know anything about the case?" I replied, trying my luck.

"Nothing that wasn't in the papers." Philip shrugged. "And like I said, I don't gossip about my patrons."

"A discretion they appreciate, I'm sure." I didn't want to push too hard and alienate him, because by all counts, Phillip was one of the last people to see Kyle Cruz.

"You said he's missing?" Philip cleared my empty glass, genuine concern etched into his face.

"I did. His partner says he hasn't been into work this week."

"*Partner* is being a little generous," Philip replied. "Lawrence is a sniveling prat who's been robbing Kyle blind for years."

I cocked my head. "I thought you said you don't gossip about your clients."

Philip managed a wry grin. "Lawrence isn't a client."

"Are you saying there was bad blood between them?"

Lawrence certainly hadn't given me that impression in the office, but then again, with his boss missing, I would have been surprised if he'd volunteered such an important detail.

Philip stroked his beard. "I don't know, man. They came in together once, had one drink, and Lawrence left in a bit of a huff. Kyle got on the juice pretty hard and said something about money missing from their accounts. To be honest, I don't know if it's Lawrence's fault, or Kyle just squandered it away. Either is equally as likely, so take it with a grain of salt but something about the guy just irked me, you know?"

I did know. Something about Lawrence hadn't sat well with me either. If he was robbing Kyle blind, that could certainly be considered motive.

But where was Kyle now?

"I hear you, but for the time being, Kyle is my main concern. What else can you tell me about that night?"

Phillip ran his fingers through his beard. "Well, he wasn't alone. He left with a woman."

"Wait, what?" I sat up. "He wasn't alone?"

"No, something about walking the girl home. I only caught the tail end of it before the two of them left. Frankly, I was a little surprised. She was much younger than him."

"Why didn't you say something? He's been missing for days."

"How would I know that?" Philip replied. "He was happy and healthy when he left here. I wouldn't fret, Darius. He's done this before. It wouldn't be the first person he picked up in my bar and spent the next few days drinking and shagging. He's good at splashing around the cash and luring them in. This one certainly went all googly eyed over him.

"I don't suppose you have a picture of her, or camera footage?" I asked hopefully.

"Sorry, man, footage wipes every twenty-four hours. Only have it in case there is an incident. People prefer it that way, you know."

I needed something to go on. "I don't suppose you can tell me anything about this woman?"

He poured a coke, without me asking for it, and set it on the bar. "She was young, probably early twenties. I think she said something about studying. Pretty young thing, big brown eyes. Dark hair, nice figure, but not a gym junkie or surgical addict, you know what I mean."

I did, but it wasn't much to go on. I was looking for a naturally attractive twenty-something year old student on the Gold Coast. One who hadn't had Kardashian-level work done.

There had to be thousands of women that might fit that description.

"Sorry I can't be more helpful. It was a Sunday night. We were swamped."

"I don't suppose you caught her name?"

Phillip's brow furrowed. "I can't remember, man. She didn't say more to me than her drink order. She'd never been here before."

"What did she have?"

"A margarita or a martini, I can't rightly remember Do you know how many drinks I serve each night?"

I didn't answer. I just opened my wallet, took out a twenty and my business card, and slid them into the tip jar.

"If you think of anything else that can help, give me a call."

"Sure thing," Philip replied. "Hope you find him."

"Me too," I replied, as I got up out of the chair. "You said they walked home?"

Phillip pointed to the beach. "Right out the same door you walked in."

It was something. I scooped up Max's lead, checked for any surprise nuggets—there were none in spite of the fact he'd been eating all night—said goodbye to Phillip.

"Like I said, come back anytime," he called after me.

I'd paid him sixty dollars for a rum and coke, and two straight cokes. I was probably the most profitable customer in the place; no wonder he wanted me back. Still, it was good music. Much closer to my age and taste than other bars I'd been in.

"I just might do that," I replied with a grin. "Let's go, Max."

I headed for the door. It wasn't much, the faintest whiff of a lead, but at least I now knew where Kyle Cruz had last been seen, and he hadn't been alone. What was the chance that Kyle would go missing the night he hooked up with a strange young woman, at a bar she'd never frequented before, but he was known to be a regular at?

It felt like a set up. Unfortunately, I had nothing but my gut to go on.

I stood in the doorway. Only seventy-two hours ago, Kyle had stepped out onto this beach and never been seen again.

I thought of the creature I'd encountered in the water. Surely, he hadn't crossed paths with the beast?

That would have required a drunk-as-a-skunk ex-Olympian to take a midnight swim in the Broadwater.

He would have to be a complete idiot, and I was fairly confident there was only one of those in town.

Refuel and Research. Wednesday, April 26th 0935hrs.

I PULLED OPEN THE door of Paradox, and the refreshing scent of freshly brewed coffee washed over me. It had been a while since my last visit. The day of my failed attempt to ask Courtney out, actually.

When she smiled up at me, I found myself wondering why I'd waited so long. She was easy on the eyes, and friendly. But good at breaking hearts, if I believed her colleague, Tommy. He also doubled as my new research assistant and seemed both skilled and efficient.

Courtney beamed as I approached the counter. Surely one date couldn't hurt?

I considered what was going on in my life and thought better of it. In the last week alone, I'd been chased, stopped a kidnapping, almost had my father kidnapped, and been shot at. Not to mention my run-ins with Benjamin Marino. Whether Courtney was good for me or not wasn't really the question. I was most certainly not safe company for her. Particularly not with the Djinn toying with me and those around me.

Besides, I had a lot on my plate. A bucket of cases, and little more than a hint of an answer to any of them.

I sighed, frustrated. With the Djinn, I had nothing to speak of. Then there was Kyle Cruz, the missing coach and my friend's missing cash. I'd found neither sight nor sound of him. All I knew was that he had left the Watering Hole just after midnight on Sunday in the company of a fetching young brunette and hadn't been seen since.

Last, but not least, I had Geoff and his mermaid menace. While I wasn't ready to concede beautiful merpeople were traversing the Broadwater on a nightly basis, I had run afoul of something in the Broadwater. The way it had dragged me down into the depths concerned me. Had it been playing with me?

There were enough mysteries in my life, I didn't have the bandwidth to add a woman as well, unfathomable mysteries that they usually proved to be, at least to me. That was a job for another day.

I strode toward the counter. My wounded foot protesting in my boot, but I'd be damned if I was going to hobble in front of her. Courtney's smile promised mischief, and one day, if I could deal with the Djinn, perhaps I might want to take a chance on that mischief.

Carl's encouragement rang in my ear. I could almost hear him. "Who cares, Darius?" he would have said. "A night of casual rambunctious fun is just what the doctor ordered."

His doctor's advice was likely more syphilitic than sound, so I erred on the side of caution.

"Heya Courtney, how are you?" I called, trying not to sound like a crazy man who'd been arguing with himself since he walked in the door.

"Darius, it's good to see you," she said. "It's been a while."

She leaned on the counter with one hand as if waiting for an explanation.

"You wouldn't believe the week I've had," I replied. "I could have sorely used a coffee."

Courtney nodded along. "So we heard. You caught the Casper Killer! I knew you would."

"Right place, right time," I answered as Tommy emerged from the kitchen.

He took one glance at me and Courtney and intervened in his usual flamboyant manner. "Courtney, dear, can't you see Darius is run off his feet? Get him a latte with three sugars and let him be on with his day."

I smiled apologetically, trying not to offend Courtney. I didn't need her spitting in my coffee. "That would be perfect."

She rang up the order. I swiped my card and slid into one of the booths to wait for it, setting the duffel I'd been carrying beneath the table.

Tommy made a show of fussing about the food display before making his way over. As he wiped down the booth counter, he whispered, "Those funds cleared in time for the weekend. Thanks for that."

I leaned back against the soft pleather seat and moved my arms out of the way. "Don't thank me. It was pay for a job well done. You were most thorough, and it helped immensely."

"I saw the report. You move fast, Darius."

The Casper Killer really hadn't given me much choice.

"Well, with the rate he was dropping bodies, we were running short of time and targets. I put two and two together and managed to get to the judge before he could. You helped save her life, you know. You should feel good about that too."

He slid into the seat opposite me. "You wouldn't believe the rush I got just watching the report. I've been giddy about it all weekend. This is what you do every day?"

"Day in day out," I replied. "But it's not always that glamorous. I mean, don't get me wrong, we're always helping people. Just usually there aren't any news crews."

"Well, if there's anything else you need me to look into, just hit me up."

"As a matter of fact, that's why I'm here. I'm working a few cases at the moment. My hands are pretty full, and I could use your help. Want to earn a few extra bucks?"

"Sure, I get off at lunch. I could work on a few things this afternoon. What do you need me to do?"

"A few things, Tommy. First, there was a case that concluded last week in the local courts. Allegations of harassment against a local swimming instructor."

"Kyle Cruz. I saw him on the news." Tommy chuckled at his own rhyme. "What's he got to do with you?"

"He's gone missing, and I've been tasked with tracking him down. Last thing I know, he was leaving a bar called the Watering Hole at the Spit around midnight Sunday. Never showed up to work on Monday and hasn't been seen since. He was apparently in the company of a young brunette college-aged student, identity still unknown."

"And you want me to find him?" Tommy pulled out his phone and tapped away, making notes as we went.

"I want you to get me everything you can on that court case, and any other allegations that might have been made against him. I'd like to find the girl who was last seen with him at the bar, but without an ID that's probably a needle in a haystack."

"You think she had something to do with his disappearance?"

I shrugged. "Right now, I have no idea what happened. But her case was thrown out of court and only days later, the man she had accused of harassing her vanishes without a trace. Someone had an axe to grind with Kyle Cruz and while she could also be a victim, I don't want to dismiss her without at least talking to her first."

"Fair enough," Tommy replied. "She certainly had motive."

That she did. I wasn't quite ready to send him hunting mermaids. Instead, I reached below the counter and grabbed the duffel off the floor. I set it between us and unzipped it.

"What's this?" Tommy asked.

"It's the remains of a disguise worn by someone I met with last week. They are doing their level best to keep their identity secret, but I want to find them."

"How did you come by it?" Tommy replied as I lifted the women's blazer out of the bag. "Surely you didn't steal this off some hapless woman?"

"She was anything but hapless." I tapped the table for emphasis. "Tommy, she is quite dangerous. And I didn't steal it. She left it for me. She's taunting me."

"Ah, you've found a nemesis, I see. Who is this Moriarty that's mystifying you? A jilted lover? An angry client?"

"If I knew that, she wouldn't need a disguise, would she?" I replied.

Tommy's cheeks flushed a little. "Fair enough. You want me to find her?"

I held up a hand. "I don't want you tracking her, not yet. I just need anything you can find about these outfits and where they came from."

"I assume you have searched them for trace DNA?" Tommy mused. Someone had been doing their own study.

"They're clean," I replied. "I was hoping you might be able to help me track down where they were purchased."

Tommy shook the blazer. "I hope you aren't just asking me because I'm gay?"

He fixed me with a stare. I wasn't sure if he was being serious.

His sexuality hadn't factored into my consideration at all.

"I'm asking you because you clearly have more fashion sense than I do, and I wouldn't know where to even begin."

A compliment never went astray.

Tommy didn't say a word, but his smile told me he'd heard me just fine. And more than likely, agreed with my assessment.

He looked at the logo of the jacket. "This, my friend, is a Kaio, a popular brand but not particularly uncommon. There're probably five stores within a hundred kilometers of here. But if she's clever and knew she was going to leave it behind for you to find, she will have bought it secondhand off Gumtree or Marketplace. No security footage to contend with."

That wasn't very promising at all.

"This gold chain is interesting." Tommy appraised the belt Mary Baker had worn. "Not solid gold, at least not the belt, but this buckle. It appears to be real. An expensive prop for a throwaway disguise. Not sure where you'd start with tracking that, but it's something, at least more useful than the jacket."

It also told me the Djinn had money to burn.

Tommy raised the wig. "This is interesting."

I leaned in. "How so?"

"It's incredibly high quality, Darius. It even looks and feels like real hair, not that shiny sheen cheap store garbage. This has been hand-made. Which makes it the most trackable item of the lot."

"You're an expert on wigs, Tommy? You never cease to surprise me."

"I have a few friends that are experts in this department. I'll run it past one and see if we can't narrow down where it was bought."

That sounded a little promising. "Thanks, Tommy, you're a gentleman and a scholar."

"And I make a mean scone, but who am I to boast?" he said as he got up.

"Well, if you find anything, just send it through. If you need anything to expedite matters, let me know. I have an allowance for disbursements as long as they remain reasonable."

Tommy nodded. "In the meantime, I better get back to work. I'll let you know what I find."

I zipped up the bag and slid it across the counter. "You can hold onto this, but don't let it out of your possession."

"Noted." Tommy hefted the duffel off the counter and headed for the kitchen.

"Your latte is ready," Courtney called, her eyes locked on me. I suspected my coffee had been done for some time. She'd just been watching me and Tommy.

I headed to the counter to retrieve my coffee. It was warm but not hot. If Courtney wondered why I'd been talking to Tommy, she didn't ask. She just gave me a little wave.

Tommy was wheeling a mop out of the kitchen, but stopped in the middle of the shop. "Darius, look!"

He pointed at the TV on the wall. I hadn't paid it any heed since I'd walked in, but now a breaking news banner was flashing along the bottom of the screen.

The volume was muted, but the subtitle and banner were only too clear.

Kyle Cruz. Former Olympian found dead by fisherman.

Swimming with the Fishies. Wednesday, April 26th 1000hrs.

IN LESS TIME THAN it took a fart to rise to the surface of a bath, my missing person case had become a homicide. And this one was starting to stink just as badly.

First, Kyle had vanished days after taking my friend's money. Now, he was dead. Sonny's chances of ever getting his money back were diminishing by the minute.

I pointed to the TV. "Tommy, can you turn that up?"

"I've got it," Courtney called, raising a remote. The hustle and bustle of the popular coffee shop was drowned out as the newsreader's voice filled the room.

"Kyle Cruz, homegrown Olympian, has been found dead in the Broadwater this morning. Our reporter Jai Washburn is on the scene. Jai, are you there?"

The screen split. On the left-hand side was a picture of Kyle in his younger days standing on an Olympic podium, a gold medal around his neck as he punched the air. On the other side of the screen was a live feed of a reporter standing on the all too familiar sandy beach of the Broadwater.

"I am, Cindy. I'm here with the man responsible for locating Kyle's body."

The shot panned out, revealing the familiar face of Captain Cronkwhile.

I groaned. Clearly, the pair of us were operating on crossed frequency. His search for mermaids and sea monsters had turned up a body for Sonny's case, while I'd almost been drowned by something I still couldn't explain.

"Ah yes, I was patrolling the Broadwater in search of sea beasts when I found the body. Hidden beneath the deeps, it was. But I've got good eyes for these things."

Jai did his best to keep a level expression, a feat of acting that might have won him an Oscar if it wasn't for his left eyebrow creeping up. "Sea beasts, you say, sir? Like a shark?"

"No, boy." The captain flailed in the direction of a body laying beneath a blanket on the sand. "No shark I know has opposable thumbs. We're dealing with something else..."

His voice trailed off in a deliberate attempt to add an air of mystery.

"What exactly are you suggesting, Captain?" Jai asked, before leaning in with the microphone.

"For weeks, I've been receiving reports of mercreatures in the Broadwater. This only confirms it."

Jai shifted back away from the captain as if concerned the man's crazy might rub off on him. "Merpeople, you say? What leads you to that, uh, unorthodox conclusion?"

"The manner in which the body was found," the captain answered. Either he didn't notice the reporter's obvious skepticism or he didn't care. "All trussed up like an offering to Poseidon. The creatures are trying to send a message. We've dirtied their domain, and mark my words, they aren't happy about it."

"You think this attack was motivated by environmental concerns?"

"Environmental concerns?" The captain shook his head. "How is it you lot can report on a teenage bully as gangs of violent youth roaming the streets, but when it comes to the health of the planet, you clam up tighter than the Illuminati?"

"I, uh..." Jai paused as his brain overloaded on live TV.

The captain had given him too much to work with. He simply didn't know which piece of lunacy to deal with first.

"I can assure you we treat environmental concerns very seriously," Jai said.

I moved closer to the TV as I tried to identify which stretch of the Broadwater they were broadcasting from.

The captain was not mollified. "It's not the first time I've seen such violence and I doubt it'll be the last."

Jai moved the microphone back in front of his own mouth in an effort to take back control of the meandering interview. "You are genuinely convinced a mermaid did this? Not another human being with an axe to grind? Looks like he was drowned, though how and why, we can only guess."

Captain Cronkwhile pointed a finger at Jai's chest. "You doubt me now, I know. But just wait till I catch the creature, you'll see."

"I guess so," Jai replied, beaten into submission by the captain's bravado.

The captain stepped forward into center frame and addressed the camera. "Don't worry, citizens of the Gold Coast, Captain Cronkwhile will drive the beast out of the bay and back into open waters where it belongs."

The camera man panned away and back to Jai. "As you can see, a most unusual case is unfolding here on the Gold Coast. But you can rest assured the Queensland Police Service are on the case."

"As am I," Captain Cronkwhile shouted from somewhere off screen.

When the reporter paid him no heed, the captain stomped through the background of the camera shot, trudging down to the water where his powerboat was resting on the sand.

Without hesitation, he pushed it out until it was floating in two or three feet of water and climbed aboard. With one hand on the engines, he backed out into the channel and fired up his boat.

"Mad as a hatter, if you ask me," the newsreader said.

The assessment didn't surprise me. Robert Kensington of Channel 9 News was quick to decry anyone he didn't see eye-to-eye with. His disagreeableness made for good ratings though, and he did quite well with people tuning in, if for no other reason than to see what he would say each night.

Old Bob had been fairly critical of my own performance, and I'd genuinely caught the murderers I was chasing.

Oh well, if nothing else, perhaps Captain Cronkwhile would give them someone else to hound and rail against for the next few days.

The newsman moved on.

"The sooner you can get me that info, Tommy, the better," I said, already heading for the door.

I needed a phone, badly, but I'd obliterated mine at the national park yesterday. So I climbed into the tank and raced back to the office. Flying through the door, I headed for my room.

"Not so much as a good morning?" Glenda called without looking up from her book.

"Sorry, Glenda," I replied as I glanced at the romance novel she was reading. She couldn't be more than a dozen pages from the end. "I didn't want to interrupt you while you were at the best part."

In truth, I needed to be at the Broadwater ten minutes ago, and didn't really have time to shoot the breeze, but my best chance of getting access to that crime scene was by calling in a favor with my newfound allies at the detectives department.

"Mighty kind of you, Darius," she replied. "One of these days, I'm going to give you a raise."

"I'm your boss, Glenda. You work for me," I called as I strode into my office. "Not that you'd notice."

"What was that, dear?" Glenda called. "You're mumbling again. If you'd rather I went home for the day, it can be arranged."

The cheek on her.

I cleared my throat. "I said, we both know you prefer reading here where you can control the temperature rather than at home, putting up with your sister."

"She's a dear, but the old biddy interrupts me every five minutes," Glenda said. "And she runs that air conditioner night and day, even in winter. It's almost like if she turned it off, she might melt. If anyone in this city is a witch, Darius, it's her. You ought to arrest her."

"For excessive air-conditioner use?" I answered. "I'm afraid I don't really have the authority to arrest anyone. So you're out of luck. I see more bingo and gin in your future."

"A pity," Glenda replied. "On the first count. On the second? Well, a good gin never goes astray."

"I've been trying to ring you all morning," Glenda called.

I pulled my shattered phone out of my pocket and held it up. The screen was useless, and I was fairly sure I'd splintered whatever electronics were inside it. Being sandwiched between a hundred kilos of me and a rock had been bad for its wellbeing.

Holding it for her to see, I said, "Sorry, no phone. I broke it yesterday when I was chasing a perp."

"One you can't even arrest?"

She was baiting me, but I wasn't biting.

"That's the job, Glenda. It pays the wages and keeps you in the lifestyle to which you've become accustomed. Why were you phoning me?"

"A woman called the office this morning. She said she wanted to talk to you. Apparently, she's been emailing you for days about a mermaid."

I fired up my computer and looked at my shattered phone. Fortunately, I kept a spare here, my old smart phone before I'd upgraded to a model with a better camera. It was five years old and double digits worth of editions behind the current market leaders, but it would have to do.

"A mermaid, I said," Glenda called again.

"I know. I'm already on it," I replied as I removed the sim card from my current phone, slid it into the old phone, and set the shattered model aside. I sincerely doubted the warranty would cover this level of clumsiness, but nothing ventured, nothing gained.

"Has the wife hunt grown so desperate, you're turning to the sea, Darius?"

It was a good one. I couldn't help but grin. "I hadn't thought of that, but now that you mention it, maybe that's what I've been doing wrong all these years. Searching for a soul mate when I should have been shopping for a magical mistress."

"I thought I sent you to lunch with a perfectly lovely woman last week."

I stopped dead. So she had intentionally mixed up the appointment with Mary Baker and Holly Draper.

"So you did. Thanks, by the way, it was lovely. But ghosting Holly Draper almost got a judge killed. So perhaps next time we could let me filter my lunch dates."

"Just looking out for you, Darius. One of them writes a gossip column for the paper. The other was a practicing psychologist, and a woman. Both of which you sorely need in your life."

I didn't want to tell Glenda that Mary Baker was a sociopath and likely a murderer. I didn't want to put her in any danger.

"So you want the mermaid woman's number or not?" Glenda called.

"If she's been emailing, then I'm sure I'll have it here."

My phone problem solved, I jumped onto my emails. I remembered seeing one mentioning a mermaid when I was sorting through them last week. I'd noted it but set it aside in favor of chasing the Casper Killer. Now, however, it could prove pertinent to the case at hand.

What fascinated me about it now, though, was the timing. This email had arrived days before Kyle Cruz had even gone missing.

Which meant either her mermaid sighting was unrelated to the Olympian's disappearance or perhaps the captain was right, the creature had been frequenting the channel for some time and Kyle was just its latest victim.

I was more interested in the location of her sighting though, on account that it might give me a pattern I could follow. I knew where Geoff had seen the creature, and I knew where I had been attacked. If I could find and collate any other accounts and cross-reference them, I might be able to pull together a broader picture of the creature's habits.

If there was a mermaid frequenting the Broadwater, I was going to photograph it for a rather handsome payday from Geoff, before getting even with it for my foot.

I was in a hurry, but given I planned to talk with the detective, I needed to bring something worth trading.

I opened my emails in the hope they contained something of use. There were literally hundreds of them and I didn't have the time to read them all, so I filtered by mermaid. To my surprise, the emails were from more than one email address. Geoff's I recognized immediately, and discarded on account of the fact it predated our meeting and I anticipated I knew most or all of what it contained. I scrolled to the next one. Beatrice Ingleburn. She had to be the woman who called the office.

Opening the email, I read swiftly.

Dear Sir,

I have seen you on the news and wanted to report a most unusual sight I happened across the other evening. I awoke late Sunday night from a terrible dream and was in the process of fixing myself an aperitif when I looked out the window and spotted a creature in the water.

Not a shark or dolphin, I've seen plenty of those in my time. No, this was like that Ariel creature out of the Disney movie. Only it was very real. She had red hair and a scaly tail where her legs should have been. I went to call the police but didn't want them to think I was crazy.

Still, I know what I saw, clear as day. A mermaid swimming down the canal. She was quite swift, and after several strokes, she vanished into the depths. That's when I saw her tail. Should you have any questions don't hesitate to call by. I live at 72 Gibraltar Drive Surfer's Paradise.

I'm not very good with technology. I tried to take a picture of it but all I got was the attached.

Sincerely,

Beatrice Ingleburn.

I opened the attachment to find a picture of half of what I presumed was Mrs. Ingleburn's face as she stared wide-eyed into the camera.

I could only assume she had been trying to take the photo when she accidentally pressed the button that reversed which camera the phone would use.

"Well, that's unfortunate," I muttered. Had she actually managed to snap a picture of the mermaid, I might have taken care of Geoff's case immediately. He didn't want me to catch the creature, simply prove its existence. Any unedited image ought to suffice.

Her sighting had occurred the night Kyle disappeared. That couldn't be a coincidence.

Though I suspected hearing the captain on the news today might serve to encourage Geoff while he waited.

The third email was from one Terence Sharp.

Mr Kane,

Thrice this week, I've been fishing in the Broadwater, reeling in a catch when some other creature has stolen it right off my hook. The first two times, I thought it was just larger prey but the third time it was early in the morning.

I had buried my rod in the sand while I fetched another cold one from the cooler and the creature took it all.

My whole rig. Hook, line, sinker, and rod. Dragged it into the Broadwater in a flash of silver, never to be seen again.

I have lost a fish or two before, but I've never had my rod stolen and suppose it to be the act of a larger creature, perhaps some sort of sea beast or merperson. What other reason would they want my rod? I was fishing off the promontory at the Spit just before dawn. No competition and plenty of action in the water. Now that I'm retired, I can sleep during the day, leave all the other suckers to take what's left.

Thought you ought to know in case you want to look into it. The whole affair has left me rather miffed, and in need of a new rod.

Terence.

Attached to the email was a picture of Terence's rod. It was rather substantial, the kind of rig you could comfortably reel in a small shark with. I reassessed my initial assumption that he was drunk at the time.

His rig looked well strung and wasn't new. Terence was no novice, but it wasn't exactly actionable information. Certainly nothing that would win over the strong-willed Olivia Hart, more a smattering of facts. Each of which might prove useful, but for the time being were like pictures of a puzzle whose place I couldn't yet discern.

I needed more information if I wanted to get Sonny's money back for him. Given my missing person had become a homicide, there was only one place to get it. I just had to hope Hart was feeling particularly charitable, and there was no time like the present to test my chances.

My new-old phone was still charging, so I called Hart from my land line. A little old school, but then again, so was I.

Hart answered on the fourth ring.

"Detective Hart speaking." She was brief, almost curt.

"Olivia," I answered, talking as if we were old friends. "Darius Kane. How are you?"

"I might have guessed that was you. Something wrong with your mobile?"

I looked at my ancient relic that was still charging.

"It's seen better days. Have I caught you at a good time?"

"Not at all," she replied. "I'm in the middle of a case but given what that lunatic has been spouting on the news, I'm sure you already know that."

I drummed my fingers on the desk. There was no good way to beg a favor, and I imagined she would see through any ploys I might try, so I got to the point.

"So you did get the Kruz case? Excellent."

"Don't tell me," she said with a laugh, "you're working it too?"

It seemed we were destined to spend more time together, if one believed in such things. I didn't; I figured it was just the misfortune of spending most of my time chasing murderers.

"Ah, yes. But when I started, it was just a missing person. It would appear things have deteriorated."

"A trend when you're involved, it would seem." Hart wasn't pulling any punches. I wasn't liking my chances of getting a favor out of her.

"And here I was calling to share the information I had out of the kindness and generosity of my—"

"What do you want, Darius?" Olivia cut me off. "And what do you know?"

I didn't have much, but I knew how to make the most of what I had.

"I have the last location he was seen alive and a smattering of interesting details that might assist in your investigation. I've been running down leads for a few days. I could save you some time."

"And what do you want?" Olivia asked with a resigned sigh.

"I want to see the body," I replied, trying not to sound too eager.

"You don't ask much, do you?" Olivia laughed.

If Kyle had been killed in a manner that suggested a mermaid or other supernatural creature might have done it, then I wanted to know.

If he'd been murdered by more mundane means, I wanted to know why. Was that why Lawrence had been acting so suspicious? Did he know his business partner was already dead?

Hart held the cards. Was she ready to deal?

"We can help each other," I said. "Isn't that what you suggested the other day?"

Olivia was silent as she mulled over my offer.

"I guess that can't hurt. Come down to the Broadwater just north of Sea World and we can swap notes. You best hurry. The coroner will be down soon."

North of Sea World? That was right where I'd been walking with Max. I couldn't have been more than a few hundred meters from where they discovered the body when that beast hit me in the water.

A shiver ran down my spine. Maybe Captain Cronkwhile wasn't as crazy as he seemed.

"Darius, are you still there?" Olivia's voice echoed down the line.

"Yep, sure am," I replied getting to my feet. "Just gathering my things."

"Good, get a move on, but when you get here, we need to talk. I need a favor."

"I'll be right over."

I hung up the phone and stared down at my desk.

A favor. What on earth could Detective Hart want from me?

Mermaids and meal tickets. Wednesday, April 26th 1115hrs

THE BROADWATER LOOKED A whole lot less sinister when I wasn't drowning in it. On a clear day like today, it was quite picturesque. It was one of many reasons I enjoyed living on the Gold Coast.

Today, that natural beauty was diminished by the body barely concealed by a sheet: Kyle Cruz's remains and concrete evidence that he wasn't shacked up with a mistress like everyone had supposed.

I crossed the sand heading toward the police.

Reporters were being held at bay up on the beach, and I could see why. It was the sort of thing that made for grim front-page news. Not to mention how much harder an investigation became when details were leaked by the press.

I was more than a little curious to hear what Detective Hart wanted from me, but after being ambushed by that creature last night, I needed every bit of information I could get. I'd been less than a few hundred meters from this very place. That couldn't be a coincidence. Had Kyle met the same creature and lost?

My breath caught in my throat as I remembered the intense building of the pressure in my ears when the beast had dragged me mercilessly into the depths, its vice-like grip locked around my wrist.

I shook my head to purge the all-too vivid memory.

"Darius," Detective Hart called as she spotted me beelining toward her.

"Olivia, good to see you again. I only wish it were under better circumstances."

"You and me both," she replied, placing a hand on my back to steer me toward the sheet. The friendliness of the gesture wasn't lost on me, nor was the soft pressure of her hand on my body. I wasn't quite sure what to do about her hand, but I went along with it.

Olivia had gone from wanting to charge me, to handsy and friendly in a matter of days. At this rate, we would be in bed by the end of the week.

The thought caused me to smile, just a little.

I very much doubted that would happen, but the meteoric shift in her attitude had me wary. Was she just trying to win me over with her charms?

Remembering where we were, I set a neutral expression. Wouldn't do to be standing here smiling like an idiot while looking down at the body of the man I was hired to find. However, the thought of Olivia Hart in much less than a pantsuit was a particularly difficult image to dislodge.

Focus, Darius. She'd eat you alive the second it suited her. Like a spider.

And just like that, my libido vanished faster than Kanye's career prospects.

Thanks, arachnophobia, I knew I could always count on you.

"Was it really found by that weirdo in the boat?" I asked, referencing the captain, but not wanting to raise the fact I'd met him before.

"Unfortunately," Hart replied. "That one has more than a few screws loose. Surprised the two of you don't know each other."

"I met him the other day," I replied. Lying seemed liable to backfire, so I opted for the truth. "He wanted to work together to catch some mermaids, but I blew him off."

"Really, I thought that sort of thing would be right up your alley."

I couldn't tell if she was making fun of me or not, and her expression was deadpan.

I shrugged. "If someone were paying me, sure. I've got bills. But this loon wanted to split the proceeds and kudos when we found one. A mythical creature that's never been photographed? I wasn't born yesterday."

"I see," Olivia replied as we neared the body. "How did you get on Kyle's case and what do you know?"

"A favor for a friend. They paid to enroll their daughter in his swim school. The upfront tuition fees are truly outrageous. Kyle took their money and then he just went and disappeared. They asked me to find him. He was missing, and I presumed he was either laying low, or had done a runner."

"So no leads on who might have wanted him dead?" Hart replied.

"Perhaps. Look, I started this just trying to help my friends get their money back. I wasn't expecting any bodies, so I'm still playing a little catch up."

"Perhaps money was the motive," Olivia replied. "Perhaps someone else found him and wanted their cash back. How much did he charge?"

"Two seasons for twenty-five thousand if paid upfront. Thirty on a payment plan. Believe it or not, they consider that a discount."

Olivia shook her head. "You're kidding me? Hard to believe any lessons are worth that sort of coin. But then again, I'm not an Olympic swimmer, and parents pay ridiculous money to see their kids succeed in sports."

Sonny and Lucille were proof of that. I just hoped I could recover something for them, though that seemed less likely by the second.

"What can you tell me about where the body was found?"

Olivia pointed to a buoy floating out in the water. It was about fifty or sixty meters out from the beach and only part way across the Broadwater.

How had the body got out there?

"The body was underwater. Weighed down so that he wouldn't float away on the tide," she added, drawing her notebook out of her pocket.

There was always a chance Kyle's death had nothing to do with a sea creature, and someone else killed him and dumped his body in the bay.

"Cause of death?" I asked, curious if I could get any leads from their groundwork.

"Drowning," Olivia replied, without hesitation. "A little bit ironic given everything we know about his skillset."

There was a certain cruelty to his fate. It was not one that I would expect. Gunned down by a cuckolded husband, or murdered by a drunk in a bar brawl, perhaps, but not drowning. Perhaps that was a clue in and of itself.

Perhaps the killer, if there was one, was trying to send a message. But that also seemed a difficult premise. They would have had to catch him with his guard down, lure him into the water, and best him on his own battleground.

The more I thought about it, the more I realized how sinister the nature of his death sounded. Drowning a professional swimmer not only removed him from the equation, but it destroyed his reputation.

That thought led me to believe that there might be a personal motive to the attack.

"Okay, Darius, level with me. What do you know?"

I hadn't even got a look under the sheet yet. She was horse trading and wanted to ensure she wasn't left out in the cold.

"Not a great deal, at least not yet." I needed to choose my words carefully. I wasn't in this to catch Kyle's killer; I was trying to help Sonny. If I pointed the police squarely at Lawrence, my chance of getting their cash out of him seemed less likely.

Olivia raised a finger. "You told me you knew the last place he was seen alive."

"I was getting there. He was seen leaving the Watering Hole just after midnight on Sunday night. He was in the company of an attractive young woman in her early twenties. From the conversation the barman overheard, she was a university student."

Olivia produced a pen and scribbled furiously.

"Apparently, he frequented the Watering Hole. It was his favorite place to find female companionship."

"Was it now?" Olivia asked. I could almost see the cogs turning in her head.

A pattern of behavior made murder much easier to plan and carry out.

"I also know that his business partner appears to be struggling with him. On a previous occasion, the pair were seen arguing, but if you speak to Lawrence, he'll be sure to explain it away. Still, it wouldn't surprise me if there was something more to it."

I needed Olivia to apply some heat without dropping the weight of the entire police service on him.

"So you're not putting any stock in mermaids?" Olivia asked, her eyes searching me for any hint of deception.

I didn't know what I'd seen in the bay, but I certainly wasn't going to tell Olivia I'd been attacked by a something within spitting distance of this very crime scene only last night. I much preferred when the detectives weren't focused on me as the prime suspect.

"I'm not ruling anything out, and I'm certainly receiving a lot of outreach reporting or at least purporting to have seen mermaids in the Broadwater. Still, I'm in the habit of disproving these things, not encouraging them. So, I'll believe it when I see it."

"Very open-minded of you," Olivia replied with a smirk.

"I'm an investigator. I don't pretend to have all the answers and have seen some things in my life that are difficult to explain. But never once have I proved them to be paranormal."

"Yet you're a paranormal investigator." She put the notepad away.

"There could always be a first," I replied with a smile. "In the meantime, I solve problems the police really can't afford to focus on."

"Like murder," Olivia answered with a hint of a chuckle.

"This started as a missing person, but I go where the work takes me. And now, I'm going to have to see the body. Is that going to cause you any trouble?"

Olivia looked around, searching the beach for anyone paying us too much attention. "I'm running the scene. Gibson is tied up, so there's no one to pull rank here. I suppose I can give you a quick look. After all, you've been a good boy."

I let the comment slide. If she was mocking me, I wasn't giving her the sense of satisfaction. If it was a term of endearment, I didn't want to encourage her.

"I'm beginning to enjoy this spirit of cooperation, detective." My grin turned a little cheeky.

"Behave yourself," she replied. "It's never too late to get the cuffs out."

"I'm sure there's a great many men who would line up for that privilege." The words were out of my mouth before I could help myself.

So much for not encouraging her.

"They do, daily, Darius. Unfortunately, it never ends like they're hoping."

I laughed. Not particularly appropriate at a crime scene, but I couldn't stop myself, the earlier images of a spider returning oh so swiftly.

"May I?" I nodded in the direction of the blanket. Several other lumps under the sheet distorted the shape of a human body. Something was awry.

"As far as killings go, this one is clinical, bordering on sadistic," Olivia said as she pulled back the sheet.

Kyle lay on the sand. Beside him, a twenty kilogram weight was connected to a chain and a carabiner that I assume had been attached to him. It would have been to keep him submerged and out of sight.

Kyle's hands were bound together, and not a clean job. Rather, they were a tangled mess of fishing line and hooks buried in his flesh.

Several hooks had torn his flesh as he'd struggled against them.

I had a strong stomach but knew at a glance when I was witnessing a cold-blooded execution. And one that had been intended to maximise his suffering.

The weight would have pulled him to the bottom, drowning him while he bled from a series of lacerations on his hands and arms.

Every moment he fought against his restraints, he would have tortured himself.

It was more savage than anything I'd anticipated. I wasn't sure where a mermaid would find a twenty kilogram plate, but it was rusty and looked like it had been submerged for some time. The collection of fishing lines and hooks was an unusual touch.

It was almost as if Kyle had been drowned with whatever detritus could be found around the Broadwater.

I nodded for Olivia to drop the sheet. "Someone wanted him to suffer."

"Intensely," she replied. "With that captain spouting off about it to the press, this one is going to drift up the priority list. We won't let the media near it, but he discovered the body so I can't stop that from spreading. No doubt he got pictures and is already shopping the story around. I saw him soliciting the press when we arrived. By tonight, I expect most of these details will be in the news. We have until then to make some headway. Otherwise, things will grow complicated."

I nodded along as she spoke, but I didn't see how this situation varied from every other bizarre case she worked. Still, it had to be terribly frustrating to be scrutinised by the press on these high-profile cases.

I didn't particularly enjoy the attention, though it was good for business.

In the back of my mind, I knew the media could turn on me, just as easily. It was the reason I decided to work with Holly.

One of a few reasons, I corrected myself. Her obvious intelligence, good looks, and pleasant company all contributed to that decision-making algorithm.

"Well, if I come up with anything, I'll let you know," I replied. "I see no reason why we can't pool our resources. I don't need the perp, just my friend's cash back and that seems unlikely until the whole matter is settled."

"I need whoever is behind this part." Olivia nudged the body with her boot. "Or I'm going to wear it from my boss."

There was a trace of something in her voice. Stress, perhaps?

"What do you mean?" I scratched the back of my neck. There was something more to this case that I wasn't seeing.

"Have you noticed the sort of cases we're crossing paths on, Darius? A ghostly killer, mermaids in the Broadwater. These are the sort of cases they give junior detectives they want to put in their place. If I buy into the folklore, it damages my professional reputation. If I fail, I look less capable than Scooby-Doo. If I succeed, all I manage is to keep my head above water a little while longer. It's lose, lose, lose."

That didn't at all line up with how she had been portrayed by Holly and others.

"I thought you were flourishing in the department?"

Olivia laughed, but there was no mirth in it. "I'm a detective, sure. A young one at that. That was an achievement, and an anchor around my neck. The moment I got my badge they started giving me the dregs. Gibson's old and nearing retirement. He doesn't particularly care if we have to chase ghosts. It's easy work or at least it's meant to be. He couldn't be bothered arguing with our superiors. So I get saddled with the rubbish cases and will be lucky if I am promoted again before my partner retires. And if Gibson sticks it out, well, I'll be chasing mermaids for my midlife crisis. Of course, if one of these cases embarrasses the department, I might need a new job."

"Who did you manage to piss off?" I kept my voice low, not wanting to attract her colleagues' attention. I'd had no idea she was a pariah.

"That's what I wanted to talk to you about," Olivia whispered. "My favor."

"Oh, that?" I replied. I hadn't forgotten, but I was happy for her to get to it in her own time. "Color me intrigued, detective. You're the last person I expected would ever ask me for anything."

I wondered what manner of case she would want me to work. Frankly, I wasn't really sure I had the bandwidth to take anything else on, not right now at least. The Djinn, Kyle, and the missing money, and Geoff and his mermaid. I had a full dance-card.

"Walk with me, Darius." Olivia motioned up the beach, distancing herself from the body and the other constables milling about, working the scene.

We walked in silence.

Finally, she stopped. "I need you to look into someone for me."

I half expected her to ask me to investigate a police officer, particularly one of her superiors who had it out for her. That was the sort of case that could backfire spectacularly, alienate those in positions of power, and draw the unwavering attention of the Queensland Police Service. There were a hundred reasons to say no. And much as I wanted to with my whole being, I had opened Blue Moon to help people. Normally, they were old women with delinquent children, dog nappers, drug dealers, or missing persons. Occasionally, they were victims like Wendy Mooney, but they all had one thing in common. They needed help and I was a sucker for a damsel in distress.

"Okay, Olivia, who is it?"

She placed her hands on her hips. "Have you heard of Benjamin Marino?"

A rock and a hard place. Wednesday, April 26th 1324hrs

I NEARLY CHOKED ON my own tongue.

I'd been expecting her to ask about a police officer. Instead, she'd named the Gold Coast's king of crime, and the one man I was meant to be steering clear of if I, in his words, knew what was good for me.

If you ask Glenda, I have no idea what might be good for me. My mother would probably agree with her.

"You could say I'm aware of him," I replied, my jaw smarting even as I said it. His goon's sucker punch had hurt both my jaw and my pride.

Olivia nodded. "That's good. You know he puts up that ridiculous front as a businessman and property developer, but everyone with half a brain knows he is dirty as sin."

I'd only spoken to the man twice, but her assessment was on point.

"At least a handful of my cases have led back to him and his organisation, but every time I try and go after him, my superiors warn me off, close the investigation, or indicate that we shouldn't waste the resources until we have concrete evidence."

"He's a protected species," I replied, running my hand through my hair hard enough my nails dug at my scalp. If he had allies in the department, he was far more dangerous than I'd originally anticipated.

"Exactly." Olivia's cheeks were flushed. "How can I get the evidence to force their hand if they won't investigate him or give me the resources to do it myself? They're letting him run free, but the longer he does, the more bodies turn up."

Marino was a scourge on the world, but I was a private investigator, not a vigilante. I knew how I would have liked to solve the problem, but that sort of thing was frowned on by civilized society.

"What would you like me to do about it?" I asked. "I don't have any authority."

"But you do have eyes, and the QPS don't pay your wages, so they can't control you. I was hoping you could do some digging."

I jammed my hands in my pockets. "If he's as protected as you say, this could get us both in strife."

"Are you serious?" Olivia stared up at me. "You broke into a sitting judge's bedroom on nothing more than your gut instinct that you were right. I didn't say it would be easy. Just that I needed the help, and you clearly have the skills to avoid getting caught."

"That sounded dangerously close to a compliment," I replied. "Admit it, I'm growing on you."

"Like salmonella," she replied, puncturing my ego with pinpoint precision. "But it's my third favourite bacteria. So, what do you say?"

189

If she was going after Benjamin Marino, she was going to need all the help she could get.

"Let's just say I share your assessment, but I doubt he ever pulls the trigger himself. Going to be tough to find something that will stick."

"But he is giving the orders," she replied, pointing at the Gold Coast across the Broadwater. "And he is expanding aggressively here. Sooner or later, he's gonna bite off more than he can chew and when he does, I want to take him down."

Hart's desire to bury the hatchet and her sudden overt friendliness made sense now. She didn't just want to work together on cases. She wanted off-the-books assistance to take down the Gold Coast's criminal kingpin. It was the sort of collar that would make her career. The sort of arrest no one in the department could minimize or make go away.

Her glass ceiling would be shattered into a million pieces.

It was also about as safe as sleepwalking through a minefield. Not only was Marino not to be toyed with, but I didn't entirely trust Olivia. Her motives could range from earnestly trying to clean up our town, to more selfish motives of advancing her career, no matter the cost.

I couldn't really say that though. It felt like a sure-fire way of alienating her. And I could use all the allies I could get.

"I'll see what I can do. I can't promise anything, and I have my hands full right now, but he's already crossed my radar and I suspect he will again. I'll keep an eye out and see what I can find. Discreetly, of course."

She smiled, and the combination of those big blue eyes and her deepening dimples were awfully hard to say no to.

"If you could avoid mentioning anything around Gibson, that would be great."

I nodded. "I'll keep it discreet, don't you worry."

"Thanks, Darius, I appreciate it. I know it's not your bread and butter, but it will make a difference around here."

"I hope so." I turned to leave, but she called after me.

"Darius?"

I paused. "Was there something else?"

"You mentioned Marino already crossed your radar? How so?"

Marino had warned me not to say anything to the police, but what could it hurt? Hart wasn't going to spill it to her colleagues. Not until she had something irrefutable.

"Marino was trying to buy Mooney's garage off him, but Mooney turned him down. I figured it made him a potential suspect, but he came up clean."

"There's a first time for everything."

I paused. My curiosity just wouldn't let it go.

"Salmonella is your third favorite bacteria. What's the first? Botulism? E. Coli? Compact and deadly, I could see them winning over a discerning detective like yourself."

"Tempting," Olivia mused. "But no. It's syphilis."

"Wait, what?"

"We both spend our days dealing with liars and cheats. I like to think it's sweet karma for those I can't put behind bars."

I wasn't even going to begin trying to decipher that. It was just further reinforcement that try as I might, women were an unknowable mystery that I might never understand.

"I guess I'll have to settle for third. See you around, detective."

Cutting across the beach, I avoided the reporters loitering at the cordon. I had nothing for them and didn't have the time to spare.

With Kyle Cruz dead, I needed to make a stop this afternoon.

Sonny and Lucille.

They'd probably already seen the news and had to know this development hurt their chances. I needed to call in and see how they were going.

Either they would already know and would want to talk, or they wouldn't and deserved to know how his death would affect the case. So I headed over to the Faletulu residence.

The whole ride, I wondered what I was going to say. By the time I pulled into their driveway, I still had nothing. I parked behind the battered old Tarago that served as their family's people mover. It was an old eight-seater model, though probably closer to five or six given none of the Faletulus were small.

They took after their dad on that account, and were just as comfortable on the rugby field as singing in the church choir. The latter was Lucille's influence, and the family could manage to sing just about anything in beautiful four-part harmonies. They were good people, and they deserved better.

I trudged up to the front door and knocked. It was an old brick and tile four-bedroom home, typical of the neighborhood. They were all built in the late eighties but this one had seen a lick of paint or two since then. The roof tiles were beat, a few in need of replacement. The yard was mowed and tidy, but the house, like the Tarago, was well loved.

Sonny and Lucille were doing it pretty tough, raising four kids on one income. I didn't know how they managed to do it, let alone put aside enough money that they could pay for Leilani's swimming coaching.

I felt like a doctor delivering a terminal diagnosis and I didn't know that I had it in me to break their hearts.

Footsteps sounded on tile flooring, and one of the younger children appeared, pushing the curtain aside and smooshing her face up against the glass. That would be Fia, short for Fiafia, which meant happiness. A fitting name that matched the nine-year-old's disposition well.

"It's Darius," she called, alerting the rest of the house to my presence.

Sonny came to the door and opened it for me.

"Come on in, man," he called. "You're right on time. We're just about to have some dinner."

I would have laughed but I wasn't in a joking mood. It was just like Sonny and Lucille, struggling for their next dollar but still no hesitation whatsoever in feeding an unannounced visitor on their doorstep.

"No, man, I'm all good. I just thought I'd come by to talk. Have you seen the news?"

Sonny nodded slowly and glanced down at the tiles. "Yeah. Come on through."

He led me through the house to their kitchen where Lucille was stirring a pot of soup. It reminded me of the ones the army would use to feed a regiment. A couple of French bread sticks sat on the table, waiting to be cut and buttered.

"Darius!" Lucille called, resting the ladle on the bench. "It's good to see you."

She gave me a hug.

"You're here about him, aren't you?" she asked as she let me out of her embrace. "I'm sorry about all this. We didn't mean to bother you."

"No bother at all. So you know he's gone?" I said, toning it down in case Fia was still loitering within ear shot.

"We did and we called Lawrence as soon as we saw it." Sonny leaned against the kitchen bench. "We figured there would be a rush of people trying to get their money back. I wanted to be at the top of the list."

I sat down on one of the raised barstools at the bench. "And how did that go?"

Lucille gripped the ladle tight enough her fingers turned white. "He said there was nothing he could do."

Her voice was halting, and I could see the effort that was going into keeping herself from not breaking down in tears.

"What do you mean nothing he could do? You only just paid them," I replied. "There's been no services delivered. You have to be entitled to a complete refund."

"We would be," Sonny replied. "If they had any interest in carrying on the school. Instead, they're filing for bankruptcy. Liquidator will be appointed by the end of the week. He told us he'd like to help, but there is nothing he can do."

"Well, that's a load of horse shi—"

"Language, Darius," Lucille called, cutting me off mid-sentence.

I winced as Fia shot off down the hall.

"Sorry," I mumbled. "But nothing happens that fast. His body is still on the beach. I just saw it."

Sonny shrugged. "That might be true, man, but I don't know what else we can do. Even the courts can't get blood out of a stone, and we're not the only ones stuck in this boat."

The house was cool, the south-easterly breeze saw to that, but my blood felt like it was boiling. The more I considered the meeting with Lawrence, the more I realized I'd been handled.

No doubt, he'd told me what he thought would get me out of the office and stall me long enough to initiate the bankruptcy. If Lawrence handled the accounts, he would have had to already known the status of the bank account long before today. He would have known if the business was insolvent.

The whole situation made him look guilty as sin, though I couldn't see the wiry Lawrence managing to drown an Olympic swimmer. It seemed beyond Lawrence or whatever pretty brunette had lured him out of the bar.

Lawrence had the motive, but the means? I wasn't sure about that.

"We appreciate you looking into it, Darius, but with Kyle dead, there's not a lot we can do. Still, we're grateful for your efforts and will fix you up for your time." Lucille was as stubborn as her husband.

"You'll do no such thing," I replied. "Sonny's helped me on two cases already. Helping you is the least I can do."

I looked at the simple meal she was putting on the table to feed their four children. Behind her, the pantry stood half empty. While my friends would understand I had come up short, it simply wasn't good enough.

Not for them, and not for me. They'd been sold a dream and fleeced by a nightmare, and Lawrence had happily assisted in the process.

"Darius, we've already talked to the police and a lawyer, both family friends. Even they said they don't like our chances." Lucille wiped her cheek. "Still, no use crying over spilled milk. We'll get by."

I was sure they would survive. They had each other.

But I couldn't let it go. After all the times Sonny had come through for me, I couldn't leave it at this.

I might not have been able to save Kyle, but I could take another look at Lawrence. Philip the bar keeper was pretty sure Lawrence was padding his own pockets. If that was true, he could still be sitting on my friend's money.

"There's plenty of food here, Darius. Why don't you pull up a chair and join us for dinner?"

I smiled. "I'd really love to, Lucille, but I have an urgent errand to run. You both hang in there. I'll see what can be done."

I stood up, unable to sit any longer. I was full of nervous energy and frustration.

"Dinner time," Lucille called.

The children piled out of their bedrooms. Sonny's eldest, Kaipo, was first. Leilani wasn't far behind. Iosefa and Fia brought up the rear.

"Let me get out of your hair," I replied, "You enjoy tea, and I'll be in touch as soon as I know more."

"Thanks, Darius, we appreciated you looking into it. We know it's not your usual sort of case."

Sonny walked me to the door and gave me a big hug.

"I'll make this right, Sonny. I don't know how, but I will."

"Don't let it eat at you," he replied. "We could use the money, but we still have each other, and that's what counts. This is just one of those lessons, man. You just gotta learn from it and move on."

I said my goodbyes and headed for the tank. He was right. There was a lesson here, but he wasn't the one that needed to learn it, and I had no intention of moving on. I had a killer to catch.

Cold Reception. Wednesday, April 26th 1710hrs

I SAT IN MY car outside Sonny's house, feeling like a failure.

My friend had asked me for a favor and I'd been too late. Kyle Cruz was already dead, and even if I managed to solve his case, the business was bankrupt. They weren't getting their money back. Catching a killer might take them off the streets, but that wouldn't help my friends.

Lawrence might have been the brains behind the swim school, but if he wasn't even the director of the company, it felt almost certain that we would discover that the deceased Kyle bore all the responsibility for the business's debts.

I felt terrible, but I was running out of options to help my friends. The more I thought about it, the less innocent I supposed Lawrence to be. It was all just a little too neat for my liking.

There was a ding, and it took me a moment to realize it was my old phone. I didn't even recognize the tone. An email alert flashed on the message bar.

Tommy. It was just after five; he worked quickly. I considered leaving the email until I got home, but since I didn't have better plans for my evening, I would spend it working anyway. I was sure Carl would have something to say about my social life, but he wasn't here now.

I skimmed through the email. It contained a number of affidavits and submissions for court proceedings.

Among them I found Kaley Winters' address and a picture snapped by one of the court reporters.

She was a young woman, in her early twenties, blonde and rather attractive. One glance at her told me it wasn't such a stretch of the imagination that a womanizer like Kyle might have said or done something inappropriate.

The fact that Kaley's family had taken him to court in the first place indicated they were more inclined to justice than vengeance, but then again since the courts failed to dispense justice, perhaps that prompted action on their part. I didn't relish the thought of talking to them, but it felt more and more necessary by the minute.

It wasn't a good look; Kaley could be the victim here. She'd had her swimming career damaged, suffered through a court case, and received nothing. I was confident accusing her of murder would be received poorly, but my only chance of helping my friends was to shake the tree until all the facts fell out.

I couldn't dismiss the possibility that she was involved without speaking to her.

I was going to need a great deal of tact and to be careful with my questions, but if I could rule out the Winters, I could redouble my focus on Lawrence.

Punching their address into my phone, I reluctantly fired up the ignition. Maybe the Winters could give me some insight into the school's business practices that would help me drag the truth out of Lawrence.

The last line of Tommy's email read, *Got a lead about the wig, be here at nine and we'll chat to Fred.* I made a note in my calendar and pulled out into the street. Unlike the Faletulu's, the Winters lived in exactly the sort of house one would expect you to own if you paid fifteen grand a season for swimming lessons.

A beautiful two-story rendered brick and colorbond home on Fiesta Avenue, right on the canal. Its own pier stood out back. From here, I couldn't tell if they had a boat. The houses were jammed so close together, there was only a few feet between the side walls of the house and the neighboring fence. Land here was worth a fortune. On either side of the house was a large fence blocking any access to the backyard.

Parking in the driveway, I made my way to the front door and knocked.

I was still trying to figure out what I would say, when the door swung open and Kaley Winters stood before me in the flesh. She was about five foot six, though the heels she was wearing added a couple of inches. She was dressed ready for a night on the town. At her age, I imagined the nightclubs and bars of Cavill Avenue were a likely destination.

"Hello, can I help you?" she asked, tucking a ringlet of her blond curls back behind her left ear.

The house was well furnished with polished porcelain tiles and ivory coloured walls. One side of the hall was lined with family pictures, mostly Kaley standing on podiums or having medals draped around her neck. One of them was older, black and white rather than color, and featured a woman who bore a striking resemblance to Kaley, standing on a second-place podium. Perhaps her mother, judging by another portrait that also hung on the wall.

"Oh, hello," I started slowly, still gathering my thoughts. "It's Kaley, isn't it? I was hoping you had a moment to talk."

Her face sank into a frown. "Who are you? How do you know my name?"

Way to go, Darius, creeping the poor girl out.

I winced. "My name is Darius Kane. I am a private investigator here on the Gold Coast. I know your name because of the court case and the newspaper articles you've been in over the past few weeks."

"Fat lot of good that did me." She scoffed. "All that time and effort, and he gets off scot free. How's that for justice? I get kicked off the squad for making a *baseless complaint* and the court protects their homegrown golden boy."

Her manner told me she hadn't yet heard the news. Either that or she was an exceptional actor. I wondered how she would react to the news.

"Kaley, I'm not sure how to tell you this, but Kyle Cruz is dead. And at the moment, I'm not sure his squad will be swimming in November at all."

Kaley's eyes bulged. "Dead?"

"The police fished him out of the Broadwater this afternoon. He drowned."

"Wait, drowned?" Her shock seemed genuine enough. "Like someone killed him?"

I nodded. "That's exactly what I'm telling you."

"And you're investigating his death?" she asked. Realization flashed across her face. "You don't think I did it, do you?"

Her cheeks turned red. "First the courts won't believe me, now you think I'm a killer."

"Whoa, whoa, whoa." I held up my hands. "I am not working for Kyle, his family, or the school. In fact, I am trying to help a friend who was in the process of enrolling his daughter in the school."

"Oh." Kaley's face softened a little.

"They had recently signed up, paid their fees, and then they heard your story and had second thoughts. But the school won't give them their money back. I'm just trying to help them get to the bottom of things."

"I don't really see how I can help with that," Kaley replied. Her sympathy seemed genuine.

"Anything you can tell me about Kyle, Lawrence, or the school might help me work out what's going on. I'm just trying to help my friend."

Kaley thought it over as she vexed her top lip between her teeth.

"Kyle ran the lessons. I didn't really have anything to do with the school. Kyle might have been a good coach, but he hit on the girls all the time. Any of them will tell you that. I was just the one who made the mistake of challenging him on it. So he cut me from the squad with some lies about my attitude and performance as the reason and we took him to court."

My opinion of Kyle Cruz was dropping by the minute. "And you don't know anything about him ending up in the bay?"

She stared up at me. "Nothing whatsoever. That was news to me."

I had no reason to doubt her, and as far as I could see, there was no way she could have successfully lured Kyle out of the pub. He had just been in court fighting her for weeks. Even with a wig and belly full of beer, he wouldn't be stupid enough to fall for such a flimsy disguise. So if she were involved, she would have needed an accomplice, perhaps another confident swimmer from the squad? Someone Kyle had also hit on relentlessly.

"And were you at home on Sunday night? I only ask because the police *will* come to see you. You're going to want to have an answer for them that you can corroborate."

"Me, why?" Kaley's voice rose an octave.

"You have the biggest axe to grind and have been heard publicly railing against him. I recommend you have an answer to that question when they show up."

"I was out with my friends all Sunday night. My friends, and the staff from a dozen clubs could verify we were there. So the police can have their alibi. It's no skin off my nose. I had nothing to do with him."

Kaley stopped abruptly, the way people do when an unpalatable thought crosses their mind.

"What is it, Kaley?" I asked, trying to hunch a little to seem less physically intimidating.

"I don't know who did it, but I will say that if he harassed me, he certainly harassed others. Maybe one of them found a different way of saying no."

That was both the understatement of the afternoon, and an angle I would have to explore. Before I left, I had one more question for her.

"Did you ever happen to witness any difficulty between him and his business partner Lawrence?"

"Kaley?" a voice called. A stunning blonde woman in her forties rounded the corner from the kitchen. She had an apron on, but it did nothing to hide her exceptional figure. From the strong shoulders beneath her halter top, it was easy to see where Kaley got her good looks from. She noticed me in the doorway.

"Who are you?" She strode down the hall, her heels clicking against the porcelain.

"Mrs. Winters. My name is Darius Kane. I know your case was thrown out last week, but I've been investigating Kyle Cruz and his school on other matters. I was wondering if you had any information that could be of use."

"Kane...You're that charlatan that is always chasing ghosts and soaking up the press. Go on, get out of here. Stop bothering my daughter. Have you no shame? She's had to deal with that awful man. Now she has to fend off gold digging con artists as well?

"Mrs. Winters," I started, hoping to calm her down. "I assure you—"

She cut me off. "Get out of here, now! Before I call the police."

"I'm trying to help," I said, but clearly, she was an avid channel 9 viewer.

"I don't care. We're about to sit down to dinner and don't have any more time to waste on Kyle Cruz, that school, or answering your questions."

I backed out of the doorway. "Not to worry. You may not have to answer my questions, but the police are going to have a few of their own. Good luck with them."

"The police, what for?" Mrs. Winters shook her head. "We're the victims here."

"You were," I replied. "But Kyle Cruz is dead so I'm sure they'll stop by anyway."

"Dead? Since when?"

"The police fished the body out of the Broadwater this afternoon." I scratched behind my ear. "But I'm pretty sure he's been there since Sunday night. Don't worry, I'm sure they'll get to the bottom of it."

Both of the Winters women were quiet, but Mrs. Winter slid Kaley aside as she placed her hand on the door. "Well, good riddance to bad rubbish. That man harassed my daughter. I'm not going to lose any sleep over it."

"Ma'am, I'd consider how you phrase that when the police show up. That's what they would call a motive. Anyway, I've taken up quite enough of your time. If you think of anything unusual about the school or how it conducted business, please let me know. I'll leave my number."

I held out my card, but Mrs. Winters snatched it before Kaley could.

"We shan't be doing that." She looked down her well-constructed nose at me. "Kyle Cruz and his stupid little school have already taken up quite enough of our lives. Don't come back."

I tried to manage a smile, but it was forced. "I shan't bother you again."

The door slammed behind me with far more force than I thought was necessary.

I'd never met Kyle Cruz but after speaking to plenty who had, I was starting to think the Winters had suffered from a grave miscarriage of justice. They weren't hurting for money, but poor Kaley might have had a promising career lampooned by this whole mess.

Her mother had interfered with my ability to ask Kaley anything about Lawrence, so I was going to need to dig a little deeper into the school.

In the tank, I headed for home. Max was overdue his dinner, and I wasn't particularly in the mood for cooking. Fortunately, there was a Hungry Jacks on the way home. It wasn't exactly fine dining, but it had a drive-through and I had a hankering for a hamburger.

My cases were moving along about as fast as peak-hour traffic on the Gold Coast highway. Kyle was dead, and I had more questions than answers. The Djinn was going to have to sit on the back burner, but I was curious what Tommy's friend had to say about the wig, because I could certainly use a lead right now.

Then there was my missing mermaid. Geoff had spotted it from his office on Pisa Avenue. Mrs. Ingleburn had spotted it not much farther along the river from Gibraltar Avenue, but Terence's rod had been stolen from the far end of the Broadwater, the tip of the Spit.

If there was a mermaid out there, it was racking up some serious distance, but why? If it was responsible for Kyle's death, how had he come across its radar? I didn't even want to believe it existed. There had to be some other explanation, but the more people insisted they had seen it, the harder it was becoming to refute their testimony.

If the mermaid hadn't killed Kyle Cruz, it left Lawrence as the most likely suspect. And he was also the only one that could make my friends whole.

I was going to need to make another stop this evening.

An inside woman.
Wednesday, April 26th
1745hrs

MY FIRST STOP WAS the office just in case Glenda had taken any messages of note. She kept them on paper, old school, much like she was. That was how she liked it. Not particularly helpful for me, but when you weren't paying market rate for your receptionist, you were lucky to get messages at all.

My efforts to convert her to email had failed repeatedly, and the look in her eye the last time I tried told me I would have had more success taming a wild bull with a paper clip than winning this particular war of wills.

That was the price of not hiring a proper secretary. At least that's what I told myself, but in reality, I enjoyed having her around.

I parked the tank out back and headed up to the office. At this hour Glenda would be long gone. She didn't drive in the dark, so I could be sure I would have the place to myself.

What I wasn't expecting was to find a young woman sitting cross-legged on the ground, her back resting against the door. She was wearing jeans and a T-shirt and an open hoodie, which was probably why it took me a moment to place her. Beneath the frazzled blonde hair and puffy red eyes was a familiar face.

"Uh, Brandi, isn't it?" I called gently, not wanting to alarm her. The last time I'd seen her was when she'd greeted me at Kyle Cruz's swim school.

She looked up. "Oh, Mr Kane it's you."

Brandi wiped her eyes with the back of her jacket. "I'm sorry. I'm a little bit of a mess."

"You heard what they did to Kyle?" I asked, hunching down in front of her.

Brandi nodded. "Who would do such a thing?"

She was the first person I'd met who seemed genuinely upset that Kyle was gone and she might have valuable insight into the swim school's operation.

"I don't know, Brandi," I replied, "but I am trying to work that out. Would you like to come inside and talk about it?"

I stood up, opened the door, and flicked on the light. Given Glenda wasn't in, there was no need to bother with my office, so I guided Brandi to the lounge in the lobby and pulled Glenda's seat around the desk so that I could sit with her.

"What can I do for you, Brandi?"

I'm not a psychologist and I'm certainly no expert on giving grief counseling. But I had received it, back in the service, on two occasions. She'd just lost her boss. Clearly, she needed someone to talk to.

"I just can't believe he's dead. Who would do such a thing? Everybody liked Kyle."

She might not have been the most observant of souls.

I took a deep breath. "But someone must have had a grievance with him. First the court case, now this?"

"You don't think they're related, do you?" Brandi asked. "I met Kaley Winters when she came for her interview. She seemed lovely. I don't think she'd do anything like this."

I heard her out but thought perhaps she might not be the best judge of character. "You know, Brandi, not everyone is what they seem. I'm afraid somebody had a problem with your boss. Can you think of anyone else who might want to kill him?"

She shook her head vehemently. "He was a great coach. His students won. The parents loved him. Now he's gone and I don't have a job. What am I meant to do?"

I leaned back in my chair. I had so much on my mind, I hadn't really thought about the fallout for Brandi. There wasn't anyone to teach the lessons, and Lawrence had filed for bankruptcy. He must've let her go at the same time.

"I haven't been paid in three weeks and now the business is finished. I have to pay rent and I don't mean to sound selfish given what's happened to Kyle, but I have my own problems."

"You haven't been paid in three weeks?" I asked. That was fascinating. The school had at least appeared to be profitable. Why wasn't she being paid? "Were there money troubles?"

"I don't think so. We have always been paid monthly. I figured I would at least get paid up until yesterday, but Lawrence is saying the money is tied up in the liquidation. But it's not there. It's gone."

How could she know that? She just manned the phones and front desk. "What do you mean the money is gone?"

Brandi looked down at her clasped hands. "Lawrence says the accounts get frozen when a liquidator is appointed for the bankruptcy. I logged in and checked them anyway. I had the details. Kyle needed me to move some money around for him last year. I never told Lawrence. But this morning, the accounts are almost empty, and have been for months. Everything that has been deposited into them, simply gets emptied out days later."

"Do you know who else has access to these accounts?" I leaned in close.

"Lawrence, of course, and Kyle. But Kyle never worried about those sorts of things. As long as Lawrence sent him his monthly pay, I doubt he ever checked the books."

"And you still have access?" I tried not to let my excitement show when she was feeling so down. "Do you think you could access them here?"

I pointed to Glenda's computer, not that she ever used it.

"I could try." Brandi sniffed. "I'm not sure how that will help. There's no money there."

"Money might be what got Kyle killed. Those accounts might help us understand why." I got off the seat and started wheeling it back to Glenda's desk. "Here, you can use this."

Brandi wiped her eyes again and trudged to the computer. She wasn't in a hurry, and I couldn't risk spooking her by being overeager.

She sat down and the computer whirred as it booted up. My mind was moving quickly. Everything was telling me Lawrence could be behind this whole mess. He had the most to gain. He also had access to the accounts. And as far as I could see, his only defence seemed to be that the business would fail without Kyle, so he would never murder him.

That wasn't going to sound compelling in a courtroom. But maybe he'd fleeced enough from the school's accounts that he didn't care. Would he really have his partner murdered?

Money was a powerful motive. One of the oldest.

Brandi opened a browser and logged in to the school's online banking portal. The screen refreshed and the school's accounts, or rather account, flashed up the screen.

They only had one.

"You mind if I take a look?" I asked, reaching for the mouse.

"Sure, I don't know what you're looking for, but you have a better chance of finding it than me."

Taking over, I started scrolling through the transactions. I was no financial analyst, but the pattern didn't need one. New money would go into the account, about a third would be left in the account to cover payroll and other running costs, and then the balance would be routed out of the account the next day.

"Any idea what this account is?" I asked, bringing up the details for where the money had been sent. It wasn't even with the same bank.

"No idea," Brandi replied. "I really didn't have much to do with it. I just answered the phone, took messages, and booked new student appointments."

Transactions rose up the screen as I scrolled further down.

"What's this?" I asked, pointing to a recurring transaction for over a thousand dollars. I recognised the name. It was a popular insurance brokerage, Zerkal. They were a massive insurance conglomerate. If it was a policy premium being paid monthly, it was an expensive policy.

"I don't know." Brandi bit her lip.

She wasn't going to be much more help on this, but she did know her boss a lot better than I did. "Kyle was single, wasn't he?"

"He preferred the bachelor lifestyle." Brandi crossed one leg over the other.

That was putting it rather diplomatically, and she was still defending her boss.

At first, I thought it was the swim school's public liability insurance. But as I skimmed through the transactions, I found a separate policy at a far lesser premium. Even more interestingly, the large insurance payments appeared to have started only thirteen months ago, whereas the smaller policy continued back as far as I could access the bank records.

Given he was single, I believe it unlikely that Kyle would be the sort of individual to carry a heavy life insurance policy - he wouldn't be around to benefit from it.

My guess was that Lawrence took out a hefty insurance policy on his partner in the event something terrible happened. To prove that I was going to need documentation.

"What are you going to do with this?" Brandi asked, pointing at the computer.

"Brandi, I've been looking into the swim school to try and help my friends recover the money they paid three weeks ago, but no one's hired me to find Kyle or solve his case. I'm afraid this one is in the hands of the police. But rest assured, I know the detective on the case. She'll run this to ground."

Brandi still looked troubled.

"I'll have a word with her about the unpaid wages. Perhaps she can note it with the liquidator for payment."

Brandi perked up a little.

"Thanks, Darius, I really appreciate it. But aren't you going to go after his killer? That's what you do, right?"

I nodded. My principal interest was in getting Sonny and Lucille's money back. That didn't seem likely unless I could track down where the swim school's money had gone. Perhaps there was paperwork in the office that might help.

"You wouldn't happen to still have a key to the office, would you?"

"No." She sniffed. "Lawrence took it from me right before he..."

Her voice trailed off into a sob.

"Let you go?" I added, trying to spare her the pain.

She nodded, and I couldn't help but feel sorry for how this whole mess had left her.

Reaching into my pocket, I drew out my wallet. "I can't help you with your rent. I don't have that sort of cash."

I pulled out three folded twenty-dollar notes that were in it. "Take this, make sure you've got something to eat."

"I couldn't do that," she whispered.

"Of course you can. Grab some groceries, something that can tide you over for a couple of days while things get sorted."

Brandi tucked the bills into her pocket, then gave me a big hug. "You're too kind."

"It's okay. You'll get through this," I replied. "In the meantime, you better go home and get some rest. Don't worry, I'll share this with the police."

She paused at the door. "You should get some rest too, Darius. You look like hell."

I tried not to laugh. She was probably right, but given what she'd just shown me, sleep was the last thing on my mind.

"That's exactly what I plan on doing," I replied. It was a lie, a little white one, but I wasn't in the habit of informing people when I was preparing to break the law. Not that I thought Brandi would rat me out, but still, it was better to be safe than sorry.

I printed a complete copy of the bank records and jammed them in the drawer for when the browser logged itself out.

The bank records would need more scrutiny later. I headed to the computer in my office, brought up a map of the Gold Coast, and traced the Broadwater all the way back up the Nerang River.

Then I pulled up my email, searched for references to mermaids, and plotted all the locations raised in the various sightings.

Staring at the pattern, I realized I had been attacking my search all wrong. I'd started in the Broadwater because I'd assumed the creature was coming in from the sea.

What if I was wrong?

The Broadwater was vast; the river was narrow.

Perhaps I would have better luck locating my prey there.

An inside woman.
Wednesday, April 26th
1830hrs

I PARKED IN THE driveway, not wanting to pull into the garage because I needed something from the chest against the front wall and it could be a tight fit with the tank in the garage.

Making my way inside the house, I scooped Max up and gave him a good pat. His forgiveness for being left at home would need to be hard-won, so I carried him around the house with me as I got ready for my evening.

It was going to be a long night and I wasn't doing it on an empty stomach, so I headed into the kitchen to fix the meal no man could fail: spaghetti.

After setting a pot of water on the stove, I spooned premium dog food into Max's bowl with the side of biscuits.

While he ate, I jumped in the shower and washed off the grit and grime of my day. All the while, my thoughts ran over the cases.

Everything kept leading me back to the same conclusion: Lawrence had the most to gain from Kyle's disappearance. Protest as he might about his reliance on Kyle,

I suspected the other insurance payments were his Plan B. After all, Kyle was far from reliable, often going on benders for days at a time. Lawrence seemed the sort of meticulous planner who might prepare against a day when his partner might party too hard or seduce the wrong wife.

Then there was the money missing from the accounts. Only a select few had access to those, and Lawrence would have certainly noticed if Brandi was stealing from the business.

The empty account was why Sonny and Lucille hadn't been able to get their money back. They had booked an appointment to talk with Kyle, but their money had been drained from the account only days after they paid it. Maybe Kyle needed it to pay his mounting legal fees. Or perhaps Lawrence had taken it.

Someone knew where the money was.

After the shower, I slid into a set of dark slacks and an open collared white shirt. I added a nice pair of dress shoes, combed my hair, and wondered if for the second time in two weeks I was going to end up on a *not* date with Tommy.

Back in the kitchen, I threw a handful of pasta into the pot. A handful being the sort of precise measurement standard my cooking expertise was built on. I grabbed the frypan and some mince from the fridge. I cooked it while mulling over the case.

Pulling the pasta off the stove. I strained it, loaded a portion onto my plate and the rest into a Tupperware container for later.

Piling the pasta sauce into the mince I stirred it and let it simmer.

Storing the rest of the spaghetti in the fridge, I left the dishes in the sink. They were a problem for tomorrow.

Heading into the garage, I opened the deep storage chest that rested against the front wall and rummaged through it.

When I left the service, I had to return all service issued weapons and equipment accumulated over the years, but in truth, I felt naked without them. So I'd started collecting gear in case I needed it.

The chest was where it lived when it wasn't being used on a case. Unfortunately, what I wanted was right at the bottom: my dive gear. I wouldn't be heading particularly deep, so I opened the black storage bags I kept it in and separated out what I needed: a rebreather, goggles, my neoprene wetsuit, weight-belt, a pair of flippers, and an underwater scooter.

They were prepped and ready to go, but I checked them twice anyway. It never hurt to be prepared. Then I remembered my last experience in the Broadwater and pulled out my diving knife.

I loaded everything in its own bag and slung it over my shoulder, before shutting the chest.

Content that I was now far better equipped to chase my mermaid, I loaded the bag in the car.

It went in the back seat with a picnic blanket over it. The gear wasn't cheap, and I didn't want any passersby to smash the window and grab it while I was talking to Tommy.

As I pulled out from the house, Max stared forlornly out the window, but there was no chance I was risking my partner with whatever was swimming laps in the river and the Broadwater.

He was far too snack-sized.

It was after eight and the address Tommy had given me was on the southern end of the Gold Coast. Making my way across town, I eased through the evening traffic. It wasn't particularly thick, but the streets were never empty either.

The Gold Coast Highway isn't what you might expect from its name. The old roadway ran parallel to the beach and in its heyday, it might have accommodated traffic quite well. But I'm talking about back in the sixties when most of the area was single or two-story residential houses.

Fast forward to tonight with hundreds of high-rise hotels and apartment buildings packed together and the quantity of traffic has exploded. Unfortunately, the road can no longer be widened to accommodate it.

That didn't stop them from racing the Indy through the tight city streets every year, practically shutting the place down, but save for those race cars, everyone else crawled through the city.

On the plus side, the high-rises did make for a spectacular skyline at night, beautifully lit buildings, with the ocean crashing against the beach only a few hundred metres away. That was something.

My phone informed me that I was close to my destination. I circled the block twice, looking for a spot and eventually found one. Parallel parking the tank was never a fun job, particularly in the city where spaces felt a good six or eight inches shorter than they ought to be.

I followed my phone's directions to the address Tommy provided. Bright neon signs announced the building as Giovanni's. It was quite clearly a nightclub.

"Darius, over here," Tommy called.

He was waving from his position at the front of a considerable line. I walked past a dozen patrons, looking apologetic. I wasn't a fan of cutting in front of queues, and loathed when others did it to me. But I also didn't have all night. It didn't escape my notice that everyone else in the line, bar a few, were men.

I suspected, based on the name, the vibe and the fact that Tommy frequented it, that Giovanni's could well be a gay club.

"He's with me, Ted." Tommy pointed at me for the benefit of the massive bouncer manning the door.

Ted moved the rope to allow us in. Even from the entrance, the lively hip-hop from inside washed over us.

"Capacity crowd tonight, Tommy. You have a good night." The big bouncer waved us in. Whoever was performing was certainly popular. We headed inside, down a small corridor, before the club opened into a large dance floor. Around the dance floor were two dozen small tables, each with two or three seats, almost all of which were full.

Booths lined the walls, and a bar stood in the corner. Tommy dragged me across the dance floor, nimbly avoiding those moving to the music of a particularly sultry rendition of Beyoncé's Naughty Girl, sung by a remarkably talented lady with a voice that might have been even better suited to singing jazz and blues, yet deftly navigating the hip-hop tones.

Tommy led me to a table with one other person already sitting at it.

He stood up as we approached, not quite reaching my shoulders. He had short blond hair that had been spiked with a copious amount of gel and he was smiling broadly.

"Paul, I presume." I reached out to shake his hand, figuring he was Tommy's wig expert.

"No, I'm Brad, Tommy's boyfriend." He turned on Tommy. "Don't you tell him anything?"

Tommy tried to utter an apology, but it was on me, not him.

"I'm sorry, Brad." I shook his hand. "Of course he does. I simply got my wires crossed. I knew we were meeting Paul. I just didn't realize I'd have the good fortune of meeting Tommy's better half as well."

I turned to Tommy, eager to curry favor. "Haven't you done well for yourself."

Tommy muttered something about being an asskisser, but Brad beamed. It never hurt to pay a compliment.

"Aren't you a little charmer." Brad placed his hand on his chest. "Tommy told me he's been helping you on some cases. You'll have to sit and tell us all about them."

I leaned in as the singer's voice grew louder. "Of course, maybe when things are a little quieter."

"Of course, of course." Brad slid into his seat.

I grabbed one facing the stage and Tommy sat between me and Brad. When Brad's eyes were focused on the stage, I nudged Tommy.

"I thought you said we were meeting Paul?" I whispered.

He nodded toward the stage. "We are, and he gets off in just a minute."

I followed his gaze all the way to the singer currently belting out Beyoncé's hit.

The closer I looked, the more I realized the singer I'd initially taken to be a rather talented woman was, in fact, a talented man, who was not only belting out Beyoncé's hit with flamboyant aplomb, but was somehow managing to do it in a dress and heels.

I'd liked to have blamed my misread on the dim lighting, but had to concede it was more likely down to Paul's well-executed costume. I had met a few cross-dressers in my time, but he was the sharpest.

I leaned back in my chair and enjoyed the rest of the number. Paul sang and danced his way across the stage, finishing to a rousing cheer from the bar and those on the dance floor. He hung up the mic and headed for the set of stairs that would take him off the stage.

"That's our cue," Tommy said, resting his arm on Brad's. "Stay here, darling. We will be right back."

Brad didn't look pleased about being left behind, but I didn't want him exposed to any information about the Djinn, particularly if he was already curious about my cases.

I followed Tommy past another security guard and down a short hall to a dressing room. Tommy knocked.

"Who is it?" the familiar sonorous voice called.

"It's Tommy. Can we come in?"

"Of course, dear, it's open."

Tommy eased open the door. We found Paul sitting at a small dresser, a brunette wig in one hand. His bald head had a light sheen of sweat, and I found even greater respect for him. Dancing in full drag and a wig, in the humidity of the Gold Coast couldn't have been an easy feat.

"That was spectacular," I began, and I meant it. Some people could be a little funny around cross-dressers, but I could appreciate talent wherever I found it.

"Why thank you, but the pleasure is all mine. Darius Kane in the flesh."

"Oh, Darius," Tommy cut in. "I should have mentioned, Paul is a fan."

"A fan?" I raised an eyebrow. "I wasn't aware I had any fans."

"And modest too." Paul laughed as he set his wig down on the mannequin's head. "Your work on the Casper Killer case was all over the news. Tommy told me he was doing some work for you, but I didn't believe him. That'll teach me."

He slapped my chest lightly.

"Well, I'll take all the help I can get. Tommy mentioned you might know something about that wig?"

"I do." Paul bent over, no easy task in heels, and lifted the bag I'd left with Tommy onto the desk. "Most of it is cheap garbage. I wouldn't be seen dead in it, but this is a masterpiece."

He fished out the wig and held it aloft.

"What makes you say that?" I asked.

I was hoping to take away something that would prevent me from being so easily fooled in the future.

"The look and feel of it, for starters," Paul replied, running his hand through it. "It's so soft and smooth, because it's made from real hair. Red is not particularly common. This vibrant piece would not have been easy to source. There's only one aficionado on the Gold Coast that could make one of these. Madame Kisar at Burleigh. If this isn't one of hers, I'll eat my heels."

"Madame Kisar?" I confirmed, noting the name in my phone. "I don't suppose she has a website or phone number."

"Just a card," Paul said, reaching into his purse to produce a small business card embossed in gold lettering. All it contained was a name, phone number, and an address at Burleigh Heads.

Burleigh was the southernmost point of the Gold Coast, a beautiful hill overlooking the sea that backed onto the Tallebudgera Creek.

"Tell her I sent you, and she'll take good care of you." He smiled. "I'm an old client of hers."

"I appreciate it, Paul. More than you know." I tucked the card in my wallet and pointed to the bag. "Do you mind if I have those back? They are evidence in a case."

"Of course." He handed over the bag and the wig, and I packed it back inside gently. "You have a real talent, Paul."

Paul smiled. "You are too kind, Darius."

"Only giving credit where it's due," I replied, "and I appreciate your help. Now if you'll excuse me, I'm afraid I have another matter I need to attend to this evening."

"Oh, a case?" he asked, looking up at me.

"It is an ongoing investigation. Unfortunately, I can't say a great deal about it right now."

"Intriguing," Paul replied. "Before you go, could I ask you for a favor?"

I lifted the bag to my shoulder. "Of course. What can I do for you?"

He held up a napkin and a sharpie. "Would you mind signing this for me?"

I'd never been asked to sign something before in my life. I was actually a little flattered.

I placed the napkin down on the bench. "Of course I can."

Pulling the lid off the marker, I scribbled a quick message.

Dear Paul, the Queen has nothing on you! Darius.

I handed it to Paul and a smile crossed his face. Not a stage smile, or some contrived delight, but genuine happiness, the sort that comes when you compliment someone on something they have spent great effort mastering.

"Have a great night," I called, heading for the door.

Tommy walked me out.

"I'm sorry I can't stay," I said. "I'm looking into the death of that swimming coach. It's rather time sensitive."

"That was a nice thing you did for Paul," he said softly.

"No nicer than what you've all done to help me. Please give my best to Brad but I'm going to have to slip out without saying goodbye."

"Oh, he'll be fine. He can be a little high maintenance at times, but he really is pretty great."

"I have no doubt," I said. "Have a good night, Tommy."

Back in the car, I hurried to Surfers Paradise. I still had a few more stops to make, and my evening was quickly vanishing.

Rolling past Kyle Cruz's swim school, I found the lights were off and there was no sign of anyone inside. No police tape either. That was a relief as it meant the cops had either been and gone or hadn't got here yet. Of course, it wasn't the crime scene and would feature on a long list of places they would need to visit as they gathered evidence.

I circled the block, making doubly sure no one was about. I'd made that mistake at Mooney's garage. This time, I was more careful.

I might have been on better terms with Detective Hart and Gibson, but I wasn't naïve enough to think that wouldn't change if they caught me where I ought not to be.

Content no one was watching the building, I pulled into the rear laneway and slipped on a black jumper and balaclava.

This part of town is only lightly trafficked, so I didn't expect any disturbances. From the back of the tank, I pulled out a small crowbar and slid it up my jumper's sleeve. It wasn't enough to avoid a disciplined observer, but a casual passerby wouldn't notice it. I made my way along the empty lane.

Fortunately, they were all commercial premises, no restaurants with kitchen staff coming and going from the alley. I found the door that led to the back of the swim school and did one last check of the surroundings.

No one.

I slipped the crowbar out of my sleeve.

"Rightio, Darius," I said. "Here we go again."

Shenanigans and Sea Monsters. Wednesday, April 26th 2230hrs

WITH A LITTLE LEVERAGE from the crowbar, the rear door of the swim school buckled like a politician during question time. I pulled it open.

Making my way inside, I looked around for any hint of an alarm or cameras. I hadn't seen anything when I'd passed through the office.

There was nothing but silence.

Frankly, it was about as much resistance as I'd expected from Kyle and Lawrence. With no money on the premises, there was little worth protecting. I doubted any of their clients paid in cash.

I wandered through a small kitchen area into the office proper. Ignoring Brandi's desk, I went straight for Kyle's office. It had a desk with two chairs on one side and an equally nice chair on the other. On every wall hung pictures of Kyle standing on podiums, having medals draped around his neck.

The other photos were students. They outnumbered Kyle's by a factor of ten to one. Whatever else he was, Kyle could swim and was an even better coach. It made me wonder how someone or something had got the better of him in the water.

No doubt this would be the room he brought prospective parents to convince them of the efficacy of paying his exorbitant fees. Surrounded by evidence of his prowess, they were far more likely to stump up the money.

There was almost nothing else in the room. Kyle likely did little work here. Most of his time would have been spent in the pool. I looked underneath the tables for drawers or anything that might have been stashed out of sight, but there was nothing.

I headed for Lawrence's office. A desktop computer sat on his desk opposite the door. On the wall behind it a large-framed picture of Lawrence and a woman standing on a beach dominated. Beneath it stood several filing cabinets. I went for those first, but they all were locked.

If the back door was no match for a crowbar, the filing cabinet's lock fared even worse. I popped all three of the locks in less time than it took Max to finish his dinner. Pulling open the top drawer, I leafed through the files. They were well organized bank records. I skimmed enough to confirm they belonged to the same account I saw earlier.

I ignored those as I already had them and moved on through the drawers. There were accounts receivable records of different parents on payment plans, and a series of outstanding invoices.

Surprisingly, little in the operation appeared to be dealt with electronically. Or perhaps Lawrence just was one of those pedantic people who enjoyed having a paper backup of everything.

In any case, it was far easier to access these than try to breach a password on his computer. I skimmed through the drawers until I found a folder labeled *Insurance*.

It was exactly what I was looking for. Unfortunately, it only contained records of the smaller policy, the one covering their general liability insurance. There was no hint of a second policy in the paperwork contained in the filing cabinets.

The fact it wasn't there made it all the more suspect. I scoured all the other drawers again, feeling rather frustrated. My gut told me I was onto something, but my time wasn't limitless. I couldn't afford to camp out here. If someone wandered past the back door and spotted the damage, they might well call the police.

I realized I'd skipped the most common hiding place of all. Pulling out the bottom drawers, I set them on the floor. Then I lifted the flooring out of the filing cabinet and searched for anything that might have been stashed beneath them. Nothing.

If Lawrence was hiding something, he was doing a good job of it.

I was about to leave when I raised my eyes back to the wall. The picture.

The one of Lawrence and his partner, glasses raised toasting each other on the beach. I'd looked at it a dozen times.

It was not particularly unusual, other than that it was the only photo in the place, and it wasn't where it could be seen from the desk.

That struck me as unusual.

Leaning forward over the drawers, I lifted the frame off the wall. Behind it was a wall safe. It was about nine inches wide and five inches tall.

My crowbar wasn't going through that, not in any sort of a hurry. So I did the next best thing.

Most people who lock their valuables in a safe figure once that door closes, they will be protected from all but the most determined intruders.

What they fail to take into account, in most instances, is the fact that the safe has been installed in a simple commercial wall, the sort of internal and flimsy structure that was little more than a few bolts attached to studs.

I looked at the wall and took a deep breath. Then, drawing back, I buried the crowbar in the plasterboard. It sank deep, ringing as I found the stud. In a matter of minutes, I'd exposed enough of the safe's external structure to find where it had been bolted in place and it was simply a matter of applying enough pressure with the crowbar to pry it free. With a crash, the safe struck the filing cabinets.

Not exactly discreet, but I was on my way out. I lifted the safe onto the desk and caught my breath.

The computer caught my eye. Best to be thorough. Opening its case, I looked around. I wasn't an expert, but I knew what a hard drive was, and yanking out the wires that led into it, I pulled the hard drive out of the rack and slipped it into my pocket. If there was any evidence linking Lawrence to anything that could be construed as a motive, I planned to have enough information to shake him until Sonny and Lucille's cash fell out.

That was what the police would call blackmail. An unsavory business, but when someone comes after my friends, I'm not above doing what is required to make things right. Grabbing the safe with one arm, I raced out of the swim school.

Back at my car I opened the toolbox. In the bottom there is a false floor, useful for keeping things hidden that others might be looking for. Setting the safe and hard drive in it, I re-secured the floor and tossed some loose tools and rags on top of it. No one had any reason to think I was connected to the swim school, so I was fairly sure the police wouldn't come looking for it, but just in case they did, I wanted to be certain they wouldn't find anything.

They would have the devil's job finding it back there and it wasn't going to be there long. However, it was nearing midnight, and I still had another stop to make.

I headed for the Sundale Bridge. It crossed the Nerang River at the mouth of the Broadwater. I was determined to get to the bottom of the sirens and sea monsters plaguing the Gold Coast's waterways. I couldn't keep up with the beast I'd encountered over a long distance, but hopefully it wouldn't come to that. After all, I didn't need to catch it. I just needed evidence to convince Geoff's business partners he wasn't crazy.

My previous attempt, I'd ventured into the water spontaneously. Tonight, I was prepared.

I was concerned by the inconsistencies between the accounts in my notes. Geoff and several of the correspondents in my email were quite insistent that the creature was a mermaid. They even went so far as to insist that they had seen a scaled green tail.

My own experience in the Broadwater had been with a large silver mass, with plates like steel, not soft scales.

Then there was Terence, the fisherman who insisted his rod had been dragged out to sea just before dawn. If I combined the various accounts, I could trace it moving south down the Broadwater and into the Nerang River.

The beast I confronted was charting that same course, but my best glimpse of it made me believe it was far larger than I supposed a mermaid might be. Could there be two creatures in the Broadwater? Perhaps one or both of them came and went from the bay, perhaps snagging Terence's unfortunate line on the way out.

There was only one way to be certain.

I parked my car near the bridge and climbed out. With my wetsuit on I pulled the hood up over my head. Adding gloves and boots I ensured I had no skin exposed except for my face. In the murky waters, I would be all but invisible.

I tucked the diving knife into my weight belt and fastened it around me, then rested the goggles on my head and carried the rebreather and flippers to the river.

The underwater scooter would help me power through the water with minimal effort. The creature I'd encountered was capable of doing at least ten to fifteen knots, and I couldn't match that under my own steam.

Sitting on the concrete edge of the canal, I fastened the flippers onto my feet, held the scooter in one hand, and pushed myself into the water. I sank into the darkness and fastened the rebreather onto my face.

It was dark in the depths, and visibility was poor. If it wasn't for the lights beneath the bridge, I would be able to see nothing at all.

Anything making its way in from the Broadwater would have to pass beneath the bridge and I hoped with the visibility afforded by my current position that I could ensure nothing slipped past me.

I had hours of air providing I didn't squander it.

Last time, the beast caught me by surprise, this time I was the hunter. I settled into the muck at the bottom of the river mouth and waited. Dressed in black, laying face down on top of the scooter, I could see nothing but the flash of my goggles each time I raised my head to scan.

Stakeouts are mostly about patience. That was where a lot of people drop the ball. My time in the service had got me used to discomfort. Whether I was in a car with my feet on the dash, or face down in the murky sand and soil of the Nerang River, I could hold my ground as long as it took.

The lights of the bridge penetrated the water, but I rested just outside the illumination they cast.

And in the deep I waited.

The whole affair reminded me of an operation I'd undertaken some years earlier. We were storming a ship that had been seized by hijackers. We'd waited in the water for hours. Intelligence had told us the ship would need refueling.

We'd lain in wait beneath a refueling tanker who had no idea we were even there. The moment the ship pulled up and killed its engines to refuel, we stormed the vessel and released the hostages. Twelve pirates were killed in the exchange.

It was part of a worldwide response to the increasing frequency of marine piracy.

They hadn't taken an Australian vessel since.

That fact brought me some solace when I lay awake at night pondering my choices. This was different though. There were no orders demanding I be here. No brothers in arms watching my back.

Hell, no one even knew I was down here. If anything went wrong, I wondered how long it would take them to find my body. Would it be days, like Kyle Cruz?

Or would the tide carry me out to sea and my body be lost forever? The mystery of the missing paranormal investigator.

Aren't you all sunshine and rainbows tonight, Darius.

I tried to snap myself out of my morose thoughts.

Something silver shot through the water beneath the bridge. The lights glimmered across it as it dove deeper beneath the water.

It cruised past me. I powered up the scooter and kicked hard, stirring a plume of muck and dust behind me.

I powered after it, closing the gap. The creature was doing a shade over five knots; the scooter could manage nine.

I eased off the throttle to not overtake it. For the first time, I saw my sea beast up close, face-to-face. Or rather, the fuselage of what appeared to be a four-meter-long miniature submarine.

It had fins and a propeller at the back. Minor wing-like fins on its fuselage allowed it to dive, surface, or maintain stability in the water. Two large mechanical arms stretched off each side of the vessel, and each had a claw-like hand.

Its thumb, or whatever you call an opposing digit on a robot, was snapped at right angles.

I'd found my beast from the Broadwater.

That had to be the appendage I'd broken to get out of its grip. From where I swam, I could see the canopy mounted to face forward. The pilot couldn't see me. The fuselage behind the pilot didn't really allow for a shoulder-check.

There was no way the pilot could not have known he had grabbed me. Which meant whoever was piloting the submarine had tried to drown me on purpose.

Somehow, that rankled me more than a sea beast trying to take a chunk out of me.

I went after the sub. I had to know what it was up to. Submarines are inherently expensive, the fact that it had tried to murder me in the bay meant it wasn't just some millionaire out for a recreational dive.

The vessel looked like the sort designed to perform exploratory operations in marine diving exercises. Only it wasn't in the ocean; it was skimming along the river bottom doing its level best to avoid detection, and if I had to guess, carrying some sort of contraband.

At this depth, it could pass under other ships and they wouldn't even know it was there. I could barely feel its presence and I was looking at it. I followed the sub all the way to a wharf attached to a commercial property on the river. If I had to guess, we were somewhere along Monaco street, but this wasn't how I was used to getting around the Coast.

The sub rose to the surface, and I trailed in after it. Reaching a buoy in the river, about ten meters from the wharf, I rose through the depths. I couldn't get any closer, not until I knew what I was getting myself into.

Hiding behind the buoy, I scoped out the warehouse.

It was substantial, and unmarked.

The canopy of the submarine opened, and a man stepped out. Two people came out of the warehouse to greet him. Or at least I thought that was their intention. Instead, they went to the submarine, opened a cargo compartment, and started unloading black watertight cases from it.

I had no idea what was inside them, but my best guess was drugs or weapons. Someone was moving illegal goods through the Broadwater. They'd damn near killed me when I discovered them. Had they done the same to Kyle?

In my mind's eye, I could still see his body wrapped up with fishing line, a heavy weight strapped to his back before he was thrown in the water.

The coroner was confident he'd drowned and that was probably right. If the sub had found him, it might have dragged him through the water until he drowned and then they simply disposed of the body back in the Broadwater several kilometers from the submarine's base of operations.

Had Kyle died because he'd stumbled onto this?

But what of the girl in the bar? Was she really just an enamored paramour?

If it was the submarine that killed Kyle, where was all that money going from the school's accounts? I'd assumed Lawrence was plundering it. Could he be involved? Or was that just a coincidence?

Another figure stepped out onto the dock and approached the driver of the submarine. I would have ecognized his smug face anywhere: Benjamin Marino.

Embezzlers R Us.
Thursday, April 27th
0045hrs

BENJAMIN MARINO WAS A businessman if you believed the nonsense he touted.

He was about as clean as a plasterer's radio.

I watched the two of them exchange words. I couldn't quite make out what was being said, but Marino seemed to be interrogating the guy in the minisub.

The submarine pilot, a short sandy haired man with an almost jockey-like physique, shook his head vigorously. It seemed to satisfy Marino, who headed back inside.

If the submarine and Kyle had crossed paths, it was quite possible Marino feared he'd already been discovered. I couldn't afford to get any closer, so I raised the waterproof gopro from its pouch on my belt and snapped a series of photos of the warehouse, the submarine, and the driver.

If Olivia was looking for evidence that Marino was up to something shady, these pictures were a good start. Whether it was actionable enough was the issue. I had no way of knowing what the sub delivered in its containers.

At this distance the photos I took would not be particularly good quality, but they would have to do. I eased back into the water. I'd been trying to avoid a conflict with the mob boss, but given that seemed unlikely, it was nice to at least have an ally in the fight against him.

I needed to watch my step though. If the department was shutting Hart down every time she tried to get a warrant, it meant someone in the food chain was on his payroll.

Slipping quietly away, I made my way back to the bridge and my car without incident. There I stashed my scuba gear in the back, rolled my wetsuit down to my waist, and wrapped a towel around my torso before climbing into the driver's seat. It had been a most eventful evening. I'd uncovered a hidden safe that more than ever I was convinced held something that would reflect poorly on Lawrence. I'd also found an explanation for what might have killed his partner, though it seemed unlikely the two had any correlation whatsoever.

I'd successfully found one beast of the bay and while it certainly wasn't mythical or paranormal, it was just as dangerous, if not more so.

Marino's smuggling operation wasn't the evidence Geoff was looking for, and it didn't fit his description, so I was back to square one there.

If Marino's goons weren't responsible for Kyle's death, someone had to be working with Lawrence to dispose of his partner. Maybe I just needed to draw them out, threaten to expose them. A dangerous course, but possibly my only play left unless the safe contained a veritable smoking gun.

Then there was the Djinn. I opened the duffel on the passenger seat, just to be sure everything was still inside, including the wig. It was, and I breathed a sigh of relief. I would run down that lead as soon as I could sneak down to Burleigh for a quiet chat with Madame Kisar.

First, I needed sleep badly.

I took off in a hurry to get to my bed. At an intersection, the light turned yellow. I was too close to stop, so I didn't. The second I cleared the intersection, blue and red lights flashed on the side of the road. The siren started as I rolled through the intersection.

My heart beat a little faster as I weighed my position. It was less than ideal. None of my scuba gear was illegal but diving in the Broadwater in the dead of night was certainly more than a little suspicious. Now here I was practically running a light. A bored police officer might suppose I was a thief trying to break into one of the expensive houses along the waterfront. It wouldn't be the first time someone had made a water-based ingress into a multi-million-dollar property.

I hadn't, but I had burgled a swim school, and I didn't particularly want to risk those items being discovered in my possession. They would be more than a little damning.

The lights and sirens whirled, and I pulled over, fabricating as convincing an excuse as I could muster on short notice.

The squad car slid in behind me.

As I looked in the rearview mirror, I breathed a sigh of relief. Olivia Hart was climbing out of the police cruiser, and Gibson wasn't far behind.

"Well, that ought to help my chances," I muttered. Unless of course they'd already discovered the break-in at the swim school, in which case, sitting here in a neoprene wet-suit in the middle of the night wasn't going to allay their suspicions.

Detective Hart made her way down the side of the tank and knocked on my window. I rolled it down and tried not to look guilty as sin.

She leaned against the cab. The one advantage of the much higher ute was that she wasn't looking down on me.

"Darius Kane, I thought that was you. Recognized your truck from Mooney's place last week."

"And you pulled me over just to say goodnight?" I leaned toward the window and dropped my voice to a whisper. "If you aren't careful, Gibson's going to get all jealous."

She smirked but didn't take the bait. "And where are you headed in such a hurry?"

"Home, detective. Some of us need all the beauty sleep we can get."

She raised an eyebrow. "Perhaps you're not doing it right."

My heart skipped a beat. She was either flirting or taking a shot at me, and I wasn't rightly sure which. Her eyes traveled down my bare chest to the wetsuit and towel.

"What on earth are you wearing? And is your hair wet? Have you been swimming?"

"Just doing what I can to stay fit," I replied. "Besides, I like to wind down after a long day. Helps me sleep better."

Her skeptical expression told me she wasn't buying it for a minute. Her gaze went to the bright red wig poking out of the top of the duffel in the passenger seat.

"Look, detective," I started. The last thing I needed was the pretty detective thinking I was a cross-dresser. My dating prospects would drop from a long shot at last call to a snowflake surviving on the surface of the sun.

"Darius." She pointed at me. "If I discover you've been dressing up as a mermaid and swimming about in the canal in an effort to drum up work, I will drag you down to the station and book you myself."

I laughed. It seemed Hart still had plenty of skepticism left in her system.

"What's so funny?" she asked.

I gripped the wheel. "Just wasn't where I was expecting you to go with that. Those are evidence in one of my cases."

"So, this redheaded mermaid that people are reporting in the bay is definitely not you?" She narrowed her eyes at me. "In spite of the literal mountain of evidence to the contrary?"

"Detective, if you'd seen my email, you would know I don't need to stir up business. I'm getting the same reports and trying to run them to ground. Besides, the wig's dry isn't it."

Hart shifted her weight from one foot to the other as she was forced to concede the point.

"Mermaid chasing. That's a step down from the Casper Killer, isn't it?"

I shrugged. "The fact some of those sightings happened the same night Kyle went missing, I find more than a little suspicious. I was just out seeing what evidence I could turn up."

"Find anything interesting?" she asked. "Anything that might help us?"

I picked my words carefully. "Not yet, but I'm close. Also, I might have turned up something on that other matter. The one you asked about earlier."

She got the hint, loud and clear.

A car tore through the intersection behind us heading south. Gibson's eyes followed it as Hart leaned in close.

"Let's talk later," she whispered. She backed away from the tank. "Saved by the stupid, Darius. Take it easy on the way home."

I tipped my imaginary hat. "Good luck catching him, detective. Seems to be in a real hurry."

I counted my lucky stars that the car had blitzed past when it had. While Detective Hart was completely off base in her assumption, I didn't particularly want to tell her what I'd been up to and if Detective Gibson was shutting down her investigations into Marino, I couldn't rightly tell her what I'd discovered while searching the bay. Not while he was listening.

I made it home without further incident and after a quick shower, promptly passed out, face down on the bed.

It was almost 9:30 AM when I finally dragged myself to my feet. Fatigue filled my legs and thighs. I might have had the sea scooter, but I'd still swum several kilometers on the back of a long day.

It was time to see what I'd uncovered.

Grabbing Max, I loaded him in the car. No doubt the robbery at the swim school would have been reported by now, and I had to know what was inside that safe. Not to mention the hard drive.

I had a murderer and a mermaid to catch. With any luck, I would find them both with the right bait.

Skipping breakfast, I was bound for the one place that would have the tools I needed and could use without arousing any suspicion. Funnily enough, when you show up to a workshop and ask people to cut into a safe, they tend to ask questions. Fortunately, my father was an accountant with tremendous overconfidence in his ability to use power tools and due to an abundance of spare time and lack of budget constraints, he would have what I required.

As I climbed out of the car at my parents' house, mum ran to meet me. "Darius, I didn't know we were expecting you this morning?"

She said it in a tone that conveyed she was confident it wasn't the case but was nonetheless pleased to see us.

"Sorry, Mum. I meant to call ahead but got a little distracted. I don't suppose you could look after Max and feed him some breakfast? Poor little buddy is probably starving."

My mother looked down at my beagle. If anything, Max was carrying a few extra pounds.

"Starving? I certainly doubt that, but come along, Max. I'll fix you something in the kitchen."

I set him down and Max skipped after my mother.

"Is dad about?" I called after her.

"Where else would he be?" She looked back over her shoulder. "He's in the garage tinkering away. Worst thing that man ever did was retire. One of these days, he's gonna get himself killed."

Maimed, perhaps, but death by one's own radial saw was pretty rare.

I removed the false bottom of the tool chest and hefted out the safe in one hand and the hard drive in the other. Wandering around the garage, I found the side door open. My dad was grinding away at a piece of steel, sparks flying everywhere.

"What on earth are you doing?" I called.

"Just fixing a new latch for the gate," he called back. "The old one seems to have busted."

"You know you can buy one of those for like two dollars at the hardware store?"

He appraised his handiwork.

"Then I wouldn't have the satisfaction of making it myself." He noted the safe. "What have you got there?"

"It's evidence in a case I'm working. The owner was rather reluctant to part with it."

My father winced a little. "And you want to store it here?

"Don't be silly, Dad. I want to open it. So why don't we put that grinder to good use?"

His curiosity got the better of him, and he cleared the bench.

It took half a dozen blades and the best part of two hours to grind through the hinges, but eventually the door could be removed.

The safe was practically bursting at the seams with paperwork.

"What's all this then?" my father asked.

"Let's find out." I poured the papers onto the table, and we started sorting through them. Paperwork from Zerkal, the insurer, had me interested, along with bank statements for a company I'd never heard of. Sunny Tides Proprietary Limited?

"What on earth is that?" I asked aloud, holding up one of the papers.

"I don't know, but we can soon find out," my father replied. "If it's a company, we can just look it up on ASIC."

ASIC was the Australian Security and Investments Commission. It regulated companies throughout the country.

"We can do that?" I asked.

My father nodded. "For a couple of dollars, we can run a search and find out who is behind it."

"Really?" That felt like something that could be easily misused. It also seemed like exactly the sort of thing that would come in handy for an investigator.

My father nodded. "We used it all the time, back when I had the practice."

I was doubly glad I had come over now.

"Let me get my laptop. I'll be right back." My father slipped out of the garage, heading for the house.

I kept filtering through the paperwork. The bank account for Sunny Tides showed sizable deposits occurring with increased frequency. I suspected that if I matched them up with the swim school's account, they would match perfectly. Easily three quarters of a million dollars was sitting in the Sunny Tides' account.

My father reappeared with his laptop and pulled up the ASIC website. "Here we are. Sunny Tides."

The screen was full of an assortment of details, including office holders and an address. Lawrence's name was nowhere to be found.

"Who is Ophelia Trask?" my father asked.

I shook my head. "I have never heard of her before."

Dad scrolled through the lines of text. "Well, she's both the director and shareholder of this company and would be in sole control of the money in those accounts."

It had to be his partner. If Lawrence wanted to avoid suspicion, he would have to hide his ill-gotten gains in someone else's name. So he'd opened Sunny Tides in his partner's name. Ophelia had to be the wispy woman from the picture in Lawrence's office.

"Now the company has only been around for two years," my father mused. "Still quite young. No website or other business activities listed. That's unusual."

"Why do you say that?"

"They aren't going to much effort to hide what they're doing. No false trail, no logged tax returns, just a pile of stolen cash. It's just lazy. They ought to take a little pride in their work."

"Lazy would seem the operative word to describe these particular operators. What do you make of this?" I slid the insurance policy across the desk.

"Key man policy," my father said, with barely more than a glance. "Benefits to pay out in the event that the individual named in it dies or is compromised. The policy is meant to allow the business to pay out its creditors."

He flipped through the policy. "Kyle Cruz? Isn't this the chap that was found in the Broadwater?"

"One and the same. I suspect his business partner has been lining his own pockets for some time. Then Kyle got wind of it and his partner disappeared him in the bay."

"Well, that doesn't surprise me," my father replied, "but this is a two-person job. He's working with Ophelia Trask."

Almost certainly, but my father hadn't seen the picture. No, he'd gleaned it from something here.

"Why do you say that?"

My dad tapped the policy. "Because these bank details listed on the policy might have the school's name, but the BSB and account number match this other account. The one for Sunny Tides Proprietary Limited."

"That seems like a pretty clear motive to me. How big is the policy?"

"Three and a half million dollars," my father replied. "Or two times annual income in this case."

The number boggled my mind. Kyle was crushing it. Both him and Lawrence should have been raking in a fortune. What had changed? Greed?

I plugged in the hard drive. "Anything on here we can use?"

My father started clicking through the different directories. "There are thousands of files. This could take hours. There are the school's accounts and client data going back several years. I'm sure with a few weeks and a pot of coffee, I could pick it apart."

I didn't have weeks. If Lawrence and Ophelia were behind this, they might run as soon as that insurance policy paid out.

"I still don't understand how they took out the policy without Kyle knowing about it."

My father laughed. "That's an old trick. If he was inattentive enough to let them steal three quarters of a million out of the company bank account, chances are they just stacked a pile of forms in front of him and had him sign them with the regular expense reports."

"Is that common?" I asked.

"More common than you'd think." My father leaned back on his stool. "The more signatures there are, the less attention most people pay. The sweet spot is about seven down the pile, never the last one. They always read the last page. It helps them feel better for ignoring the rest."

"Thanks, Dad. This has been... most enlightening."

"What are you going to do with all this? Turn it over to the police?"

I couldn't. Not yet anyway. I still needed to get my friend's money back. Fortunately, now I knew just where to find it.

"Soon, Dad. Just got a few things to take care of first."

My phone started to ring. It was Geoff Kinsella, no doubt looking for a progress report. I hadn't so much as given him a call since I'd taken the case.

"Sorry, Dad, I've gotta take this." I stepped away and raised the phone to my ear. "Hi Geoff, I was just going to give you a call."

"Oh, really?" There was a note of doubt in his voice. "Why is that? Have you found the creature?"

I hadn't found a mermaid, at least not yet. But I suspected he knew that.

"I expect I'll have the proof you need shortly," I replied. "I'm narrowing things down."

Geoff sighed. "I'm running out of time, Darius. My partners have scheduled a meeting tomorrow morning at ten o'clock. I think they're going to try and remove me from the partnership."

"Well, stall them as long as you can. I suspect I'll have all the evidence you need," I replied. "But that's not why I wanted to talk to you."

"You wanted to talk to me?"

There was one thing that had been bothering me all week. Someone just kept showing up where they didn't belong.

"Am I the only one you've put on this case? Or are there others?"

An awkward silence filtered down the phone line.

I pressed the advantage. "It was you who hired Captain Cronkwhile, wasn't it?"

At first, I'd thought his coming to town was coincidence. But the fact he was trawling the Broadwater at the precise time Geoff claimed to have seen his mermaid, and then had stumbled across Kyle's body was one too many coincidences for my liking.

"I did," Geoff said. "He has something of a reputation for finding sea creatures. Want me to call him off?"

I couldn't afford for him to show up at the wrong time, at the wrong place. It could ruin everything I had planned.

"On the contrary, he may be just what I need to wrangle my prey. I'm going to send you some instructions. See that he gets them."

"That's rather cryptic," Geoff replied.

"It's better this way." I paced the garage. "I'm your private investigator, not your client. Probably best we maintain some plausible deniability."

"I see. Very well. Send me the instructions, I'll send them on, with my encouragement that they be complied with."

"You'll have them shortly. I'll be in touch soon." I hung up.

The captain was a wild card. If I could rely on him, he might be just the backup I needed. Or he could torch my whole effort. Perhaps I ought to send him on a wild goose chase, just to be sure.

The beginnings of a plan formed in my mind. I had evidence, motive, and a suspect. Not to mention a line of mermaid sightings stretching from the Broadwater up the Nerang River. I made my decision and texted Geoff the details for the captain.

Then, I dialed Lawrence's number. It was listed as the contact number on the insurance policy.

"Hello," Lawrence answered. "Who is this?"

His voice held that uneven timbre people use when they didn't know who is calling. I didn't answer; I wanted him on the back foot. I breathed heavily into the phone.

"Who is this?" Lawrence asked again.

"Lawrence," I tutted. "You never called."

"Darius? Is that you?" His voice was a little frantic.

"I swear you said you'd call if he didn't show up to class. You never did. Perhaps that's because you already knew where he was."

"How dare you," Lawrence shouted. "My business partner's been killed, his body savaged and dumped in the bay, and now you're harassing me. I'm going to call the police."

I laughed loud enough he couldn't miss it. "I'm surprised you haven't already. I heard there was a break-in last night."

The sharp intake of breath was unmistakable, even down the phone line. "That was you?"

"I never said that," I replied. "But if the police were to come for a chat, they're going to find all sorts of interesting things here. Bank records for a company that Ophelia controls. Transaction logs between it and the swim school showing money being purloined from the company accounts."

"Wait, how did you—"

"Patience, Lawrence. It's not question time." I shut him down hard. "Most interestingly, they'll find an insurance policy on your partner set to be paid into an account he had no knowledge of or connection to. It all paints a very damning picture and with the transactions logged on your machine, I'm confident they'll know exactly who to arrest."

"What do you want?" Lawrence growled.

"Me? Nothing, really. I'm just a concerned citizen. But my friends would like their twenty-five grand back."

"The swim school is insolvent. Receivers have been appointed. I have no power over the company's assets."

"Oh, you misunderstand me, Lawrence. If the school is insolvent, you knew before last week. You took their money. You can make them whole. If it helps, I know where you can find three quarters of a million dollars. Just run it past Ophelia. I'm sure she'll prefer that to jail."

"I didn't have anything to do with Kyle's disappearance," Lawrence stammered.

"I don't particularly care, Lawrence. I'm not the police. Bring the cash in a waterproof case and meet me at the Broadbeach Aqua Park at six PM."

"The Aqua Park? There'll be people everywhere," Lawrence complained.

"That's the point," I replied. "You won't try anything and we'll both know neither of us are wearing a wire."

"At least we can add extortion to your repertoire," Lawrence muttered.

"Keep it up, Lawrence, and it will be a hundred thousand."

"Fine, I get it. If we see one hint of the police, we're out of there. Come alone."

"Six PM, Lawrence." I hung up the phone.

"You better not be going alone." My father thrust his finger into my chest.

"Of course not, but I'm happy for him to think I am. Can you and mum look after Max? This is bound to get interesting."

"Interesting." He shook his head. "There are times I'm not entirely certain you're my son."

I gathered up the insurance policy and headed for the door. "You'll have to take that one up with mum. Good luck!"

Climbing into the tank, I picked up my phone. It was time to call in some reinforcements.

Sirens, sea monsters and scoundrels.
Thursday, April 27th 1815hrs

THE GOLD COAST AQUA Park is located on the opposite side of the Broadwater to the Spit. Together with the Sea Pool, it occupies the beach front for the Parklands. The Sea Pool is a massive netted off section of saltwater surrounded by pontoons where people can play in the surf, confident that sharks or other sea creatures won't interrupt their rest and relaxation.

Next to it, the Aqua Park provides a great time for any who enjoy inflatable mazes, bouncing castles, or ninja warrior courses. It features a massive interconnected series of inflated obstacles and mazes, and I was waiting at the very end, furthest from the shore with a commanding view of the Broadwater. It might seem an unusual spot for a clandestine exchange, but I wanted one with access to the water and enough passing sea traffic to prevent foul play. Plus, the aquatic setting created a natural buffer against electronic listening devices should Lawrence try to turn on me and bring in the police.

I was, after all, in possession of material clearly stolen from his office.

Given the nature of who I was meeting, I would have preferred body armor and combat fatigues. Instead, I was wearing just my board shorts, and carrying a waterproof case. There wasn't a snowflake's chance in hell that Lawrence would approach if I was armed, so I stood on a massive inflatable at the extreme edge of the Aqua Park, unarmed, alone, and trying to ignore the drizzle of rain that was spoiling what should have been a beautiful afternoon on the water.

The inflatable was octagonal with a climbing pyramid in the center. Usually, kids would be climbing and wrestling each other off the elevated platform at the top. But between the inclement weather and me calling in a favor with the park's operator, the inflatable was deserted.

I had swum out to the obstacle after sending Lawrence the specifics and had been waiting for the better part of an hour for him to show.

To my left, Holly was out there somewhere on one of the Sea Pool's many pontoons, lurking in wait for her story.

Sighing, I checked my waterproof watch once more. Maybe Lawrence had thought better of showing up. Perhaps he'd simply taken Ophelia and run for the hills. He had to know the police would at least take an interest in him with all the evidence in my possession. Perhaps he thought he could outrun them.

I leaned on the inflatable watching the approach, until the sound of an engine cutting out drew my eyes back out to the seaway. There, drifting on the water toward me, was a twenty-foot boat. Lawrence stood at the wheel in an open collared casual white shirt, khaki slacks, and a pair of thongs. At his side was a fetching brunette woman in a sarong tied over her bikini. In one hand she held a clutch. She seemed particularly perturbed at being here.

What I found most interesting, however, was that she in no way resembled the woman in the picture from Lawrence's office, save for her height.

Ophelia, I presumed, but if she was, then I had a suspicion as to where some of the embezzled funds had been spent. She had clearly invested in herself, you might say.

They drifted alongside the inflatable and killed the engine.

"Get in," Lawrence called.

"Not on your life," I shouted back, as droplets of rain splashed on my face. I pointed to the pontoon I was standing on.

"Show me the cash, I give you what you want, and we both go our separate ways."

I waved the case containing the insurance policy and a number of other select and incriminating documents.

"If you try anything else, I leg it back to shore and ensure these go to the detective in charge of the investigation. I'm sure she will have an abundance of questions for you both."

"I didn't kill him, you know," Lawrence called. "The money was just me planning for the future. It was inevitable the school would fail. Kyle was a dumpster fire waiting to happen. I know how it looks, but I worked hard to build the school. I just wanted to make sure I wasn't left empty-handed."

"So you embezzled money from the company, gutting its ability to operate or deliver on its obligations, leaving your clients in the lurch while you skip town with a multi-million-dollar insurance policy tucked away safely. One call, you know, that's all it would take, and the proceeds of that policy will be frozen by your liquidator."

"But you're not going to do that, are you?" Lawrence replied. "Because you want this."

He waved a waterproof Samsonite case. "Twenty-five grand. Just give us the evidence and we'll give you the cash."

"Come on over," I replied. "I'm not going anywhere."

The wind whipped along the Broadwater. Lawrence was a little hesitant to leave the safety of his boat. I understood his reluctance. I could break him in half, and he had no leverage other than the money he was holding.

"Fine," he replied. "But let's make this quick. I have places to be."

He stepped off the rocking boat, onto the inflatable, the small case in hand.

His companion followed him onto the inflatable pontoon, swaying as she tried to keep her balance.

I didn't offer her my hand. "Ophelia, I presume?"

She managed a smile but screwed up her nose. "You'll have to forgive me. I normally dispense with the pleasantries when I'm being extorted."

I laughed. "No, you probably reserve those for when you're committing the felonies, like embezzling or murder."

"I said, we didn't do it," Lawrence snapped. "For all we know, Kyle slept with some mobster's wife and was dumped in the bay when he was caught in her bed."

"Perhaps," I replied, unzipping the case and showing him his hard drive and the documentation I had lifted from the safe. "But you don't have to worry about me. Like I said, I'm not the police. I just want my friend's money back. All of it."

Lawrence opened the case. Bundled neatly inside it, in tight wads of fifties, was the cash. I counted the rubber bands, noting that it ought to be five stacks of five thousand, but I wasn't going to sit here and count it. I just wanted to be sure the stacks weren't stuffed with paper.

"Fan the bills, please." I nodded to the case.

Lawrence raised an eyebrow. "Are you serious? I suppose you want me to count them out as well?"

"You'll forgive me for not giving you the benefit of the doubt. You've robbed both my friends and the company. So, fan the bills.

Lawrence grumbled but picked up the first wad of bills. He fanned them slowly so that I could see nothing else had been used to fatten out the stack.

"And the rest," I said, still holding the evidence firmly in my hand.

Lawrence went through the piles, one by one, fanning them in front of me. When I was satisfied that each contained one hundred, fifty-dollar bills, I nodded, and he closed the case.

"We give you this, and we never hear from you again?" Lawrence held out the case.

"That's the deal," I replied, as I offered him the evidence.

Kyle handed me the case, not letting go of it until I had released the case full of incriminating evidence.

There was just one question gnawing at me.

"I just have one more question for you," I replied.

"What is it now?" Lawrence clutched the evidence as if he feared I might try to steal it back.

"You always figured he would lose the court case, didn't you?"

Lawrence's brow furrowed. "What do you mean?"

I shrugged. "While I was waiting, I read the policy. It's fairly broad, probably why it was so expensive, but it covers any circumstances under which he would no longer be able to teach. If he was found guilty of harassing one of his clients, he'd lose his blue card, and certainly any ability to work with the Olympic teams ever again. You never figured on having to kill him. You thought his own philandering would get the job done."

"For the last time, I didn't do it," Lawrence replied. "We were friends, but I knew what he was."

I nodded. "I believe you, Lawrence, but I wasn't talking to you. I was talking to Ophelia."

The brunette screwed up her face. "Me? What do you think I had to do with it?"

She was used to playing the victim, and it showed.

"Darius, what are you banging on about?" Lawrence asked. I could hear the fatigue in his voice and almost felt sorry for him as I realized the truth.

"I just wasn't sure whether you were in on it or not, Lawrence. But you weren't, were you?"

I turned to Ophelia. "It was a clever plan. After all, Kyle hasn't seen you lately, has he? The botox, the new nose, not to mention a nip here, a tuck there. I bet you were all smiles when he hit on you in the bar, weren't you? Using his own proclivities against him."

"Wait, what bar?" Lawrence looked from me to Ophelia.

"I bet you weren't home Sunday night, were you, Ophelia?" I turned to Lawrence as the itching sensation at the back of my neck went wild. "What did she tell you,

Lawrence? That she just ducked out to check on a friend, or was it a girl's night out?"

"Ophelia, what is he talking about?" Lawrence turned to his partner, uncertainty etched in his furrowed brow.

I piled on the pressure. "The only problem, Ophelia, is the bar keeper is gonna recognize you. How long do you think it will take him to ID you as the last person who saw Kyle Cruz alive?"

"Good luck proving that," she replied. "There were dozens of patrons there. It'll never hold up in court."

"So it was you." My smile broadened as she confirmed my suspicions. "Oh, it won't be that hard now that we have your accomplice. You really shouldn't have called her today."

"Her, who?" Lawrence was turning a little red in the face.

I ignored him, zeroing in on Ophelia. "Sure, you got him nice and drunk, but he wanted more. So you lured him out of the bar with sultry promises, brought him down to the beach, and baited him into the water."

Ophelia was shaking as I plowed on.

I raised my voice. "You might not have been the one who drowned him. No, that takes a real malice and you're not the sort to get your new nails dirty, so you had help. Fortunately, there was someone that hates Kyle Cruz a whole lot more than you do."

"I have no idea what you're talking about," Ophelia answered, her voice breaking as she fiddled with her clutch.

"I wondered why the mermaid sightings moved their way up the river. Surely such a creature would come in from the sea."

"Ophelia what is he talking about?" Lawrence asked. "What did you do?"

"Nothing, Lawrence. Shut up, grab the evidence, and let's go."

I winced. "I think the pair of you are in for a mighty uncomfortable boat ride wherever you are headed. Non-extradition, I hope, because she was happy to have Kyle killed for the money. I hope for your sake she's still into you, Lawrence, because the second Ophelia thinks she can do better..."

I dragged a finger across my throat.

"I would never harm Lawrence," Ophelia shouted over the rising wind.

"But you would kill his partner and friend if he stood in the way of three and a half million dollars."

Ophelia ripped open the clutch and produced a compact pistol. A Ruger LCP tiny enough to fit in the small purse. She pointed it directly at my chest.

Hart had told me neither of them were licensed to carry guns. We could add another charge to their rapidly growing rap sheet.

"You should have taken the money and run." Ophelia shook her head, the rain running down her face. "But you had to be clever, didn't you?"

"Occupational hazard," I replied with a shrug as I tried to appear nonchalant. She was clearly nervous, and I didn't want her feeling threatened enough to pull the trigger.

"Ophelia, what are you doing? Where did you get that?" Lawrence's voice was hoarse as his world view crumbled.

"I told you this was a dumb idea," Ophelia shouted. "We should have taken the money and run. We could have fought the insurers for the rest, but no, you wanted to see what he had to say."

"See, we're learning things about each other already." I smiled. "But I'm a paranormal investigator, not a therapist, so you will need to sort out your relationship issues on your own time."

"Shut up," Ophelia snapped. "And get on the damned boat."

"Oh, I don't think I'll be doing that," I replied. "You'll shoot me and dump me in the bay the second we're out of earshot of the beach."

"I'll shoot you now." Ophelia's voice was shrill.

"You might," I replied, my voice calm and level, in spite of my racing heart, "but it's a lot different pulling the trigger yourself. I know, I've done it. Your hands are already shaking, probably your first time firing a gun. That's why you picked that super cute little Ruger. It goes with your clutch, I know, but it also only fires .380 ACPs. They aren't going to be nearly enough to stop me."

I pointed to a scar on my right shoulder. "A hijacker stood right where you are weighing the choice you have before you, and he made the mistake of pulling the trigger. I am here. He is not."

"What if I shoot you in the face?" Ophelia replied, raising the weapon.

"Ophelia, don't!" Lawrence shouted.

"He's right," I said. "The last thing you want is to murder me right in front of the paparazzi."

"You're bluffing. There's no one here," Ophelia said as she looked around the park. "No one on the beach can even see a thing. Conveniently, there are dozens of these massive inflatables blocking the way."

"You're right, that's why I told her to set up on the Sea Pool. If you look over there on the pontoon, that's Holly Draper. With any luck, you'll be on the front page of the Bulletin first thing in the morning."

"You set us up," Lawrence growled.

"No, I took precautions, and right now, she's snapping pictures of you about to murder me. Good luck disputing that in court."

A steady thrum of engines accompanied the distinct sound of a jetboat's hull slapping against the waves. A large black speedboat was cruising right at us.

"And that..." I pointed to the rapidly approaching boat. "That is my good friend Captain Cronkwhile, an accomplished mermaid hunter. I had him waiting for your accomplice. Mermaids don't do great with nets."

Ophelia's face fell as I mentioned the mermaid, confirming my suspicion that she was in league with the creature spotted in the bay. I was bluffing about the captain having caught the creature, but she couldn't know that.

"I wonder who'll turn on you first," I mused out loud. "Lawrence, or your mermaid friend?"

Ophelia turned, moving the gun from me to Lawrence.

"I didn't have anything to do with this," Lawrence stammered, though I wasn't entirely sure whether he was talking to me or her.

"A bit late to back out now, Lawrence. You're what the police call an accessory. You have Ophelia to thank for that."

Lawrence's jaw drooped as he started to realize just how bad the whole situation made him look.

"I only did it because you never would." Ophelia's voice was shrill. "He was destroying the school's reputation and would have taken you with him. I made sure that didn't happen."

"You killed him," Lawrence said.

"Get on the boat," Ophelia shouted. "We need to go."

"I don't know that I'd do that, Lawrence," I said, entirely unhelpfully. "Chances are, she'll bury you now that you know the truth."

She brandished the gun at me. "Shut up!"

I pointed at the captain's boat. He was steadily accelerating toward us.

"I think that maniac plans to ram your boat," I muttered.

Ophelia turned, the gun sweeping out over open water as she weighed the threat the captain posed.

I had to give it to him. His suicidal charge even had me convinced.

"Now, Sonny!" I shouted as I lunged for Ophelia. I trapped the pistol before she could point it at me.

The captain wheeled hard to starboard, spraying a massive fan of water at us, before circling away from the pontoon.

That was when a hundred and sixty kilograms of angry Samoan muscle took a flying leap off the top of the inflatable's climbing tower. It was like watching a less hairy Donkey Kong hurtle through the air toward us. And Sonny wasn't aiming for the water.

I was already heading off the inflatable as Sonny hit it.

The gun went off, the round striking the water somewhere as the entire inflatable violently ejected everyone but Sonny.

Ophelia and I were tossed out into the ocean. Lawrence sailed sideways into his own boat. There was a sickening thud as his head struck the hull. Ophelia lashed out at me with one hand, but I kept both of mine on the pistol, pulling the trigger and discharging it into the water.

Contrary to popular opinion, most guns will fire underwater just fine, at least for a round or two. Sometimes more. As we sank into the Broadwater, I tore the gun from her grip and let it sink.

I was far more at home in the water than she was. As we plunged downward, she flailed, which confirmed my opinion that she wasn't the killer, only the facilitator.

I grabbed her as she struggled, and started swimming back to the surface. I had no intention of letting her drown. She would make some poor soul in Numinbah Women's Correctional Centre miserable, and I was determined that she would live long enough to see that cell.

I dragged her back to the boat to face justice. I grabbed the ladder on the back of the hull and something sharp bit into my thigh.

I growled as I shoved off the boat, letting go of Ophelia. She was now the lesser of two evils.

"She's here. You grab that one. I'll track the mermaid," I yelled to the captain before letting myself sink below the waves.

Beneath the inflatable, I could make out the flashing of a bright green tail as it swam away from me.

My thigh burned as I kicked hard after the creature. Its massive tail allowed it to plow powerfully through the water.

At first, I thought the creature was running, but no sooner was I beneath the inflatable, than she whirled about, and came for me.

Her ivory nails were wicked sharp and cut through the water ahead of her terrifying visage. She had red hair billowing about her, and a bony maw full of wicked pointed teeth. Her upper body looked like that of a human but was covered in a tangled mass of seaweed. From her waist down, her body tapered into a powerful scaly green tail. It propelled her through the water as she charged at me, wicked claws ready to rake across my exposed flesh.

We were both trapped beneath the inflatable and unable to surface for air. As she drew closer, I feinted forward only for her to lash out at me. Her nails dug into my arm, drawing more blood, but I seized her by the wrist and twisted it hard.

A plume of bubbles marked her tortured howl.

She might have been quick, but I was stronger. The other hand peeled down my other shoulder. Saltwater poured into the myriad of cuts, but ignoring it I turned her and grabbed her free arm. I was now behind her with her back trapped against me. As the creature thrashed, I pointed her own dagger-like claws toward her. They sliced against the scaly body, except instead of blood and muck pouring from the wound, it parted like foam rubber.

The entire tail was a prosthetic. Judging from the feel of it against my skin, the seaweed might be real, but the torso piece was also a costume.

The murderous mermaid lunged forward, sinking her teeth into my arm.

I yanked my arm out of its mouth, pushing it away, and drove my elbow into the side of its skull.

The mermaid went limp. I grabbed the creature's tail and dragged it along behind me as I kicked towards the edge of the inflatable.

As I surfaced, a thick rope landed beside me in the water. I grabbed the loop and secured it around the bottom end of the prosthetic tail.

Pulling the rope twice, I shouted. "Reel her in!"

The mermaid managed one more swipe at me before the captain activated the pulley on his jetboat and the mermaid was unceremoniously yanked through the water after him.

I dragged my battered body back onto the pontoon.

By the time I cleared the water, the captain was bringing the boat around. Ophelia was sitting in the back, being held in check by the captain's assistant and the captain was manning the pulley as he reeled in his prize. The prosthetic tail appeared at the water's surface. I climbed into the boat to lend a hand and together we pulled the mermaid out of the water.

The creature coughed and spluttered as she landed in the back of the jet boat.

Only it was no mermaid at all. It was a human in a series of incredibly lifelike prosthesis. She wore a padded wetsuit over her torso which she'd covered in seaweed. The hair was almost definitely a wig. I could tell courtesy of the feel and my recent education.

Her hands had bony nails that had been wired onto prosthetic fingers and were fashioned from bits of steel. Fake teeth made her very human mouth look like a maw. Altogether, if you were more than a few meters from the murderous ensemble, I imagined it would be rather compelling.

"I'm afraid she's less mermaid, more murderer," I said, placing an arm on the captain's shoulders. "Turns out we make a decent team after all."

"You're alright, Kane." The captain chuckled. "But who is she, and how did you know she'd be here?"

"That, captain, is a trade secret, but granted we'll both be supplying the evidence to Mr. Kinsella, I imagine he'll have no trouble paying both our bills.

I reached down and pulled off the wig. "As for who she is... Meet Mrs. Winters, an accomplished swimmer in her own right. She took silver in the '96 Olympics. Of course, she never got much coverage on account of the handful of gold medals Kyle brought home. The country made him a hero, didn't they, Mrs. Winters?"

At first, I'd thought it was a coincidence that they'd participated in the same Olympics, and that she'd subsequently enrolled her daughter in his school. Now I saw the carefully calculated retaliation.

"That sicko hit on my daughter," she hissed through the prosthetic teeth.

I nodded. "Almost certainly. I bet he hit on you too. But that's why you sent her there, right? You knew his reputation and you wanted to destroy him. When the court case didn't, you took matters into your own hands."

"You have no idea what it's like," she spat.

"It's tragic, is what it is." I sighed. "It's also a crime. You can explain the rest to the police."

One person's jealousy had cost another their life, would land at least three others in jail, and leave the real victim without one of her parents. I felt sorry for Kaley, though given the circumstances, she might arguably be better off.

"Where to?" the captain asked.

I pointed to the Sea Pool. "Bring us alongside that pontoon, good sir. My colleague will have all the evidence we need."

"What about their boat?" his wiry assistant asked.

"Sonny will bring it and Lawrence. I imagine the police will want to talk to the lot of them, and the boat might help clear some of the school's debts."

We taxied up alongside the pontoon, the rain still drizzling down.

Holly was waiting for us in a shapely halter one piece swimsuit, holding a water-proof camera.

"Darius, you're bleeding?" Her voice rose in panic.

"I've had worse," I replied, examining my arms. They looked like I'd gone two rounds with Edward Scissorhands. "But I've brought you a mermaid. As promised, one story right for the front page."

Holly snapped a picture of Ophelia and Mrs. Winters with me in the background. I didn't particularly want to be on the front page, but I doubted Holly was going to give me much choice in the matter. Whether I liked it or not, apparently, I sell papers.

Holly stepped into the boat. "Tell me everything."

It wasn't far to the shore and there wasn't nearly enough time to fill her in.

"Patience, my young padawan. Let's hand these crooks off to the authorities, and I promise I'll tell you all about it over some coffee, or perhaps some bandages once we get somewhere warmer."

When we reached the beach, the boat was swarmed over by Hart and Gibson along with a dozen other uniformed officers. Sonny taxied in beside us, beaching Lawrence's boat with a good deal less prowess than the captain had.

"Darius, you're a hot mess," Hart replied, shaking her head. "So these are our killers?"

Holly made a choking rasp and leaped off the boat.

"Holly," I called after her. "Just let me give them my statement, and we can catch up later."

Holly shrugged and headed for the carpark. She didn't look particularly happy about having to wait, but there was no one scooping her for this story, so she had nothing to worry about.

"Was that," Olivia asked, "Holly Draper throwing a temper tantrum?"

"Oh, don't start, detective. I needed evidence, and Holly Draper takes a mean picture."

"I don't know why you see the need to feed the beast," she replied. "The Bulletin makes our lives miserable."

Was that jealousy, or simply professional contempt for Holly's poor coverage of Hart and her department's work in recent times? It was difficult to tell, and I certainly wasn't going to ask. I was also battered and bleeding, and had buckets of salt in the wound, so I was ready to be anywhere but standing on the sand and getting rained on.

"Just let it be," I replied. "You have your killers and another closed case. It's wins all around."

She didn't look entirely convinced, but I pointed to the unconscious form draped over Sonny's shoulder. "Let me introduce you to Lawrence. He was robbing Kyle Cruz blind. Insists he had nothing to do with the murder, but I'll let you be the judge of that."

The detectives took notes as Captain Cronkwhile and his assistant unloaded the others.

"This is Ophelia, his partner. She lured Kyle out of the bar. Philip at the watering hole will make that ID for you. I suspect she got him drunk and tricked him into the water where Mrs. Winters was waiting. You won't recognise her with the prosthetic and wigs, but that's her under there. She's your murderous mermaid."

Olivia leaned forward and toyed with the wig. "I prefer yours, Darius. A much nicer colour if you ask me."

Sonny eyed me with confusion. "Is there something I ought to know, Darius?

"For the hundredth time, it's evidence," I said through gritted teeth. "Anyway, detective, you have your crooks, a bucket of evidence, and I'll be happy to provide a statement. If it helps add to the charges, this one tried to murder me."

I pointed at Ophelia.

"I've felt that way myself," Olivia teased.

I didn't dignify her comment with a response.

"Oh, cheer up, Darius. This is good work." Gibson pointed at the boats. "A mess, but we're not in the bedroom of a sitting judge, so I'll call it a win."

I shook my head. Pointing out to the Aqua Park, I continued my debrief. "You'll find a gun on the bottom of the seaway by that climbing fort. Sorry, I couldn't retrieve it. I was busy fighting for my life. If you have any questions, anything else at all, just give me a ring. I'll swing by the station a week from never."

"Oh Darius, don't be so sour. We're just playing." Olivia sauntered closer, right inside my bubble. "We joke with our friends, but if it's too much, we can go back to arresting you if you like."

"Hard pass," I replied, managing a smile. "But I've found a few interesting notes on that other matter. I'll reach out another time. I need to get myself patched up."

"Take care of yourself," Olivia replied. "And thanks for the assist today."

"See you around, detectives," I called as I headed for the car.

Sonny slung his backpack over his shoulder and fell into step beside me. He put an arm around me. He was one of the few people big enough to do that easily.

"So, you and the detective, huh?"

"It's just a working relationship, Sonny. There's nothing there."

He cocked his head to the side. "You mustn't have been in the same conversation I just witnessed, but I guess if you're seeing that pretty reporter, I can understand why you're ignoring that smoke show of a detective."

"Again, mate. She's just a colleague."

Sonny shook his head in disbelief. "I saw how she reacted when you got in the boat. Just a friend? Please."

"We're just helping each other out. I give her some stories, she helps me with cases. It's a win-win."

"Cases, right." Sonny looked at me sideways. "For someone who tells me they're looking for love, you'd manage to drown in an ocean of opportunity."

We passed over the sand and onto the grass heading for the car park. I wasn't sure what to say.

"Don't worry, man, one of these days you'll work it out."

Eager to change the topic, I tapped his backpack.

"I take it you've got the case?" I asked.

"I might have forgot to mention it to the police."

I grinned. "Possession is nine tenths of the law, and it was your money. Let's see anyone contest that in court."

"Thanks, man, I really owe you one."

"Rubbish." I waved him off. "If anything, this barely makes us even."

He gave me a massive bear hug and headed for his car.

I turned and took one last look at the beach. The police were busy loading Lawrence, Ophelia & Mrs. Winters into squad cars to drag them down to the station.

It was a job well done, and as soon as I got some bandages and a little rum and coke into me, I'd no doubt feel a whole lot better about how the case had gone. I hobbled over the bitumen toward the tank.

Holly sat on the bonnet, still wearing her swimmers, though she'd pulled on a cute set of denim shorts. Her dark hair was plastered to her face by the rain, and she had a first aid kit open in her lap.

She fixed me with a stare. "You, Darius, are going to tell me everything about this mermaid business."

"Or what?" I stopped short. "You're going to torture me with that?"

"I can drive what's left of you to Gold Coast hospital where you'll spend half the night waiting to be seen." Her lips crept up into a mischievous smile. "Or I can patch you up myself and we can find some other way to spend the night."

I stopped dead in my tracks. That was not what I'd been expecting. I'd clearly misread the situation and was about to protest when Sonny's words came back into my mind.

You'd manage to drown in the middle of an ocean of opportunity.

Holly was clever, driven, attractive, and for reasons I couldn't quite fathom, seemed only too willing to put up with me. I only felt I ought to opt for the hospital because Holly was so far out of my league, I couldn't see her on a clear night with a telescope.

But try as I might, I couldn't find a compelling reason to sabotage my night. So I took my key out of the waterproof pouch in my board shorts, unlocked the car, and opened her door for her.

"You're hired." I tried not to grin like a giddy idiot and failed miserably. "Get in."

Holly snapped the first-aid kit shut and slid down off the bull bar. As she climbed up into the tank, she looked out at me. "Where are we going?"

I closed the door and made my way around the car.

"To learn to swim, I suppose," I replied, not loud enough for anyone but me to hear.

I had closed two cases in one day: Sonny and his missing money, and Geoff's mermaid, though I daresay that hadn't turned out like he'd hoped. He would keep his job, but his sea-borne siren was more of a mistress of murder.

When it came to the Djinn, I'd made very little progress, but I'd also solved Kyle's murder and uncovered Marino smuggling who-knew-what into my town.

All in all, lady luck seemed hell bent on shining brightly in my direction, and for once in my life, I was going to get out of my own way and let her.

The End.

About The Author

When I set out to write *Blue Moon Australia*, I truly wanted to capture the unique atmosphere of the Gold Coast. It's a beautiful location where you can walk city streets surrounded by skyscrapers, move a few hundred meters, and find yourself standing on the golden sand. I knew I needed a story set on the Broadwater and waterways of the Gold Coast.

I tried to add a little twist with the presence of two different creatures; you'll have to let me know how I did. As for the location of the final battle, it is an actual aquatic play area on the Gold Coast. I love taking my family there; my kids are far better swimmers than me... I'm a professional doggy-paddler. It was during one of those visits that I envisioned the image of a massive Samoan leaping out of the tower to help save the day.

Another favorite part of *Sirens and Sea Monsters* is how Darius reacts to Sonny's situation. He's fiercely loyal to his friends, and despite the very real danger of the Djinn looming over his head, he doesn't hesitate to put his own problems on the backburner to take care of a friend in need.

Like all Blue Moon Australia novels, Sirens and Sea Monsters contained a few slang references for that authentic Aussie feel. Sometimes these are similar to other countries, sometimes they have a little twist on how you might use them at home.

Slang

How are you going? – Rather than 'How are you doing?' The meaning is identical, but this is how we speak. 'Hi mate, how are you going?' is probably the second most used sentence in my average day.

Going to wear it – Normally refers to a dressing down/earbashing from someone. For example. Carl bought his girlfriend a vacuum cleaner for her birthday, he's going to wear it (from her) when he gets home. The from in the sentence can be omitted but usually represents the source of the impending doom.

Tea – Most commonly means dinner here. We all sat down for tea together, usually would be a reference to dinner We discern the difference from context.

Water Police – Are literally what we call our police in boats. Different to the Coastguard, or other enforcement agencies. I'm pretty sure there are some other slang names for them, but we won't include them here.

Lass – Doesn't originate here but does see some use. Blame our convict past.

Going to squeeze him until it falls out – This was probably the #1 sentence advance readers took umbrage with. But this is how I speak and I'm pretty Australian, so I'll die on this hill. It simply meant Darius will find him and apply pressure until his friend's money is produced.

There are plenty more paranormal problems for Darius to solve, so find a comfy chair and enjoy the adventure.

I'll see you in the next book.

Sam Stokes

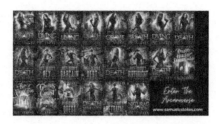

Want to see my other titles? Head to my website

https://www.samuelcstokes.com/

Or sign up to my newsletter where you'll receive exclusive short stories, giveaways, behind the scenes look into my series, and so much more. My newsletter is the place to go to never miss sales, new releases and special merch. Click the link below or type it into your browser.

https://www.books.samuelcstokes.com/jointhevips

If you enjoy social media, I have a growing group of readers who love to hang out, share their favourite reads, funny animal pictures, and torment me about when my next book is coming out.

www.facebook.com/groups/scstokesarcanoverse/

What's next for Darius?

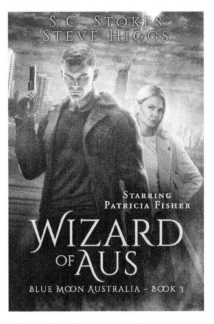

Our next *Blue Moon Australia* adventure will pit Darius against the Wizard of Aus. What happens when a murderous magician walks out of a high-security prison in the dead of night?

Crispin Taelos was at the height of his career when a double homicide sent him to prison for consecutive life sentences. Now that he's out, Crispin intends to continue performing for his beloved audience. However, the wizard's performances twist his magic into mayhem and murder.

Darius will need to catch the caped killer before the final curtain falls. Fortunately, he has a little help in the form of a rather sharp detective, Patricia Fisher, her half-butler, half-ninja, Jermaine, and Barbie, a fitness instructor eager to surf the world-famous waves of the Sunshine State.

Team up with Darius, Patricia, and the team in *The Wizard of Aus*.

Free Books and More

Want to see what else I have written? Go to my website.

https://stevehiggsbooks.com/

Or sign up to my newsletter where you will get sneak peeks, exclusive giveaways, behind the scenes content, and more. Plus, you'll be notified of Fan Pricing events when they occur and get exclusive offers from other authors because all UF writers are automatically friends.

Copy the link carefully into your web browser.

https://stevehiggsbooks.com/newsletter/

Prefer social media? Join my thriving Facebook community.

Want to join the inner circle where you can keep up to date with everything? This is a free group on Facebook where you can hang out with likeminded individuals and enjoy discussing my books. There is cake too (but only if you bring it).

https://www.facebook.com/groups/1151907108277718

Printed in Great Britain
by Amazon